THE
ASSOCIATION
OF
SMALL BOMBS

KARAN MAHAJAN

Chatto & Windus
LONDON

1 3 5 7 9 10 8 6 4 2

Chatto & Windus, an imprint of Vintage,
20 Vauxhall Bridge Road,
London SW1V 2SA

Chatto & Windus is part of the Penguin Random House
group of companies whose addresses can be found
at global.penguinrandomhouse.com.

Copyright © Karan Mahajan 2016

First published in the United States of America in 2016
by Viking, an imprint of Penguin Random House LLC

First published by Chatto & Windus in 2016

www.vintage-books.co.uk

A CIP catalogue record for this book is available from the British Library

ISBN 9780701182601

Printed and bound in Great Britain by Clays Ltd, St Ives plc

Penguin Random House is committed to a sustainable future
for our business, our readers and our planet. This book is made
from Forest Stewardship Council® certified paper.

FOR FRANCESCA

BLAST

MAY 1996

CHAPTER 0

The bombing, for which Mr. and Mrs. Khurana were not present, was a flat, percussive event that began under the bonnet of a parked white Maruti 800, though of course that detail, that detail about the car, could only be confirmed later. A good bombing begins everywhere at once.

A crowded market also begins everywhere at once, and Lajpat Nagar exemplified this type of tumult. A formless swamp of shacks, it bubbled here and there with faces and rolling carts and sloping beggars. It probably held four seasons at once in its gigantic span, all of them hot. When you got from one end of the market to the other, the wooden carts with their shiny aluminum wheels had so rearranged themselves that the market you were in was technically no longer the market you had entered: a Heisenbergian nightmare of motion and ambiguity. So the truth of the matter is that no one really saw the parked car till it came apart in a dizzying flock of shards.

Strange sights were reported. A blue fiberglass rooftop came uncorked from a shop and clattered down on a bus a few meters away; the bus braked, the rooftop slid forward, leaked a gorgeous stream of sand, and fell to the ground; the bus proceeded to crack it under its tires and keep going, its passengers dazed, even amused. (In a great city, what happens in one part never perplexes the other parts.) Back in the market, people collapsed, then got up, their hands pressed to their wounds, as if they had smashed eggs against their bodies in hypnotic agreement and were unsure about what to do with the runny, bloody yolk. Most startling of all, for the survivors and rescue workers both, was the realization that the main dusty square was rooted so firmly by half a dozen massive trees, trees that had gone all but unnoticed in all those years, their shadows dingy with commerce, their branches cranked low with hanging wares, their droppings of mulberry collected and sold—until the bomb had loosened the green gums of the trees and sent down a shower of leaves, which Mr. Khurana kicked up on the ground as he tried to uncover the bodies of his two sons.

But the leaves, turned crisp, shards themselves, offered nothing. His sons were dead at a nearby hospital and he had come too late.

The two boys were the sum total of the Khuranas' children, eleven and thirteen, eager to be sent out on errands; and on this particular day they had gone with a friend in an auto-rickshaw to pick up the Khuranas' old Onida color TV, consigned to the electrician for perhaps the tenth time. But when Mr. Khurana was asked by friends what the children were doing there (the boy with them having escaped with a fracture), he said, "They'd gone to pick up my watch from the watch man." His wife didn't stop him, and in fact colluded in the lie. "All the watches were stopped," she said. "The way they know the time the bomb went off is by taking the average of all the stopped watches in the watch man's hut."

Why lie, why now? Well, because to admit to their high-flying friends that their children had not only died among the poor, but had been sent out on an errand that smacked of poverty—repairing an old TV that should have, by now, been replaced by one of those self-financing foreign brands—would have, in those tragic weeks that followed the bombing, undone the tightly laced nerves that held them together. But of course they *were* poor, at least compared to their friends, and no amount of suave English, the sort that issued uncontrollably from their mouths, could change that; no amount of sobbing in Victorian sentences or chest beating before the Oxonian anchors on *The News Tonight*, who interviewed them, who stoked their outrage, could drape them or their dead children in the glow of foregone success: Mr. and Mrs. Khurana were forty and forty, and they had suffered the defining tragedy of their lives, and so all other competing tragedies were relegated to mere facts of existence. For a month afterwards, they made do without the

TV, which for all they knew was still sitting in the basement workshop of the electrician, its hidden berths of microchips heavy with dust, its screen screwed off and put facedown on the floor, looking into nothing. They only caught their own mugs on *The News Tonight* because a neighbor knocked on their door and welcomed them into his house to watch the news. He was friendly with them ever after.

Now Mr. Khurana, who had been a troubled, twitchy sleeper ever since he'd become a documentary filmmaker years ago, began to suffer from dreams that impressed him deeply, and he never failed to discuss them with his wife or his collaborators. He didn't mention that he was terrified during their nightly unspooling; that he slept in the crook of his wife's armpit like a baby, his body greased with sweat, his leg rotating out like the blade of a misfired fan. But the dreams were truly notable, and in the first and most frequent one, he became, for a few minutes, *the bomb*. The best way to describe what he felt would be to say that first he was blind, then he could see everything. This is what it felt like to be a bomb. You were coiled up, majestic with blackness, unaware that the universe outside you existed, and then a wire snapped and ripped open your eyelids all the way around and you had a vision of the world that was 360 degrees, and everything in your purview was doomed by seeing.

In the dream, the market—where he had been many times, his collar usually popped—was so vivid in his mind, so three-dimensional, that he sometimes lingered on details for hours of dream time. A single foot thrust into the dark cube of a shop would become gangrenous and huge with meaning; it would kick right against the inner wall of his temple, and he would wake up just before he could see the children flying through the shop front outside which they'd been found facedown, a sash of blood showing through the blackened cotton on their backs.

In the mornings he'd rouse Mrs. Khurana and they'd make eerily passionate love, using more muscle than necessary, their insides lurid with lactic acid, and then both would stack their slack bodies against each other and cry, so that later in the evening, when Mrs. Khurana returned from her

errands and began to unwrap the sheet from its bulge of bed, she'd notice
two parallel lines of salt that marked where they had lain in the morning,
shoulders soggy with tears.

But both of them were grateful for each other, for how little they remi-
nisced, how they refused to apply the butterfly effect backwards to their
lives or ruin themselves with what-ifs; that neither blamed the other for the
fact that the children had taken an auto-rickshaw, hotboxed with May pollution, to Lajpat Nagar that evening. Why bother, when the entire circuitry
of their brains had been rewired to send up flares of grief? Why bother
with talk? You lift a spoon from a claw of thick stew and you weep. You
wrap your hand around an armrest on a bus (sometimes Deepa Khurana
would ride to school with the children for the PTA) and it is as if the burning steel was riven from the earth only to remind you of the hotness at the
core, to which your children will be returned. Under the shower there is the
outline of your body for water to fall around, then a sputter and dry-
throated silence in which you are sheathed in the same soap that you remember scrubbing off the shoulders of your boys. No action is safe from
meaning. The boys had stored, between them, all the world's possibilities:
Nakul had been handsome and sporty; Tushar had been plump and
responsible—what does it matter? Who's to say that this is what they would
have remained? Who's to say, Mr. and Mrs. Khurana, that you lost something you knew?

At the cremation, which occurred on the stepped bank of a Yamuna
River canal speckled with a thousand ripply eyes of oil, tendrils of overgrown hypochondriac plants thrust deep into the medicinal murk, Mr.
Khurana noticed that outside the ring of burning flesh and wood, little
snotty children ran naked playing with upright rubber tires. Behind them
a cow was dreadlocked in ropes and eating ash and the wild village children
kicked it in the gut. He shouldn't have, but in the middle of the final prayers
Mr. Khurana stepped out and shouted, shooing, the entire funeral party
dropping back from the wavy black carpet of fire shadow. The children,
not his, just looked at him and with beautiful synchronicity dove headfirst
into the water, the rubber tires bobbing behind them, but the cow eyed him

with muckraking glee and put its long wet tongue into the earth. The prayers continued but a tremor was evident: if the chanting had sounded before like the low buzzing of bees, the vocal swarm had now cleared and thinned as if to accommodate the linger of a gunshot. The exhilaration of Mr. Khurana's grief gave way to the simple fact that he was a person, naked in his actions, and that as a person he was condemned to feel shame. He felt eyes rebuking him with sudden blinks between solemn verses. He stopped thinking of his two boys as they burned away before him in a flame that combed the air with its spikes of heat and sudden bone crack of bark. More ash for the cow.

VICTIMS

MAY 1996

CHAPTER 1

"Where are the boys?" Vikas Khurana asked. He was with his wife in his flat. The sun was setting, oiling the trees outside with light. The Khuranas lived—unusually, for a couple at the end of the twentieth century in upper-middle-class Delhi—in a joint family compound, though even this compound, which spanned half an acre of Maharani Bagh, was joint only in name: the three buildings had been diced into six flats, and the common kitchen, once anchored by the grandparents, was now a formal space, reopened only for communal occasions like Diwali or Rakhi. The family members saw each other as often as people do in apartment complexes.

When Deepa gave him the answer he expected—they were probably stuck in traffic—he glanced from the first-floor window through the folds and dust-filled crevices of the complex for signs of life. Nothing. Only Nepali servants lingering in the street with milk thermoses, dusk swirling around their crew-cut hair in the form of clouds of mosquitoes, and closer, pigeons shaking dirt off their wings, the shades on their necks—greens, magentas, yellows—stabbing in their brilliance. "Every year the mosquitoes come earlier," Vikas said. "Apparently, Vibha's son has malaria."

"That's because the Yamuna is oxygen dead," Deepa said. She was icing a cake on the dining table, dripping white frosting through a cone of paper in her hand. A talented baker, she sold her cakes to kitty parties and birthdays for extra income.

Vikas changed into shorts and went out for a walk. He'd become fidgety waiting for the boys, who'd left a while ago in an auto with their cricketing friend Mansoor. After dropping Mansoor at South Ex, they were supposed to reverse course and stop at Lajpat Nagar to pick up the TV, enthroned on the electrician's worktable after springing a mysterious green line across the screen. The TV had been out for repair for days, but Vikas had made no move to fetch it till today, when a day-night South Africa–Australia cricket match was scheduled.

He was an art filmmaker and did not keep regular hours; he could arrange his day around cricket matches if he wished.

It was a bit early for a walk. Most of the regulars were indoors, or at work; the sun burned up the roads despite the ashoka and neem and peepul trees plugging up the sky on both sides; and the sounds of traffic on Mathura Road conveyed speed and impatience, with honks traveling down the avenue like javelins thrown by ghosts.

Vikas walked pensively, uncomfortably, dismayed by the imperfection of the circumstances and his own mood. Soon, though, he fell into a rhythm and was making rounds of the park where the boys played most evenings. It was there, at the corner of that park, near a small temple abutting a garbage dump, that another walker, Mr. Monga, came up to him.

"Did you hear? There's been a blast in Lajpat Nagar," Monga said, speaking to Vikas but looking down the serene colony street for other walkers, his eyes vivid with gossip and excitement. "Why now, in this hot month, I don't know," he said, casting another glance down the alley and twitching his shoulders, shoulders that seemed deformed under the big-pored cotton of his white polo shirt. "Could be related to the elections." The Hindu nationalist BJP had come to power six days earlier, with a tight majority.

When did it happen? is all Vikas wanted to know.

"Just now, yaar. I heard because my missus had gone to Bon Ton and she was coming through Ashram and traffic was very bad, so she asked a DTC guy."

The rest of it unfolded at high speed. Vikas bolted from the periphery of the park, raced down the avenues—aware, as he ran, of the terrible flaws in the sidewalk, the tilts and burps in the blistered tiles—and got into his car and drove off. He told his wife nothing—she was busy upstairs with an order for a silver anniversary and he didn't wish to panic her. But because he had shared his fears with neither his wife nor Mr. Monga, whom he had batted off with an excuse, he was more fearful than he otherwise would have been.

Strangely, though, as he drove, his mind was not on *his* boys but on their friend Mansoor Ahmed, who was the same age as the older one, Tushar. Vikas would never be able to live it down if something happened to Mansoor, if he died on his watch—Mansoor, who had been born to the Ahmeds after seven years of infertility and whom they protected with all their parental paranoia, only letting him go out to visit the Khuranas, whom they counted among their best (and only Hindu) friends. Vikas, for this reason, had a strong bond with the boy—stronger, at times, than the one he shared with his own sons; he relished Mansoor's intelligence and sensitivity, found him more receptive to the arts and to listening, and always used him as a cudgel with which to shame his sons (Vikas had always been self-hating when it came to family). When Mansoor came over, he tried to give him a taste of the freedom he was denied by his parents. Sending him with the boys, instead of dropping him off personally, had been his idea.

Monga was right, though—traffic was horrible, and almost out of petrol, the car swung uneasily through the rush hour streets, its needle shaking near E. "Shit, shit, shit," Vikas muttered, the panic in his heart displaced by the unperturbed pace of traffic.

The boys had left together in an auto, flagging one down from Mathura Road even as the chaperoning servant kept telling them, "Move back! Your mother's going to scold you!"

"I'll scold *you*," said Tushar, brimming with the manic energy that consumed him at dusk, the city with its ferocious horns and traffic and tired efflorescence not exactly helping matters.

But when the boys got into the auto, squeezing their small brown legs together, they were quiet and serious as they expected auto riders to be.

They watched the traffic from the open sides of the vehicle, and occasionally pointed out fancy cars to each other. "Oye, the new model of the Rover Montego's come out?" Nakul, the younger one, asked.

"They make them in Oxford," Tushar said.

"Where are we going, can you please tell me?" the alcohol-scented auto driver asked.

"Let's go to Lajpat Nagar first," Tushar said. "That's OK, no?" he said, turning to Mansoor.

Mansoor grinned. He knew he was supposed to be dropped home first, but he liked being bossed around by rebellious people so he could break the rules and be let off the hook.

At twelve, Mansoor had an amazing, ingratiating grin, and a mouthful of crooked teeth that would never be fixed.

A few minutes later, the boys strolled around Lajpat Nagar together, Tushar teasing Mansoor and slapping his back and Nakul carrying himself proudly, combing his hair and fine-tuning it with his fingers like a radio. "And that's the framing shop where we got that Founder's Day photo framed," Nakul said. "We bought Sorry and backgammon from the shop behind it."

"They sell classy English willow bats there," Tushar chimed in, though he was a terrible cricketer.

Mansoor, unused to being out on his own, took in the sights and sounds. The crowds consisted of a particular kind of Delhiite Mansoor recognized immediately. This sort of Delhiite was slightly malnourished, wore shiny polyester clothes, grew a black mustache, had a fondness for stud earrings, kept his pants hitched too high, let his fingers roam his nose, used slightly loose, lackadaisical hand gestures, and had a cynical dumb face that could never seem grave (the women looked the same, but with lighter mustaches and cheap floral saris).

"Where are we going?" Mansoor was asking when an explosion ripped his sentence in two and stuffed half of it back in his mouth.

Later, everyone reported seeing a gushing white star, and there was a long silence before the screams started, as if, even in pain, people watched each other first to see how to act.

When Mansoor woke up, the market was burning. People lay in positions of repose. Mothers were folded bloodily over daughters; office-going men were limp on their backs with briefcases burning beside them; and shop-keepers crawled on their elbows while cars burst into flames inches from their faces. Through a woman's ripped kurta Mansoor spied his first breast. His own wrist was oozing blood but the sensation was far from him, like something hidden in another corner of the market.

People began climbing over the corpses with the guilty looks of burglars, their hair frazzled and wild and faces half-black. Mansoor, lifting himself up too, saw Tushar lying on the ground and staring up at the sky, his lips wet and open, his curly hair full of sand, or another whitish substance blasted off a wall. Nakul was next to him with his arm over his face like a worker dozing in the sun.

"Tushar! Nakul!" He was unable to hear himself. But when he crawled over to shake them, a sharp pain erupted in his hand and he looked up to see a torn leather shoe pressing down on it and then a disfigured man dis-appearing over him and the bodies.

"Uncle!" Mansoor screamed. But the man was gone and others—gory, bleeding—kept coming.

Then a hand gripped Mansoor's shoulder. "Get up, son," the disembodied voice said—a kindly voice, the voice of the earth, full of pity and groaning patience. But an old instinct about not talking to strangers took hold and Mansoor ran from the burning square.

By now Afsheen Ahmed had become very anxious about her son's absence and had called Deepa Khurana.

"He's still not reached?" Deepa said, cramming the phone between her ear and shoulder and gazing out the windows, her hands covered in cake mix. "They must have got stuck in a jam on Ring Road—there's lots of construction happening near Ashram. And the boys were supposed to go to Lajpat Nagar after dropping Mansoor. It could be that they went there first. They're all such independent boys already."

When Afsheen heard this, she turned cold. "Deepa, there's been a blast there."

"Rush hour is still going on," Deepa said. "They should be reaching just now."

"A bomb."

"I see," Deepa said, surprised at how stern she herself sounded. She'd always believed that misfortune was brought on by those who worried it into existence.

"I heard it on the radio. I was in the kitchen and it was playing on the servants' radio." Afsheen was now crying.

"Afsheen," said Deepa, softer.

Soon after, Deepa got off the phone and went to the landing of the flat and looked down the stairs. No sign of her husband. "Go find sahib," she instructed Hari, the servant, who took off quickly, his Hawaii slippers thwacking. Deepa washed her cake-smeared hands, absently running a palm through her hair and leaving a white streak there, like Indira Gandhi. Then she went down in her faded kurta to the gate. When she saw the car was missing, she swore loudly. Where had her husband gone and when would he return? He couldn't be trusted. He was absentminded.

She strode to the main road and hailed an auto herself. It never occurred to her to ask any of Vikas's relatives in the complex for help.

In any case, Vikas—deep in the disinfected, bloated governmental belly of the hospital—beat them all to it. He found Tushar and Nakul laid out flat on a dhurrie amid other bodies. Nakul's pretty eyes were blasted open in fright. Tushar slept peacefully, as he always had. Getting down on his haunches, rocking on his heels, Vikas pressed their cold, burned cheeks and wept, adding his fluids to theirs.

When he looked up (hours later, it seemed), Sharif and Afsheen Ahmed were standing over him—Sharif, fat and hassled-looking, with his black disordered beard, his checked shirt and black pants swelling around his belly; Afsheen, dark, her oval face ruined with tears, her slim body wrapped in an elegant chikan salwar, the whiteness of her clothes out of place on this tarmac of death. Vikas's own clothes had long ago turned the color of soot, of radically vaporized skin and bone. "I'm so sorry," Vikas said—his first words in the morgue. "I'm so, so sorry."

Mansoor was still walking.

When the explosion had happened, he had panicked and run away from the burning square and into the shacks. Then, as he searched for a PCO to call home or a stranger to lead him to a phone (he prayed for his phone number, which had vanished from his mind), the dark, sunless alleys distending with people swarming away from and toward the explosion, he panicked again. He'd never been alone anywhere in Delhi, let alone a market after an explosion.

"Did someone's LPG cylinder burst?" a woman asked.

Mansoor was unsure if he was being talked to.

"Must have been Arora's compressor," another man, this one with a terrible tumor growing out of his neck, said.

"They shouldn't have installed it. The wires here can't take the load, but they don't listen even if they're being told at the association meeting."

Another boom came from the market—perhaps an actual LPG cylinder going up in a blue column—and the men and women packed together in the alley screamed and there was a muscular pushing and everyone surged out to the main road, where Mansoor, coming across the fresh, untouched life of the city, its towering buses and belts of filth and mud, felt suddenly acute with life, with smoke.

"Bhaiya, you're OK?" an auto driver asked, walking away from his vehicle with his hands on his hips, but Mansoor instinctively moved away from him, trying to stanch the bleeding in his right wrist with his left hand.

He wondered if he had gotten his tetanus booster on time. He had always wondered about the efficacy and necessity of these injections, but now he was grateful.

The auto driver's top few shirt buttons were undone; a locket flared in the light amid the drowsy sparse chest hairs. "I'm fine, uncle," Mansoor said for reasons he could not understand.

From the jammed roads—the crowds gathering there and pooling around a stopped bus, pointing—he could tell something exceptional had happened. Then a woman who could have been his grandmother said, "A bomb just burst here."

A bomb. He had survived, witnessed, walked through a bomb blast. He couldn't believe it. He had heard of bomb blasts before, of course—they were always in the news and had been recently because of the 1996 World Cup; some of the matches scheduled in Sri Lanka had been canceled because of bomb threats by the LTTE, an organization his father called "ruthless." "In this country, they're always accusing Muslims of terrorism," Sharif had said, bringing his soft paws together—he was a fat man with unemotional features that were childlike, even pitiable, in their conviction—"when the most dangerous terrorists have been Hindus and Sikhs. You know who blew up Rajiv Gandhi? Hindus. A woman from the LTTE, the same group that set off the bombs in Colombo that so scared the Australian team. You know who killed Rajiv's mother, Indira? Her sardar bodyguards. So when people say—" He shook his head. "It makes me angry when the proof is right there, the statistics are there, and the journalists won't consult them."

"Gandhi-ji's assassin was also a Hindu."

"Yes," said Sharif. "We're very lucky that that was the case. Your Nana-ji was in Aligarh when it happened." Sharif's grandfather had been a freedom fighter, an associate of Sir Syed Ahmed Khan; Sharif was proud of this fact, and loved telling Mansoor about it. Mansoor, though not interested, liked sending his father into raptures of open-ended conversation so he could daydream about the girls he loved in school. He was, he felt, a tragic romantic hero. He stared at girls shyly and gave them poems that he claimed to have written but that he had copied from his mother's thick

Emily Dickinson anthology; she had an MA in English from LSR and had been a theater actress and a counselor at Air Force Bal Bharati School before becoming a housewife.

How far he'd come, in the space of a few hours, from that home life!

Mansoor, tired, bleeding, walked on Ring Road, past a mandi with its nauseating smell of rotten, overripe fruit and covering of blue tarpaulin. After spending a few minutes on the jammed road outside the market, listening to people speculate about the bomb, whether it had been planted by Muslims—listening, in other words, to people intent on gossiping about the tragedy rather than heeding a victim passing before them—he had made the decision to walk home. Of course, he only knew the city from the insides of an air-conditioned car. How far was home from here? Fifteen, twenty minutes? The streets with their bracing angles scrolled and zagged in his mind's eye, unfurling at whatever speed the vantage of the car provided.

By the time he was outside the mandi, he was exhausted, and worried about how he would navigate the thundering pitiless straight-shooting traffic on the main road. His body tensed; he held his bleeding wrist, disgusted by the stickiness, and walked on.

It became easy to avoid oncoming traffic; he pressed close to the edge of the mandi, often standing in the way of cursing, bell-ringing cyclists, and he only had to jump out of the way when a cow browsed toward him (he had once been knocked down in Bhogal by a bull, losing a milk tooth, and that had been the end of his mandi-going ways).

Dusk deepened, coloring the sky a polluted pink; birds wheeled restlessly overhead, as if waiting for rush hour to end so they could head down to collect their spoils. Mansoor ambled past a school on his left; crossed between hawkers smoking peanuts in black vessels on the sidewalk; dodged cakes of cow dung; and wondered, with a half smile, if his parents would be impressed with his presence of mind, his ability to navigate the city after the shock of the explosion. Then the smile fell away as he remembered Tushar and Nakul. What had happened to them? Were they—dead? And why had he run? If he were to go back and play the thoughts running through his head at the moment he had left them, they would have been something like this: They're brothers. They can take care of themselves. Or: Didn't I tell them I didn't want to go to the market? Why did they force me?

Men and women and kids and dogs passed by, unaware of who he was, why he was bleeding, why he stood in his upper-class shorts alone on a city sidewalk. Their faces were sweaty and private in the Petromax lights switched on by the street carts.

"Sir," Mansoor said to one man in his twenties, but Mansoor was too feeble and the man passed him by.

"Uncle," he said to another man who walked by, licking an ice cream. And this man stopped and studied Mansoor with eyes that were either surprised or glaring. He was middle-aged and paunchy and mustachioed and his tongue shot out to keep the sides of the softie from melting.

"Talk," the man said.

Mansoor told him what had happened: the blast, the market, the boys, the walk.

Perhaps because he lacked another option, the paunchy man with the unblinking, ambling eyes kept licking the sides of his ice cream, sculpting it into a manageable shape with his tongue.

"Where do you live?" he asked.

"South Ex," Mansoor said.

"In part one or two?"

"Two." How was this relevant?

"Your parents are at home?"

"Yes, uncle."

"And your friends' mummy and daddy?"

"At home also, uncle."

He shook his head seriously. Then he said, "Will you have some ice cream?"

The man was much more at ease with the ice cream out of his hands. Taking a hankie out of his pocket, he wiped his face and then his forehead. "There's a PCO nearby. We can phone from there."

As they walked in the direction Mansoor had come from, Mansoor having gratefully demolished the ice cream (even as he dreaded the germs he'd imbibed), the man said, "You're badly hurt, yaar. Maybe we should go to a hospital first. My car is parked nearby. Come with me."

Till this point, Mansoor had been happy to walk with the man, but as soon as talk of the car came up, he recoiled. "No need, uncle. Let's make the phone call."

"But, son, the car's right here. In the time we make the call we can get you treated."

"But, uncle, my friends are in the market."

"Let me open my car."

Mansoor wanted to tell him about the traffic jam, but something came over him and he ran.

"Son!" the man shouted.

He ran fast, kicking up dirt with his heels; when he stopped, only a little beyond where he'd first spied the man, he was winded and ashamed. He looked over his shoulder to see if he was being pursued. He felt he'd done the right thing. He had grown up in a city full of stories about kidnappings and disappearances; had heard from his mother about how one maid dressed up her ward, a two-year-old, in rags, blackened his face, and took him out on the street to beg. The parents of the child were always wondering why the child was so tired when they came back home; then one day the mother was driving on the road and   Ah!

Mansoor walked with urgency. He did not want to be pursued by the fat kidnapper. He cursed himself for not having asked a lady for help.

His house was still at least a kilometer away and he'd made little progress. Heavy black smog sat over the road. A stranded ambulance screamed in traffic. Beyond, blinking, he could make out Moolchand flyover, and beyond that, the mirage of South Extension—smoke and haze and the familiar congested approach to home.

The Ahmeds were convinced their son was dead. Leaving AIIMS hospital, where Afsheen's cousin promised to keep vigil, they headed to Moolchand hospital. One by one, in this manner, they made a desperate tour of the hospitals of South Delhi. Afsheen was sick and crying throughout. "Be positive," Sharif said, as he watched his high-strung but sweet wife dissolving. "There's no objective evidence that anything has happened." He was at the steering wheel of the car. "He might be at someone's house."

"How could they do that? How can you be so irresponsible with someone else's son? How many times have I told them I don't want him to go out?"

"They've lost two kids."

"They should lose two kids! They should lose everything!"

"Afsheen," he said. But the truth was that he felt the same way.

The hospitals yielded nothing. But that night Sharif felt he'd come closer to the reality—and suffering—of the city than ever before: the tired grief-soaked expressions of patients; the exhaustion of nurses; the crumbling medical infrastructure; the weak tube lights flickering and clicking; the way in which doctors became bureaucrats the moment they were questioned. Sharif felt he ought to wash his hands of this country, this place he had fought so hard to make his own, enduring the jibes of his family members who claimed to lead happier lives in Dubai, Sharjah, Bahrain, Lahore.

By now the tears had dried up; husband and wife sat at the dashboard in rage-filled silence. "Let's go to the police," Afsheen said, half-crazed. "We should register a criminal case against the Khuranas."

"We should have gone to the market earlier," Sharif said, slapping his forehead.

They had gone to the market briefly before coming to AIIMS, springing through the debris, calling out for Mansoor. In doing so, they'd realized they were far from the only people searching for a relative in the market: half of Delhi seemed to be out in this dung of destruction, though, in the end, the death toll would be only thirteen dead with thirty injured—a small bomb. A typical bomb. A bomb of small consequences.

"Let's go home first, in case he's there," Sharif said.

Home. The last time we'll come back and be able to call it that, he thought, pulling up in his Esteem, the dark colony illuminated with the dirty electricity of the city. But as soon as he parked, he saw two individuals outlined in the light of the front landing.

Afsheen got out of the car and ran over and hugged and then slapped her son. The servant, who was sitting next to Mansoor, got up excitedly.

"How could this have happened?" Afsheen wept. "Why didn't you phone us immediately?"

Sharif hugged his son tightly on the landing. He only now realized how tense he was, how much he loved his son. "Bring me some water," he told the servant when he was inside, trying to control his emotions, the three of them holding each other in an odd huddle.

"We have to go help the Khuranas," Afsheen said, looking up from her son.

CHAPTER 2

Vikas's concern for Mansoor had long since given way to grief over his sons. It became his priority—and his wife's—to spend as much time with them as possible, to not abandon their corpses for even a minute. It was as if, having failed to protect them in life, they felt double the responsibility to fulfill their duties in death. Still, the cremation, which happened the next day at Nigambodh Ghat, stunned them both. They howled as the boys were crushed to ashes.

The bodies had been taken away briefly the night before for a postmortem so the doctors could recover pieces of the bomb from Tushar's and Nakul's corpses. The leftover pieces—bright triangles of metal, serrated edges of bottle caps, nails—glittered in the pyre.

Deepa, weeping violently, her hair pouring everywhere, gray from smoke, screamed, "Take me away." Vikas watched with his arms behind his back, like a military man at the funeral of his entire squadron.

The members of the Khurana clan did not see each other frequently, but they took the responsibilities of family life seriously, and after the cremation, they came from their flats and gathered around the couple in their house to console and comfort them. Rajat, Vikas's youngest brother, a handsome fellow in his thirties with an unfashionable mustache and an air of self-important family-oriented efficiency, pulverized sleeping pills with a rolling pin and dissolved them in the couple's tea; that they drank this hot cocktail without noticing was a sign, to him, of how far gone they were. Bunty Masi went through the kitchen drawers, collecting knives and dropping them into a jute bag she took home. The Khuranas' close friends, writers and filmmakers and decent professional types, came together and sat in a grief-stricken huddle; the blow had been so big, it had the potential to damage an entire friend group.

Others crowded on the floor, offering homilies, stories, banalities. Everyone (save for two patriarchs) agreed it was impossible to imagine what the Khuranas were going through.

The bombing happened at six p.m. on a Tuesday. By nine p.m. a group calling itself the Jammu and Kashmir Islamic Force had called Zee TV and NDTV and claimed credit for the attack. The family members discussed the group and its intentions and fell back on their normal scorn for Muslims. "They can't live in peace, these Muslims. Anywhere they show up, they're at war," one Masi said. "A violent religion of violent people. In the Quran, it's written—no Muslim is supposed to rest till he's drunk the blood of seventy-two unbelievers."

"Kashmiris have always been filthy people. The whole winter passes and they don't bathe. That's why Srinagar stinks so much."

"The problem is they believe they'll receive seventy-two virgins in heaven."

"You're saying this, but I work with Muslims every day. All the craftsmen and weavers are Muslim. You go to their locality and each of them has twenty children."

The Ahmeds too were adjusting to this new world—this world in which their son had nearly perished and in which his two close friends had died before his eyes.

The doctor who had seen Mansoor on the day of the blast said he was very lucky: some other object or person nearby must have absorbed the shockwave. It was the shockwave that killed most people. If you inhaled at the moment of the blast, which was the natural impulse, the compressing air got inside you and tore up your lungs and you died of "massive trauma." "You, young chap," the old doctor said, slapping Mansoor's cheek in a friendly but unsettling manner, "you've only got a fracture and some stitches in your hand—things that all boys of your age get. Soldier's wounds." Then he slapped him again and prescribed a few months of physiotherapy. Mansoor was allowed to take home all the shrapnel that had been pulled out of his arm—twenty pellets—in a plastic bag.

"Should we take him to VIMHANS?" Afsheen asked afterwards, referring to the mental health institute on Ring Road.

"Tell me what happened, how it felt," Sharif said to the boy.

"You can't just ask like that!" Afsheen said. "There's a proper process for these things."

But the boy was happy as he was, at home. "Please, Mama, I don't want to go anywhere," he begged.

"See, Afsheen, what's the rush?" Sharif said.

In any case, the Ahmeds found themselves very busy with the cremation and funeral rites of the Khurana boys. Blessed with good fortune, they experienced a strong obligation to be present for their unlucky friends and they went and sat in the Khuranas' flat every day, ignoring the abuses hurled at Muslims by Vikas's relatives—relatives who were either not aware they were Muslim, or wished to harangue them in a sidelong manner.

"Only another mother can understand what you're going through," Afsheen cried in Hindi, sitting on her knees by Deepa in the Khuranas' drawing room. "Mansoor keeps saying his life should also be taken away if Tushar's and Nakul's were, and I have to tell him, No, beta, no, don't have these thoughts."

Deepa barely registered Afsheen's presence. "They were such good friends, all of them. Best friends." She sniffled again, covering her sharp nose with her bony hands, and then said, "I'm so sorry. I'm crying too much."

"Cry. It's OK to cry."

Sharif spent time with an ashen, shocked-looking Vikas. "The terrorists were Kashmiri fellows," he said, in the measured and serious way of someone unused to emotions, someone obviously puffed up by the opportunity to proffer advice. "It'll be easy to find these people. They're not professionals. The important thing is that you take care of Deepa. She needs you. I'll ask Mansoor if he saw anything suspicious at the market."

Mansoor was the one who provided the Khurana family with an eyewitness account of the boys' deaths, putting an end to morbid speculation about their final moments. But he'd been unable to explain to his parents why he'd walked away. "Why didn't you phone us, beta?" Afsheen said.

"I thought the lines would be cut," he lied.

"But promise me, if there's ever, *ever* such an emergency again, you will phone. Each market these days has hundreds of PCOs."

But Mansoor—disoriented, overwhelmed Mansoor—wasn't listening. He was thinking instead of the shattering, deafening moment the bomb exploded, the pain he'd felt in his extremities, the way Tushar and Nakul had snapped into sleep, going from on to off. What could he have done? Though he had no experience with mortality, though he had not gone over to their corpses to examine them, he had known they were dead, and had known there was nothing he could do. How to explain this? How to tell his parents the obvious thing—that walking had been his way of grieving, of indicting the entire city with his eyes?

His parents protected him from the Khuranas and the cremation and the chautha—he was a victim too, after all; his right wrist and arm, fractured, were in a cast—but one day, he was nevertheless taken to meet the Khuranas in their flat. Vikas, grief stricken but affectionate, hugged Mansoor with downcast eyes, smelling his hair deeply, wanting a full version of events. Deepa, dressed in an obscenely yellow kameez, sat on the sofa chair next to him, dazed, a hand on her head, the embodiment of a crushing headache. Afsheen kept throwing worried glances her way. "Deepa, will you have anything to drink?" she asked, even though this was Deepa's house and the servant could be heard operating the mixie in the kitchen.

Mansoor told them about the auto ride, the walk in the market, the explosion. "But did they die instantly?" Vikas asked.

"They weren't moving, uncle."

"But you know for a hundred percent sure?" Vikas said, muddling his words. "We're trying to make a case against the hospital and the police. When the bomb exploded, people phoned the fire department from the market, and they kept saying, we're coming, we're coming. But they didn't come. They phoned AIIMS for an ambulance and they also didn't come. They actually put people in the back of a police van and drove them to the hospital. They piled them on top of each other—"

"Answer uncle's question, beta," Afsheen encouraged him, realizing Vikas was getting lost in the horror of these imagined events.

"They were no more, uncle," Mansoor said.

Vikas looked at Mansoor and in that glance it was clear to Mansoor that Vikas blamed him, that this question was not about the hospital or the fire department or the police but about why he had left them to die and walked away.

Why? He didn't understand either. He saw the landscape, the dripping city with its thousands of watery, refracted lights; saw the dust on the yellow necks of the traffic lights; saw the torrid concrete undersides of the flyovers—saw it all and felt afraid, as if the city had recognized his guilt on the way home and would find a way to destroy him.

"Had they gone to pick up a watch or a TV?" Sharif asked Mansoor when they drove home in their Esteem.

"You don't listen properly," Afsheen scolded Sharif.

"TV, Papa," said Mansoor.

"That's what I thought. Because today I heard some relatives saying they had gone to pick up Vikas's watch," Sharif said. "That's all. I was just checking."

Having chased down the leads, having talked to the boy, having come to see there was no one else to blame, Vikas succumbed to shame. He felt his entire life had been a failure and that it was this failure, particularly the failure to make money, that had brought him to this point: if they'd had a driver, how could this have happened? He kept apologizing to his wife. "I told you I should have gone back to being a CA," he said, referring to the career as a chartered accountant he had given up thirteen years before to make documentaries. "I'll do anything for you."

But Deepa wanted only one thing: revenge. Having passed rapidly through the stages of grief, she had emerged at a clearing of rage and felt the only reasonable thing was to watch the boys' killers die a violent death. "Do you think they've actually arrested the right people?" she asked Vikas.

As usual, the police had made a few arrests right after the blast.

"God only knows, Deepa—I'm so sorry."

When would this pain end? Vikas wondered. He'd experienced nothing like this—had never known a pain that could slip into every fold of the body—and he could only imagine what his delicate wife was going through. She was not a healthy person to begin with—her lung had collapsed some years before, and cancer ran amok in her family—and he worried that this uprightness, this forced bright rage, was a prelude to serious illness.

The family continued to surround them. But now the advice grew more specific. Bunty Masi suggested they see a guru she visited in GK. "Talk about a great spirit. He touches your hand once and half your problems disappear. Remember how bad Mansha's leukoderma was? Absolutely gone." Pratap Tau said grief made people holy and they should consider having another child during this period. "Adoption is also a possibility," a do-gooder added (the house was full of do-gooders). Rajat offered to buy his brother and sister-in-law an all-expenses-paid tour to Switzerland. "May-June is the best time to go," he said, smiling awkwardly. "There are very nice waterfalls."

These people bewildered Vikas. But then again, they had never suffered such a loss, had never really known his kids. To them, every child born into the family was the same, a continuation of genetic material. He remembered why he had cut himself off from these people in the first place.

Deepa grew more and more adamant that they press the police to find the killers. Then, one day, to everyone's surprise, it happened: the police said they had arrested the terrorists.

TERRORISTS

MAY 1996

---

CHAPTER 3

Soon after Shaukat "Shockie" Guru received the order to carry out the blast, he went to his alley and washed his face under the open tap outside the building. Then he entered his room and sat on the bed, brooding. The room was small, foggy with dust, ripe with the smell of chemical reagents (there had been construction recently in the alley), poorly painted. The sole decoration was a poster of a slick-bellied Urmila Matondkar from *Rangeela*. Two charpais lay separated by a moat of terrazzo. The mattress under him was thin. He felt the coir through the clotted cotton.

After a while, he went back into the alley, where afternoon was announcing itself in the form of clothes hung out to dry between buildings and the particular yawning honking that comes from cars when the sun is high overhead, dwarfing human activity, and he went to the PCO and called home. It was his ritual to call home before setting out on a mission. His mother thought he was a student in Kathmandu—at least she made him believe she thought that—and he wanted to give her an opportunity to save him. She is the only one who has the right to decide whether I live or die, he often thought when he smelled milk boiling in the shops—yes, that was the smell he associated with his mother and with Kathmandu. It gave Kathmandu a sweet, plasticky flavor. Of all natural substances, milk has the most artificial smell.

Shockie was the leading bomb maker of the Jammu and Kashmir Islamic Force, which operated out of exile in Nepal. An avuncular-looking man of twenty-six, he had catlike green eyes, wet lips, and curly hair already balding on the vast egg of his head. His arms were fat rods under his kurta. In the past four years he had killed dozens of Indians in revenge for the military oppression in Kashmir, expanding the JKIF's "theater of violence," as the newspapers called it.

Now he pushed the receiver close to his ear in the PCO booth. Deep in a crater of silence on the other side of the Himalayas, the phone rang. The phone was a drill seeking out life. "You're sick," he imagined saying to his mother. "Should I come?"

His mother had been a presswali her entire life, and had developed a tumor in her stomach after years of exposure to the hot coals in the heavy, radiant, red-jawed iron, an iron that was shaped like a medieval torture device, something you might want to trap a head in. No one had been able to cure her. And yet she always refused his offer. This time, the phone wasn't even picked up (it wasn't her phone—it belonged to Shockie's cousin, Javed, who lived a few minutes from his mother in Anantnag, in Kashmir). Sweat distorted the air before Shockie's eyes in the suffocating cabin of the PCO, with its thrum of phone voices. Back in his room, he asked his friend and roommate, Malik, "Should I not go?"

Malik—a slow, deliberate, hassled man at the best of times, the sort who seems to be exhaling deeply against the troubles of the world—said, "You're making excuses." He was sitting curled up on his charpai.

"I fear that she's back to work again. My brother is ruthless and callous. He never did anything growing up and he's used to being taken care of, and she likes taking care of people." He spat. "Do you think this is a wise mission?"

"Not wiser or unwiser than anything else."

"This is the first time Javed hasn't picked up," Shockie said, unzipping his fake Adidas cricket kit bag.

A journey to Delhi to plant a bomb did not require much, at least in the way of equipment. Most of the stuff you needed you bought there. That way no one could trace you to your source. You destroy a city with the material it conveniently provides. But every respectable revolutionary needs a few changes of clothes, and Shockie, on his knees in his shabby room, folded two shirts and a pair of black pants into the kit bag. On the journey, he knew, he would have to dress in pajamas and a kurta—brown rags. He was supposed to be a farmer attending an agro-conference near Azamgarh, in Uttar Pradesh.

These agro-conferences were among the most fascinating things about India. They happened several times a year, in far-flung parts of the country. Tinkerers and crackpots showed up, hawking inventions to solve irrigation problems and plowing "inefficiencies"; a good number claimed to have invented perpetual motion machines (Shockie remembered a machine shaped like a calf with a swinging leg). The farmers, dismissed by urban Indians as bumpkins, roamed in gangs, examining the machines, discussing the finer points with the inventors. They were the audience for these raucous fairs held under tents in eroded Indian fields. The farmers were uniformly suspicious. They were taken in by nothing. Shockie—who had attended a fair to buy pipes for a large new bomb the group was building, as well as to purchase gunny sacks of ammonium nitrate and other fertilizer—was impressed. When he heard another one was happening in UP, he decided to disguise himself as a farmer in tribute. After stuffing a few old farmers' newspapers in his kit bag, Shockie patted his hair into place, as if it needed to be coaxed into traveling with him.

The next day, with Meraj, another agent, he left by bus for the Indo-Nepal border at Sunauli.

Meraj and he were both in tattered kurtas. The bus, rattling over bad roads, usually took eight hours to Sunauli. Today it took almost ten. The landscape, a wild scrawl of reddish terraces and gushing private rivers, came right up to the bus, nearly shattering it. The dug-up road heralded the air with red dust. Plants with plastic bags over their heads crossed their leaves in surrender. A baby in the back screamed the entire way. Shockie and Meraj shifted on their shared seat, trying to apply enough pressure to keep Nepalis from sitting next to them.

When Meraj, an absent-looking fellow with a disarmingly stupid face you could consider capable of nothing dangerous, picked dandruff off his hair and sniffed his fingers, Shockie said, "Don't do that."

"OK," he said, smiling nervously. But he had obviously not understood Shockie's command and soon smelled his fingers again.

"That," Shockie said.

At the border in Sunauli, a town reveling in its own filth, the policeman in the Indian immigration hut gazed at them for far too long. Shockie and Meraj remained impassive, but when they were halfway out, the policeman suddenly shouted after them. "You're meat eaters?"

"We're farmers. We told you," Shockie said quietly.

"But you're of the terrorist religion, no?" the policeman said. A dandy, his mustache was trimmed to the same depth as his eyebrows. "I've lived among you bastards and you're all Pakistanis. Now go."

Shockie and Meraj walked quickly to the Indian side, disappearing into a crowd of truck drivers. When they came across a small dhaba selling sandwiches wrapped in plastic, with a grassy patch in the back, they collapsed on the ground, breathing heavily. Meraj counted out money for ketchup sandwiches, but kept fumbling the notes.

Suddenly, Shockie burst out, "How much did they give you?"

"Two thousand," Meraj said.

"Two thousand." Shockie shook his head. "You think it's enough?"

Meraj kept smiling—but it was a vacant, expectant smile. "It's not bad."

"Nonsense," Shockie said. "Do you know how much Abdul makes at the shop alone?" Abdul was the leader of the group, a thirty-year-old who ran a carpet shop and also taught in the local school. "Fifty thousand," Shockie said.

"Where, yaar?"

"I've seen it with my own eyes. And that's on top of the dana we're getting from Karachi." Dana was counterfeit money. The Jammu and Kashmir Islamic Force prided itself on being composed entirely of native Indian Kashmiris, but received funding from NGOs run by the ISI, Pakistan's intelligence agency. "But why share it with us?" Shockie said. "We're little people. We're only making chocolate." "Making chocolate," the code for bomb making. "You know how in restaurants they have a mundu who helps the cook? That's the amount of respect we get. We're *servants*." He snapped a Kit Kat they'd bought from the dhaba. "Listen to how it snaps. What a delicate sound. It sounds like *money*. They probably spent more for this one chocolate, in setting up the factory, than they give *us* for one chocolate." He put a piece in his mouth.

Meraj watched.

Shockie said, "These small chocolates will achieve nothing."

Meraj shook his head absently.

"You're listening?" Shockie said. "Fuck it. It's useless talking to you."

This was not the best attitude to have, since they were soon on a five-hour bus to Gorakhpur, in India. A diesel-perfumed monster, its seats appeared ready to come loose from their moorings on the metal floor. Shockie looked out angrily at the landscape as Meraj drenched his shoulder with drool. How had this arid, dusty, ruthless part of the world become his life? Fighting for Kashmiri independence, he hadn't seen Kashmir in two years; he was an exile, and in those two years, he feared (with the unreasonable worry of all exiles) that Kashmir would have changed. What if it had become like *this* after all the warfare? What if the green had been exhausted and the placid mirror of Dal Lake had been smashed, revealing layers of dead bodies and desert that lay on the lake bed?

When he'd been growing up in the late eighties and early nineties, he was convinced that the bottom of the lake was choked with bodies, that each taut stem of lotus or water hyacinth tugged at the neck of a drowned person like a noose. Sometimes his friends and he boarded a shikara and went trawling, running their hands through the water, jumping back if they touched something or if they saw a small drop of red floating by.

When Shockie looked out of the window again, it was evening. It occurred to him through his sleep that maybe even Uttar Pradesh had once been as pretty as Kashmir—only to be despoiled by wars and invasions.

Gorakhpur is one of the armpits of the universe. The best thing that can be said about it is that it is better than Azamgarh, which, along with

Moradabad, competes in an imaginary inverse beauty pageant for the title of the world's ugliest town.

Shockie and Meraj disembarked and checked in to their usual hotel—a half-finished concrete building that had once been a godown and was crowned with rooms in a gallery on the first floor and now called Das Palace. (Though *they* called it Udaas Palace—Sad Palace.)

The room was even more awful than the ones they were assigned in Kathmandu. Mosquitoes swarmed through the gaps in the doorframe—the door did not fit properly. Meraj, alert after his nap on the bus, smeared his body with Odomos. "There's Japanese encephalitis here," he said, offering the tube to Shockie and savoring the name of the disease: he had once been a compounder.

Shockie accepted moodily. Alexander the Great had died from a mosquito bite, from malaria, he knew.

In the morning, when they had drunk tea served by the hunchback, the only apparent employee of the hotel, they went to visit the Jain.

The Jain sat on a cushion in an impeccable house, impeccable only on the inside, of course: outside was a heap of roiling, shifting garbage, a heap that seemed a living thing with rats burrowing through it—swimming, really, floating in an unreal paradise of gnawables with pigs pushing aside layers of plastic and rotten trembling fruit with their snouts.

But the Jain's house, built like a Gujarati kothi, was oblivious to all this. The Jain was a boulder of a man with smooth coal-colored skin and a bald head offset by two equal tufts of hair. His nose was a beautiful chorus of tiny pores. He had large dark hands, whitish on the inside. He sat on his knees on a cushion in a white kurta, the rock of his paunch balanced before him. "I had orchiopexy, you see—you know what that is?" he started. "When one of your testes doesn't descend." He must have been twenty-nine, thirty. No one in this world was very old. "For years I had lots of pain, and though I was strong, I couldn't run without losing my breath and getting a sharp pain in my torso. I used to always wonder why." The servant set down three earthen cups of tea; the Jain accepted his cup daintily in his large hands. "Now that I've had surgery I have all this energy. I can run five kilometers without stopping."

Where does the poor fellow run in this dump? Shockie wondered. But ideas of health, Western ideas, were spreading everywhere. Shockie himself was obsessed with exercise, with hanging from a rod in his doorway.

"Anyway," the Jain said, putting his large hands on his thighs, thighs the size of cricket bats, "I overdid it, so I have been advised to rest. Hence this cushion under me."

A fan turned overhead, raising a delicious current from the layers of sleeping air. It was dark in the drawing room, a welcome respite from the May heat of Gorakhpur.

The servant brought a VIP suitcase with a numbered lock and the Jain twisted it open on his lap. "Count it," he said.

Meraj and Shockie each took a bundle in their hands and petaled the notes. Shockie was sleepy and slightly delirious; the room had a fan but not much air, and the smell of fresh money made him high. He kept losing count only to realize he'd been thinking of nothing, or rather, thinking of himself thinking.

When they had finally accounted for all the money, they dumped it into their kit bag and went off.

"You see what I was saying?" Shockie said, as they waited on the railway platform for the train to Delhi. "What we get is just a tip."

The money was not for them. It was to be dropped off with an agent in Delhi, part of a hawala money-laundering operation that sustained the group.

"But this is also for chocolate," Meraj said, speaking with the dazed clarity that comes to people in extreme heat.

"Just like that, it's for chocolate? If they have so many funds, why do you think they still bother to send us on such a long journey? Use your brain for once, Meru."

The train from Gorakhpur to Delhi could take anywhere from fifteen to thirty hours, depending on the mood of the driver, the state of the tracks, accidents, and random occurrences. Meraj and Shockie settled into a third-class non-A/C sleeper compartment. Shockie was in a tired, despairing mood. He always got this way before action. It was like an advance mourning for his life. The vibrating bunks, stacked three to a wall; the mournful synthetic covers of the bunks, torn in places and looking smashed, with the webbed look of smashed things; the racing wheels underneath, like ladders of vertebrae being whipped; the sense of abject stinking wetness surrounding a train's journey through the universe—all these things filled Shockie with futility. The bogey was a jail cell ferrying him to a destiny he did not desire, his jaw on edge like the stiff end of his mother's iron.

Bougainvillea bloomed insanely here and there in the landscape.

Meraj kept waking up and falling asleep on the bunk across (they both had top bunks) and Shockie considered him with pity, surprise, even tenderness: people were closest to animals when they were sleeping and fighting for wakefulness. Or dying and fighting for life. What is Meraj dreaming about? he wondered. Probably the same thing as me—his own death—only through the obfuscating membrane of sleep. Meraj had been pulled out of a chemist's and beaten and tortured by the Jammu and Kashmir Police a few years before.

At desolate stations in the depths of the subcontinent, Shockie got out and smoked, observing the blight of mildew on the walls, kicking away the twisted, disabled beggars who crowded around his feet cawing about their Hindu gods.

At the Old Delhi Railway Station, twenty hours after they had set out from Gorakhpur, an agent met them. The agent was a tall, hippy, pimply, nervous fellow in tight black new jeans. Shockie disliked him immediately. He had the slick, proprietary attitude that small men from big cities sometimes bring toward big men from small cities. He lorded everything over them. He didn't help them with their cricket kit bags. He asked them if they had ever been to Delhi before.

"Yes, hero," Shockie said, setting his emotional lips in a smirk.

"Let's go in different directions and meet at the car. It's parked behind," the agent, whose name was Taukir, said.

"Why do you want to do that?" Shockie said.

"You never know about the police these days."

"No," Shockie said. "What's safer is that we go together."

The key to not being caught, Shockie knew, was to behave confidently.

They walked through the annihilating crowds to the car. From the high steel roofs of the station, birds raced down, avoiding a jungle gym of rafters and rods. People pressed and pushed as the trains hurtled through their routes of shit and piss, plastic and rubber burning weirdly in the background, spicing the air. The station was so bloated with people that the loss of a few would hardly be tragic or even important.

When a Sikh auntie leading a coolie into a maroon train jostled Shockie, Shockie shouted, "Hey!"

"Move!" the woman shrieked at him.

"You move, you witch."

And with that, she was gone, swallowed up by the dark maw of the train.

Invigorated, he lit a cigarette, broadening his shoulders as he brought the light to the Gold Flake hanging from his lips. He had always enjoyed the rudeness of Delhi.

A few minutes later, in Taukir's Maruti 800, Shockie gripped the plastic handrest above the window and looked out. Delhi—baked in exquisite concrete shapes—rose, cracked, spread out. It made no sense—the endlessness, the expanse. In Kashmir, no matter how confusing a town was, you could always shrink it down to size by looking at it from a hill. Delhi—flat, burning, mixed-up, smashed together from pieces of tin and tarpaulin, spreading on the arid plains of the North—offered no respite from itself. Delhi never ended. The houses along the road were like that too: jammed together, the balconies cramped with cycles, boxes, brooms, pots, clotheslines, buckets, the city minutely re-creating itself down to the smallest cell. From one balcony a boy with a runny nose waved to another. A woman with big haunches sat astride a stool next to a parked scooter; she was peeling onions into a steel plate and laughing. Before municipal walls painted with pictures of weapon-toting gods—meant to keep men from urinating— men urinated. Delhi. Fuck. I love it too.

Taukir lived with two spinsterish sisters and a mother whose eyes were dreamy with cataracts. The ladies served a hot lunch of watery daal and tinda and ghia, but Shockie was so excited he could barely eat. "No, no, bas," he said, whenever the younger of the sisters, not unattractive, gave him a phulka. The man and his house seemed very modern, with many cheap clocks adorning the walls; you had a sense that whatever money the family had earned had been spent on clothes. "When can we go to buy the materials for the chocolate?" Shockie asked Taukir.

Shockie wasn't sure how much the sisters knew; he felt proud and confident nevertheless, puffed up like the phulka he set about tearing on his steel plate.

Taukir provided several ideas for where they could go.

"Chawri Bazaar is better than all those," Shockie said.

After wiping his mouth with a towel, he signaled to Meraj and they went out to buy materials.

A car bomb is made by putting together a 9V battery, an LPG cylinder, a clock, a transformer, a mining detonator, and four meters of wire—red and yellow, to distinguish circuits. The cylinder is then put in the dicky while the wiring and the timer are packed in the bonnet.

The clock was easy to buy—they got it from a shop in Chandni Chowk, the Red Fort a merciless mirage in the distance. The 9V battery they acquired from an electrician's shop in Jangpura, where an old Punjabi man sat among sooty tables taking paternal pride in every piece of equipment. Shockie understood the fellow. He himself took a certain sensual, even feminine, pleasure in shopping for materials for a bomb; he might have been a man out to buy wedding fixtures for his beloved sister. But he had to keep his instinct for haggling and jolliness to a minimum. You had to make as little an impression as possible, and it was crucial to get material of the highest possible quality for the lowest possible price. You did not want your bomb to go *phut* when the day came—something that happened all the time, even to the best bomb makers. It had certainly happened to Shockie. One of his bombs had fizzled and let out a small burp of fire. This was in a market in Jaipur. He ran away before being caught, but two of his fingers were burned and had to be chopped off at the ends. He lost some feeling in his hand too, but it was for the best. It marked him as serious. When bomb makers met each other, they inevitably looked at each other's hands.

Taukir came along with them on these excursions, looking alternately keen-eyed and lanky and then despondent and distracted, one arm looped behind his back and clutching the other hand in that lackadaisical, half-stand-at-ease, half-chastised posture that is the hallmark of bored people at rest.

They shopped in a conspicuous group of three because the Indian police often prosecuted terrorists on circumstantial evidence, trying to damn them with statements like, "Why was he shopping alone with a shawl pulled over his face?" Thus, the revolutionaries reasoned, if you had three people carrying out a task meant for one, you defeated the police's logic with your illogic.

After two days of shopping in different parts of Delhi and arranging the materials on the floor of a room in Taukir's house—a room that obviously belonged to the sisters and mother, who had been sent away to the village the day after Shockie and Meraj arrived—Shockie said, "Now, let's see the car. It's still parked outside?"

Taukir let out a noncommittal sound.

"You've parked it somewhere else?" Shockie repeated, getting up from his chair and smoothing his curly hair, an unnatural motion for a man who liked the puffs and curls of his plumage.

"Ji, sir, that's my car," Taukir said, finding his voice.

"And where's the car for us?" Shockie said.

"Well, we have to steal it."

"I see," Shockie said. "Let me go steal it now."

Before Taukir could react, Shockie was up and heading outside the house. He came across Taukir's 800, the one in which they'd been driven from the station. Like every other vehicle in Delhi, it was a dented and dirt-spattered specimen, ruined as an old tooth.

As if conducting an examination, Shockie put his fist through the front window. The window came away, the crystalline fracture smeared with blood from his hairy arm.

"No!" Taukir screamed, coming outside. "What are you doing, sir?"

But Shockie said nothing, simply walking away, drops of blood falling on the earth.

The May heat was horrifying, violating the privacy of all things while also forcing you into yourself. Shockie closed his eyes against the ferocious prehistoric explosions of the sun. As he looked for a PCO from which to call headquarters and abort the mission—he had tied up his minor wound with a hankie—he cursed under his breath. *They fucking want freedom but this fucking cheapness will never go away.*

When Shockie had headed out for the mission from Kathmandu, he had been reassured that he would *not* need to steal a car—he had fumbled this crime before, and besides, he disliked all aspects of the job that made him feel like a common criminal.

Packets of gutka dangled in front of a shop like strings on a bride's veil. Within the shop, the shopkeeper fished out items from the shelves with a pole. Shockie was about to ask the man if he knew where he could find a PCO when his eyes fell on another Maruti 800, parked on the side of the road—an ugly little blue thing with maroon fittings, tinted windows, and colorful plastic floral designs taped to the top of the windscreen.

The street was dense with scooters and bicyclists.

In a matter of seconds, Shockie bounded up to the car, hugged himself against the onslaught of vehicles and people, and then, in a swift motion that would have shocked anyone watching this avuncular fair fellow from a distance, put his hands on the petrol cap, stuck a blade under the metal, heaved with all his might, and ripped it off.

Every muscle in his left hand—his stronger hand, after that debacle in Jaipur—was afire. Carrying the petrol cap in his hand, making heavy strides in the traffic, he walked to Taukir's house.

———————

Back at the house, Meraj and Taukir were playing cards on a sofa in sulky silence, light filtering dustily through the old Punjabi-style grilles of the house. The sofa had been put together by joining two metal trunks and covering it with a dhurrie.

"While you were sitting, I've done the job," Shockie said, coming in. He handed them the petrol cap.

"Was the car close by?" Meraj asked, turning it over.

Taukir looked away.

"Give me some water and go get a key made," Shockie instructed them.

While Taukir and Meraj had the key made at a shop (this was a flaw in the 800's design; the key used to open the petrol cap could also be used to start the car), Shockie feasted at a local dhaba and admired the women at the tables with their gluttonous husbands.

He wanted to ram his penis into their wives. He imagined pinning the dhaba owner's wife on a table and ripping off her kurta. Soon after, he went up to her and asked for another paratha. "Just one?" she said. She wore a nose ring and was obviously recently married.

"Yes, madam," he said, with the exceeding politeness of a man who has just imagined raping you.

Meraj and Taukir returned with a new key.

But in the morning, when the three men walked down the alleys to the spot where Shockie had found the blue Maruti, it was gone.

"Bhainchod," Shockie said. "I thought it belonged to that shopkeeper. It must be in the lane behind this one."

But after looking for a few hours, searching the neighborhood in an auto, they had still found nothing.

So now, their mental scores settled, they did what they would have normally done—went to Nizamuddin, a rich neighborhood; found a shabby car orphaned outside a fancy house; stole the petrol cap; had the key made (at a different shop) and returned the next day and drove it away.

———————

In an alley near Taukir's house, they removed the license plates from the stolen car, packed wires in the bonnet, and put the LPG cylinder in the back. Like a person sprinkling petals on a bed, Shockie grimly filled the dicky with nails and ball bearings and scrap. He rued the lack of ammonium nitrate—it would have been good to visit the agro fair and buy a sack. Fertilizer was more explosive than natural gas.

This part of the operation was the most dangerous—scarier than running amok in Delhi with the police possibly at your back. Bomb makers, like most people, are undone not by others but by themselves. Shockie knew countless stories of bomb makers who had lost eyes, limbs, hands, dicks to premature explosions; knew operatives who'd succeeded in blackening and burning their faces so that the skin peeled off for months and ran down their backs in rivulets and they looked like hideous ghouls, unable to do the anonymous work of revolution without exciting the pitying, curious stares of onlookers—the same looks you hoped to elicit for the craters you left behind.

Even the greats were not immune to this curse of bomb makers, Shockie knew. Take Ramzi Yousef. He flew to New York in 1993 without a visa, snuck into the country after being let go from an immigration prison in Queens (it was overcrowded), and then, after setting off practice fertilizer bombs in the New Jersey countryside, hired a man at a local mosque to drive a rented van packed with explosives into the basement of the World Trade Center.

The night the bomb went off, buckling but not capsizing the first tower, injuring thousands but killing only three, Yousef flew first class on Pakistan International Airlines over the plumes of his explosion. All good. But then he got to Pakistan and tried to assassinate Benazir Bhutto and ended up in the hospital with burns (the pipe bomb he'd been preparing exploded in his face as he tried to clean the lead azide in the pipe). The police suspected him and he had to run away. A year or two later, he found himself in Manila. His plan was now to assassinate the Pope, who was visiting, and Bill Clinton, who was coming to one-up the Pope. His comrades and he had robes and crosses with which to Christianize themselves. On a plane from Manila to Tokyo, testing out a new device, he attached a tiny explosive fashioned from a Casio Databank watch under his seat. When he got off at

Seoul's airport, the stopover, a Japanese businessman took his place. In midair, en route from Seoul to Tokyo, the seat exploded, painting the inner ribs of the aircraft with the guts of the businessman. The plane, weaving wildly through the air like a gutless firework rocket, did not crash.

So now, back in his Manila flat, Yousef—invincible, a genius of terror, perhaps the greatest terrorist who ever lived—cooked a virulent soup of chemicals on the stove. Or no. He was cooking to get rid of the evidence. But as the chemicals vanished, huge clouds of smoke appeared and his comrades and he fled the apartment in fright, leaving behind chemistry books, canisters of fertilizer, passports, wires, Rough Rider condoms.

Yousef escaped to Pakistan but was arrested later in a hotel in Islamabad as he puffed his hair with gel and stuck explosives up the ass of a doll.

A genius of terror. Shockie's heart pounded. He wanted to be like Yousef, the Kashmiri Yousef, but even Yousef, who had shocked America— who had almost toppled a building that seemed to snick heaven like a finger, who had tried to blow up jetliners over the Pacific and kill the Pope—even Yousef was fallible.

Shockie prayed as he attached the wires in the corroded belly of the car. Like so many rich people's cars, it was poorly maintained.

He blew the dust from the machinery with his mouth and inhaled the rich petroleum blackness. He made the other two men stand with him as he risked his face.

The bomb did not explode during assembly. But afterwards he was tired; he had a headache and his arms hurt—more so than when he had violently tugged the scab of the petrol cap from the rump of the Maruti—and he stayed up all night on the bed of the spinsters, his head throbbing and the city mocking him with its million nocturnal honks, wondering: What will it be for? Am I ruining it by not sleeping? Will my nerves be too shot to pull off the blast?

They drove the car to the market the next evening. They were all bathed, and they had all gone to the mosque and prayed—even Shockie, who

found prayer distasteful and feminine. They were in good clothes and disguised with thick spectacles and false mustaches (Meraj wore dark glasses,
for contrast). If anyone asked them, they were to say they had come to buy
clothes and gifts for their sister's wedding. They'd even brought pictures of
a woman in a fake marriage album (not one of Taukir's sisters but a random
pinup girl ripped from the walls of a seedy photography studio) to show
how they were trying to buy wedding bangles that matched her dupatta.

Shockie, in the middle of the night, unable to sleep, had masturbated to
this woman, completing the fantasy that had begun with the dhaba owner's
bride.

The market was packed—just as he had hoped. It was a Sunday. Driving
carefully through the obstacle course of pedestrians and cyclists and thelas,
they entered the central square of Lajpat Nagar Market—if you could call
it a square. Encroachment had softened the sides and the corners of the
market; there were buildings and shacks on all sides, and a park in the
middle with a rusted fence and rubbish collecting on the brown mound
where grass had once grown. Shockie was pleased with this choice of
venue. He'd visited Lajpat Nagar on his previous trip to Delhi and had
decided, with his friend Malik, that it would make an excellent target.

They parked the car in front of Shingar Dupatte, a women's clothing shop.

Afire with nervous tics, they came out of the car. Shockie smoothed his
hair, Meraj put on his dark glasses, and Taukir dusted off his tight black jeans.

Quite suddenly, a man appeared before them. "You can't park here," he
said.

"Sir?" said Shockie.

"My son has to park his car here." The man was the owner of Shingar
Dupatte—a short bald fellow with a mustache and a granitic head that
appeared to hold every shade of brown.

"And who's your son—the king of Delhi?" Taukir asked.

"Come on, it's OK," Shockie said.

At first he was appalled that Taukir would risk searing himself into the
man's memory with an argument, but later he was grateful: Taukir had
behaved as any rude Delhiite would, and besides, they were disguised.

Now, getting back into the car and reversing it, Shockie said, "Next time be quiet." This was already the worst mission he'd ever been on, he decided; his mind swarmed with images of the police, of torture, of life coming to a sudden end in Delhi. The only way out was to park close enough to Shingar Dupatte so that the nosy, rude proprietor—and his son—were killed. "You guys get out now and I'll park. That guy is going to come after us again and ask us to move."

They did as he instructed, and Shockie maneuvered the car in front of a framing shop.

Within the shop, he caught sight of oil paintings of mountains—things yellowy and oozy with paint; a golden Ganesh; a Christ on a cross; a Rajasthani village woman. It was like a flashback a man might have as he dies, all the odd significant objects swirling into view over the heads of humming, commercially active humans.

He parked, jumped out, and walked away. He pressed a small jerry-rigged antenna in his hand and activated the timer, set to go off in five minutes. The proprietor of the framing shop looked at him but Shockie smiled and waved back—as if he were a regular customer—and the man, seated fatly behind a counter, one of those counters that have a money drawer, looked confused and then smiled and waved back.

Shockie walked away from the central square. "Don't look; keep moving," he told the other men as he came across them in an alley. After a while they made it to the main road.

But the market—the market was noisy in its normal way. There was no disruption, no blast, nothing. "Shit," Shockie said. "But let's wait."

They threaded their way through the dark alleys, sweating, bad-breathed, anxious, melting in the heat. "It must be the cylinder," Shockie said finally, realizing the bomb had not gone off. "Let me go back and get it," he said. "Something must have gone wrong." He was ashamed. The eyes of his comrades were on him. Failure was failure—explanations solved nothing. His bravado had been for naught.

"We'll come," Meraj said.

"You should have helped when it was needed," Shockie said. "Now what's the point?"

"What if it goes off when you get in?" asked Taukir.

"Then do me a favor and say I martyred myself purposely."

The car was still there when he went back. For effect, he entered the framing shop. "How are you?" he said, bringing together his palms for the proprietor.

"Good, good. Business is fine—what else can one want?"

The proprietor was fair and doggish, with worry lines contorting his forehead. He had a serious look on his face, as if being surrounded by so many frames had made him conscious of being framed himself, of being watched.

Shockie went back to the car. As he turned the ignition, there were tears in his eyes. Instinctively preparing himself, he put a palm over his dick.

So this was how it would end. Pulling the gears, he backed out of the spot.

"I know what went wrong," Shockie said, when they were back in Taukir's house.

"What?" said Taukir, now feeling much closer to Shockie.

Shockie pointed to the yellow wires that he'd clipped from the contraption in the bonnet, picking them up in a loop the way one may pick up a punished animal by the ears. They had frayed in the heat.

"Let's just go tomorrow and try again," Meraj said irritably. He just wished the mission to be over.

"We can't," Taukir said. "The market is closed on Mondays. But Tuesday is a big day because it's the day after it's closed."

"We better send a message back to base," Meraj said sleepily. "The election is in four days." The bomb in Delhi was meant to be a signal to the central government about the elections they were organizing in Kashmir.

"Tell them that it was a wiring problem," Shockie replied. "They'll understand."

But Shockie was chastened. They were all chastened and disappointed with each other. Like men who have failed together, they wanted nothing more than to never see each other again.

On Tuesday, Shockie went alone to the market. But there was no pleasure in it. It was all anticlimax. And he could see the faces of the framing shop owner and the owner of Shingar Dupatte, how they would react when the bomb went off; and he felt sad, the way one always did when one knew the victims even a little.

CHAPTER 4

After the blast, Shockie returned to Kathmandu, retracing his steps, reading the news whenever he could.

The *Times of India* featured a picture of a blasted stray dog.

When Shockie got back to the base in Nayabazar—he had separated from Taukir and Meraj, who had gone elsewhere, into hiding—he was surprised to find himself embraced as a hero. "You killed two hundred," Masood said. "God bless you."

"It was more like fifty," Shockie said, immediately disgusted by his own lie. He tended to believe the Indian papers on this subject. They had no incentive to play down the horrors.

"Our reports say a hundred at a minimum," Masood said.

Shockie did not say anything further.

It was only when he went out for a walk later with his friend Malik that he burst out, "I'm thinking of defecting."

"Tell me why," Malik said, exhaling deeply.

Once Shockie started, he couldn't stop. He felt the leadership of the group was corrupt and in denial, prone to inflating figures to get more funding; that they were siphoning money to build big houses for themselves and sending their children abroad but not providing even the minimum for blasts in Delhi—why else had only thirteen died?—that they were ideologically weak, not realizing that one big blast achieved much more, in terms of influencing policy, than hundreds of small ones; that one of the militant leader's sons was studying in England—granted, Ramzi Yousef had also studied in Swansea, Wales, but then he was from a rich Kuwaiti-Baluchi family. . . .

But mostly Shockie felt there was no innovation when it came to bombs.

"You just have a habit of complaining," Malik said.

"That's not true."

"It's true, yaar. Even if the blast had been huge, you would have complained. Now, what do you want? That the whole country fall to its knees? This isn't America, bhai. There the people are rich and they wait excitedly for tragedy. You set off a small pataka and they cry." Malik hadn't been to the U.S., but he was a big reader, and this fluent authority brought tears of satisfaction to his eyes. "Whereas a city like Delhi—what can you do?"

"We could try Parliament, like I told Abdul."

"Leave the Parliament. There's too much security."

"What about Teen Murti or IIC? FICCI. World Trade Center. Oberoi."

"You are not getting my point," Malik said, shaking his head. "Delhi is a Muslim city, with a Muslim history and Muslim monuments. If you want to shake people, you have to attack Muslim targets. It makes our decision to attack harder. And when you look at the new construction, it's all Punjabi and awful. No one cares if it falls." Happy with this irony, he smiled broadly.

"Whatever it is, there should have been more damage," Shockie said. "I looked at it after I left. I shouldn't have done that—it was dangerous—but the bomb only made a *phut* sound and I thought better to look than waste a month of work. Nothing happened, yaar. A few buildings fell. A few people were burning." He looked at his friend, trying to gauge his response to this violent reenactment. "My personal philosophy is, if we're fighting a war, we should try to kill people, not injure them. You've seen what injury does." Malik had a limp from being severely beaten by the military years ago. It was a turning point for their friendship and their involvement with the conflict. Shockie had knifed a soldier on Malik's behalf. From that time on they had been inseparable, tied to each other even if they didn't quite want to be. Their relationship, really, was a kind of marriage, held in place by a massive history. "How is your foot?" Shockie asked.

"Fine, fine," Malik said. "Pain is all in the mind." Talking about his foot put him in a bad mood and he changed the subject. "Were you able to go to Sagar?"

Sagar was their favorite restaurant in Delhi.

"Not this time."

Now they walked in happy silence, Shockie contemplating Malik's injury and their joint past, Malik contemplating the road, the hills, the twisting smoke fires. He was a bright person with a wonderful eye for detail; the limp had slowed him down, but it had also slowed the world around him. He missed nothing and he remembered everything; when he closed his eyes he could re-create a landscape down to the smallest leaf.

This was how he calmed himself through moments of pain. He painted too—it was a good way to make use of his photographic memory.

The two men arrived at a valley packed with boulders of many sizes and a clear mountain stream and they stripped down to their underwear and swam. Malik felt the water against his penis, which had been burned and electrocuted during the torture. Sometimes he felt swimming in natural streams, with their rich purse of minerals, might solve his problems. Shockie, broad and muscled, made unnecessary strokes in the water next to him.

After they were done, they rested on flat rocks and let their bodies roast in the sun. They held hands like lovers, though there was nothing sexual about this.

How could it be that only four days ago I was in Delhi planting a bomb? Shockie wondered. And now I'm here? The birds overhead were fervent in their high-pitched complaints. A surge of brightness passed over him. He hugged Malik and briefly fell asleep.

After this excursion, Shockie went to visit Abdul, the leader of the group.

Abdul was a schoolteacher; when Shockie entered the classroom in the half-caved-in house that served as a school, Abdul was teaching the Sanskrit poet Kālidāsa to a group of rapt ten-year-old girls sitting on the floor with plaited hair and black shoes and gray uniforms, hunched over notebooks. Water leaked from the ceiling to a spot between two girls but they didn't seem to notice. Abdul's hand moved up and down the blackboard and his mouth made mechanical sounds. Set among the schoolgirls, he seemed even taller and bonier than usual, his cheekbones jutting from his face and his fingers fragile and long, an unnecessary shawl around his shoulders. When he saw Shockie, he smiled a weak smile, cut off his lecturing abruptly, and without saying anything to the girls, went to embrace him.

Shockie allowed a half smile as the man's arms went around him. He knew the eyes of twenty girls were on him.

"Welcome back," Abdul said, straightening up and thumping his shoulders. "I was worried about you. When did you arrive?"

"Just yesterday," Shockie said. "Should we go outside?"

"Of course, of course."

As they walked to the carpet shop (another of Abdul's businesses), Shockie crossed a puddle and was reminded of the deep lilac pool of mountain water from the morning.

The bomb—all bombs—seemed far away.

In back of the carpet shop, Shockie talked about the operation in Delhi. "You need to give us more funds," he said. "When I first made the chocolate, no one would eat it. I tried feeding it on the nineteenth, but the shopkeepers refused. I had to take it back and bake it again. Then only it went off on the twenty-first," he said, breaking code without realizing it. "Everything OK?" he asked, with irritation. "You look distracted."

"Yes, yes, but I have good news."

"What?" Shockie said, mildly irritated by the inattention.

"You are going to meet the leader of the Hubli Faction."

The Hubli Faction was a terrorist group based in South India. For years, the members of the JKIF had been trying to extend their links to other terrorist outfits, but without success; Shockie, who had joined the group when he was twenty, and was now twenty-six, had been a chief proponent of this networking. Still, he tried to not show too much enthusiasm. "First listen to me," Shockie said. Speaking slowly, he finished his story about the chocolate in Delhi, sprinkling it with unnecessary details. Eventually, though, he said, "Tell me about the Hubli Faction."

Abdul now gave a confusing story about how he had dealt with several middlemen to finally get in touch with an agent who was running a training camp in the forests near Hubli.

Shockie's mind was elsewhere. He was looking at the objects in this back room: rolled-up carpets, old plastic chairs, buckets. What was he doing here? Were they cracked to have such delusions of grandeur, to think they could shake up India from a carpet shop? And now they were going to meet the Hubli Faction? "When do you want me to go?" he asked.

"Tomorrow," Abdul said.

Shockie fell silent.

"What?" Abdul asked.

"Can Malik come with me?"

Abdul laughed. "You're being serious?"

"Yes."

Abdul laughed again and shook his head.

Malik had a reputation as something of a thinker in the group. This wasn't a positive appellation: he was regularly derided by the others as being effeminate, confused, contradictory, ineffectual, and eccentric. He offered the most fantastic ideas at group meetings at the back of the carpet shop. "We should write letters to the victims and families of victims of attacks," he'd said once. "After all, what these victims go through is similar to what we all have gone through as Kashmiris. Something bad happens to them, they expect the government to help them and instead the government ignores them. Yesterday I was reading in the *Hindustan Times* that most blast victims don't get compensation for two or three years. I'm telling you, all these people—eventually they turn not against us but against the government. If you want a true Islamic revolution in this country—not just fighting selfishly for our small aims—then we need to win over these people, show our solidarity with them, tell them that our hands were tied, we were only trying to expose to them the callousness of the people they have chosen to elect." There were tears in his eyes, as usual, from his own eloquence. "Only then can we depose the central government."

"Anything else, Malik?"

"Yes," he'd say, continuing, everyone watching with bemused expressions and grinning quite openly at each other.

Malik did not appear to notice. But Shockie always felt a little bad for his friend. "You aren't appreciated here," he often said. "You should have been a professor."

"But I can contribute much more as a writer here." Malik was the publisher and propagandist in the group and very proud of it.

Poor innocent Malik! Shockie thought. What could he contribute? He was only tolerated because Shockie was his protector and benefactor and Shockie was the top bomb maker in the group. And yet Shockie loved him. Being in the group meant eschewing relationships with women and this was the closest Shockie could come to re-creating the tenderness one felt toward a woman. They were roommates and Shockie often asked what Malik was reading. Gandhi, he might say. Or Tolstoy. Or Pushkin. What does he make of himself? Shockie wondered. Does he really have no idea how pathetic he is? But Malik appeared innocent about his own oddness. Perhaps the injury to his leg and penis had made him a little blind, had given him the aspect of a holy fool, as if that were the only way to deal with the horror that had been inflicted upon him—Shockie had seen this with other cripples, too: a strange light, maybe the light of death, bleeding around the edges of their dull corneas.

After his meeting with Abdul, Shockie went to his room. When he came in, Malik was praying on a mat laid out between the two charpais. He was a religious person—religion, Shockie thought, that crutch of the weak.

When he was done praying, Malik sat at the edge of the bed, and Shockie told him about the meeting with Abdul. Malik listened with his hands tight around a copy of Gandhi's *Autobiography*, nodding at odd moments.

"You're listening?" Shockie asked. Why were people never listening to him?

"Yes, yes."

"Do you want to come?"

"What will I do, bhai? You know how these people treat me."

"This is an opportunity to change that," Shockie said. "You'll get a little practice. Otherwise our missions are too dangerous for a first-timer. But you don't have to. You can keep letting these people call you a coward."

"It's not that I'm afraid," Malik said. "I think I can be more useful here." He tipped his head toward a cyclostyle machine and some letter-block printing paraphernalia in the corner of the room. As the "publisher" and "propagandist" he churned out pamphlets, posters, manifestos, and warnings against civilians and army officers to be posted on the walls of village houses and GPOs and thanas, all of them written in an overblown apocalyptic style that Abdul said gave him a headache, and that Shockie, as Malik's guardian, always edited.

"Suit yourself," Shockie said.

But he was sad.

That night he stayed up thinking of his mother and imagining a series of girls he had been infatuated with in his village. Where were they now? Was that horrible ox of a weaver really fucking Faiza? (This did not stop him from picturing the act; he liked imagining the private lives of others.) Was Sahar really a mother of two, putting oil on her round stomach? And what about Asma . . . ? In this way, he began to fall asleep. But right when sleep was coming, he got up and said, "You're lazy."

Malik, curled on his charpai, his back against the wall, reading, his toes visible and dirty, said, "What?"

"You should come with me. You have no idea how disrespected you are in the group. They mock you openly. When I told Abdul I wanted to bring you, he laughed and forbade me from doing it."

Malik said nothing.

"When you were talking about Gandhi the other day, they were all laughing. I even tried to signal to you but you were so lost in your conversation. You need to do something. Your position in the group is insecure. If something happens to me, what will you do? That's why I want you to come with me. That way we can be together if something happens."

He felt he had made such a good appeal that he was surprised by Malik's reply. "Maybe you're the coward."

Shockie said nothing.

"Inflicting violence is cowardly. We've talked about that. If we were brave we'd walk into the street and be martyred." He pointed to the *Autobiography*. "You know what Gandhi said Jews should do when faced with the Nazis? Commit mass suicide. Think about that."

Shockie shook his head. "You're cracked."

"So what? What do you think these attacks are going to achieve? Today when you were complaining about the blast not being big enough, I was thinking: It doesn't matter. It's all wrong. Blasts are a way of hiding. If you want to be a hero you have to be a martyr."

"Why don't you propose this to Abdul?"

"Maybe I will."

After Shockie went to sleep, Malik read by the milky tube light fixed over his bed. He read about Gandhi's childhood, his suicide attempt with datura seeds, the shame he felt over the fact that he was having sex at the moment his father died, his weak vegetarian constitution, his struggles with pain and sexual urges—he read all this and thought, "But this is me."

In the morning, when he woke up, Shockie was gone.

Shockie took a shared jeep taxi from Kathmandu to Bhairawa, on the border with India. At Bhairawa he boarded a bus to Gorakhpur, where he spent the night again in Das Palace.

Then, after days of traveling by train—this was his real profession, wasn't it? Traveling?—he came to Hubli.

The Hubli Faction was a small group of Keralite Muslims who planned attacks from a safe house in a forest. They took him to a clearing and wanted to talk about Marxism, revolution, Naxalites, water politics— anything but the issue at hand, which was: arms. Finally they showed him a stash of the most derelict-looking AK-47s Shockie had ever seen and grenades covered in thick dust. Nothing. It was pointless. This was playacting. The country spread around them in the form of a thousand animal sounds: crickets, bats, birds. He thought about what it would mean to die, right now, here—who would remember him? His mother, maybe; possibly Malik—but anyone else? No.

He felt lightheaded in the clearing, in the dry dusk air of the forest, with birds leaping about in the space between trees. A wood fire was going and the members of the Hubli Faction, who got their cues from Rambo, were dressed in black and smoking around this fire.

The next day Shockie took a train back to the Indo-Nepal border. He was in a contrite mood. "I must apologize to Malik," he thought. He never got the chance.

Instead, four days after Shockie left for Hubli, Malik was swept up from his lodgings and arrested.

Malik was brushing his teeth by the open tap when the police came. The four men handcuffed his thin wrists before he could put pants over his underwear.

"What have I done?" he asked.

The police would tell him nothing.

Still, once he was placed in the lockup, he began to relax.

Kashmiris were always being hassled in Nepal for bribes, one oppressed race expressing its particular brotherly cruelty toward another; and besides, the investigator who came to ask him about his recent whereabouts was amiable, distracted.

It was only when Malik caught sight of two bearded Sikh Indian policemen in the crowd of blue Nepali uniforms that he became worried.

The Sikhs were stout and talking fast and Malik put all his fingers in his mouth.

Then the station suddenly emptied and a Nepali policeman keyed open the lockup. "Am I free?" Malik asked.

"In a sense. Very much. Come with me."

Instead, Malik was led to a windowless police van parked outside in the dirt and shoved into the back. He found himself in a metallic cavern, the outside world visible only through small stripes in the metal, the paint on the inside of the van scratched by desperate inmates.

When the Sikhs got into the front and started the ignition, Malik knew he was being taken to India as a suspect for the bombing.

Crouched uncomfortably on the floor of the van, handcuffed, his back against the metallic crown of a tire, Malik watched Nepal disappearing from view, photographing it mentally for what he expected would be years of imprisonment. He had read that the only way to endure solitary confinement—if that was your sentence—was to retreat into your own memories, to open and reread the books stocked in the library of your mind.

He began to cry.

Later, through the openings in the van, through the small grille, Malik saw a clear stream of water—a thread, really; a reel of light and fluid on the earth—and was reminded of his outing with Shockie to the pond two days before. It would be his happiest memory for many years.

CHAPTER 5

Malik was placed in police custody in Delhi on a Sunday. He was tortured for ten days straight.

A month later, he was produced in a Sessions Court in Delhi and united with a group of arrested Kashmiris he didn't recognize. The men stood like scolded schoolboys before the judge, each with a personal police escort at his side. Malik had feared, after all the torture, that he might find himself facing another co-revolutionary who had broken down and come clean. But this wasn't the case.

Gaunt, underslept, hungry, dressed in good clothes (for the sake of appearances), Malik peered out at unfriendly faces in the crowd.

Where's Shockie bhai? he wondered again, as the bald, lipless judge, a man in his sixties, exchanged a few words with a lawyer. Arrested? On the run? Around the room no one looked familiar. But Malik would not have put it past his more impulsive friend to disguise himself and walk into an Indian courtroom and spray the crowd with bullets.

But what if Shockie *was* the informant? Shockie, in his whining, complaining, dissatisfied way, had talked a lot about defection, though this had been just that: talk, a way to fill the existential space between explosions.

A fat, bespectacled, avuncular, wheezing policeman in slippers (Why were all the policemen in slippers? As if they had just rolled out of bed?) clutched Malik's wrist; he smelled of sweat and gutka.

The smell of sweat had become Malik's relentless companion in the past month, in the heat of Delhi, in his small cell that he shared with ten others.

This is the difference between being free and not. Freedom (at least temporarily) from the sweat of others.

Everyone in the courtroom fell silent. The hustle and bustle of the judge's various assistants died down, and only the judge's voice and the stenographer's thwacks could be heard. The judge made a few remarks and read a list of charges against the men. Malik and the others stood in front of the judge, facing him, but all Malik could think about was his hunger. He had been fed his breakfast at six a.m. as usual, but had been given his "lunch" at seven thirty a.m. That was because you could not eat outside the jail. He was dying of thirst and hunger. "Barbarous actions . . . Civilization . . . The killing of innocents," the judge said.

"Bread. Pizza. Chow mein," Malik thought.

MR. AND MRS. KHURANA'S
RESPONSE TO TERROR

1996–1997

CHAPTER 6

Deepa and Vikas and Sharif and Afsheen were in the crowd.
When they had heard about the arrests, they'd been excited, passionately angry, each person exercising his or her fantasy of murder and revenge. Deepa imagined scalding the terrorists' faces with cooking oil. Vikas smashed their heads with blunt metal rods. Afsheen thought, improbably, of delivering injections to their eyes. Sharif, who, in person, was the most bad-tempered of the lot, was the most subdued in his imagination. Slitting their necks quickly would do the trick, he thought.

But when the four victims, or kin of victims, sat in the court and saw the terrorists, observed the state of the room in which they were being processed—the cobwebs blousy in the corners, the guano dissolving the floor, the twitchy fan above barely containing the fire of the afternoon—they became dispirited.

Vikas put his arm around Deepa's narrow frame and pressed her bones. She sat next to him on a plastic chair, tense and perched forward. She had been a good, diligent student and he half-expected her to bring out a notebook and sublimate her rage with flowering handwriting.

The men—bearded, gaunt, fair, dressed in sports windbreakers (as if they'd come from cricket practice)—looked middle-class, harmless. Unlike the criminals the Khuranas had seen in the court complex, they were not even handcuffed. Each man was held at the wrist by a paunchy policeman. One of the prisoners seemed to be on familiar terms with his escort and was laughing and showing his yellow teeth.

Were these the people who had killed her children? Deepa wondered. Their personalities did not add up to a bomb.

She became thoughtful and pensive, confused, shouted back to reality. She was aware, suddenly, that the death of her children was not a metaphysical event, but a *crime*. A firecracker set off by uncaring men in a market. She did not trust the government or the courts to do anything.

After the adjournment, the Khuranas and Ahmeds rose and went out into the heat. "If the next hearing is in September, how long does that mean the case will go on?" Deepa asked. The court complex pressed on them from all sides. In tiny huts sat lawyers amid alcoves of dusty tomes, cracking jokes. Tall British buildings hogged the sky. Men of various sizes and speeds threw their legs along the winding medieval streets, chatting, exchanging information.

Sharif, strolling plumply in slippers, said, "In the past these cases have gone on for five, ten years."

"Because the blast was in Delhi, it'll be faster," Vikas said quickly.

"I've had a lot of experience with the justice system," Sharif said. "It's all about un-law and un-care."

"The important thing is that they've been caught," Afsheen said, her dark glasses lodged up on her head. "It's terrible," she said. "What these courts look like."

In the car, after they had parted ways with the Ahmeds, Deepa said, "When the terrorists come to the court in September I want to be there to speak."

"I'll phone Jaidev and find out," Vikas said obediently. He was marveling, through the windows of the car, at the orange midafternoon indifference of the city—the dropping trees, the flat blocks of government construction stranded in the haze in the distance, the canal by the side of the road with fresh black mud shoveled out on the sides. Everything felt closed after the hearing—all the sense of expectation and possibility was gone. "I wonder how Mansoor is," he said.

"He's alive," Deepa said.

But, at home, when Vikas phoned Jaidev, a lawyer friend he knew from his evening walks, Jaidev told him what he had expected—there was little point in getting involved; the case would drag on; besides, they hadn't been present. The best thing to do, Jaidev said, would be to focus on future events, on the effects of terrorism in society, in setting up a scholarship or a debating prize at the kids' school. "There is nothing to be gained from being involved in the legal system, believe me," Jaidev said, his voice dusky with gutka. "It's barely worth it for us with the current taxation system." Though Vikas knew he made crores.

"Don't you think a mother's testimony will be powerful?" Vikas asked. He felt alienated from himself as he posed this question.

"No, no. It won't affect how quickly they prosecute," Jaidev said. "That's based simply on how much evidence they have. You know yourself, from having done your documentaries; here they arrest first and find evidence later. Now, that's not to say that the people who they've captured aren't guilty—these people are not any more competent than the police—but it depends on how they build the circumstantial case."

Vikas was at a loss. He did not know how to proceed.

The next day Deepa and he visited the Lajpat Nagar police thana, a brutish bureaucratic place characterized by the powdery paint on the walls and heavy steel desks. Upon arriving, they were surrounded by several policemen who asked what they wanted, clearly sizing up their ability to proffer bribes. They were led into an inspector's office, where, under the portrait of a dead policeman, they registered their statement.

"Anything else?" the inspector asked, squinting. He had a cold. One broken epaulet stood up on his shoulder like a praying mantis, or the wick of a candle.

"Will we get to speak in court?" Deepa asked.

"It depends on the lawyer, madam," sniffled the policeman.

They returned now to the depths of their lives, awaiting the next hearing.

The days went by, soggy with anticipation, with the implication of important things happening elsewhere. Deepa baked cakes in the kitchen, punishing herself with heat. The kitchen was the largest, most luxurious part of the flat; a space that could have easily serviced three households, not just the tiny one attached to it—a leftover of the old joint way of life. Amazing, Vikas thought, watching her, that we've been in the same house for all these years. If I had money, we'd move.

But they were tied to the house. He'd inherited it from his father. He owned the flat jointly with his siblings, and it was difficult to imagine selling it: Who would want to live this deep in a complex full of Khuranas, even if the address were a posh one? Would his siblings allow it? (It occurred to him that, in the circumstances, yes, they would.) Mostly, it was difficult to fathom the complexity of selling, setting a price, transporting one's stuff, homing in on a new place—tiring. When you came down to it, this flat was the only security they had, the only immutable thing, even if it were blood-ied from the insides with memories of the boys, Tushar waddling about in his giraffe-patterned pajamas and ordering around the servant, Nakul lounging in his hep overlarge T-shirts, surprising Vikas with his catlike stare. It was because of the house that he'd stuck to Delhi and not moved to Bombay, where the film industry was concentrated. It was easier to make documentaries if you weren't terribly strapped for cash and worrying about meeting the rent and if, by the luck of good inheritance, you had a decent address.

Foolish, he thought. I should have risked it and moved. Then this would have never happened and it would have been better for my career, which withered in Delhi, surrounded by family—people who judged my choices and my way of life without trying to understand.

Vikas had a fever. Since the day of the blasts, he'd been consumed by such what-ifs (the initial embargo on them, imposed for the sake of his wife, out of a temporary maturity that comes to a man when he feels he is in a historic phase of his life, having been lifted). Every way he turned, his past was detonated, revealing tunnels and alternative routes under the packed, settled earth of the present. For every decision there were a million others he could have made. For every India, a Pakistan of possibilities.

When things are good, you can see no other way of living; when things are in ruins, there appear a million solutions for how this fate could have been avoided. He blamed himself for all sorts of decisions: for turning down money (he'd been offered a commercial project on the strength of his documentaries but had rejected it on cranky artistic grounds), for not taking another job (his brother had offered him a position at his travel agency when he was particularly low, living off loans from the family), for cowardice (why had he been so afraid of trying his hand in Bombay, of fleeing his festering ancestral womb?). He blamed himself for selfishness (why had he persisted with this career that so clearly made his children ashamed? All the fathers of their friends were industrialists who took their kids on holidays to Jungfrau and bought them Parker pens for their schoolwork). But mostly, he felt trapped with his consequences in the flat, in this flat with its terrazzo floors and yellow post-partition walls and views across the street of the home of a technology czar, a sleek set of buildings muscled through with old, hard, thick Rajasthani-looking wood—a fashionable touch recommended by an architect, no doubt, the same one who had recommended that the pool be shielded from view of the prying neighbors. Are there any women in this house? Vikas wondered, coming to the window. He had vaguely known that the IT czar's daughter was a classmate of Nakul's, but he had never seen her or her mother—not even at the funeral rites for the boys, which the czar attended alone, looking freshly barbered and shaved in his white safari suit and designer slippers, slippers he carried in his hands out of fear of the shoe-keeper at the temple misplacing them.

They must drive up in their tinted Mercedes and be docked directly into the air lock of the portico of the Spanish-Rajasthani villa, Vikas thought.

What am I supposed to do? he wondered. How am I supposed to respond to this thing that has happened to me? A few weeks ago I was standing here, looking through this garbled, pearly whorled window for my kids on the street, seeing instead the servants skulking under the ashokas. Now they're gone, forever, no matter how long I stay here like faithful Hachiko, from their English reader. And yet I have an urge to stay here forever. An urge to punish myself by looking, by scouring every inch of tarred road and glittering gutter and veined dust-sprinkled leaf, in every season, at all times, for my boys—to look till I go blind or mad, till my brain revolts, staging a headache in the space where I am trying to insert the entire city by looking.

His heart moved like a rudder through the icy seas of his chest. Vikas was a tall man with a patrician forehead and a rude thatch of hair; he took it in his hand in wild bunches. He did not move from the window. His eyes—wide-set, mobile, vulnerable—blinked more than normal. His thighs, muscular yet thin, like pipes, burned with tension. Outside, on the street, the wind unfurled a serpent's tongue of dust through the colony, pushing the organic detritus a few feet, little bits of shattered leaf getting stuck in blisters of tar. Horns. No cars turning the corner. Leaping sunlight. No boys.

The next hearing kept getting postponed. The government would set a date only to cancel it at the last minute and propose another in a month. Deepa began to slip. "Maybe they're not even guilty," she said one day, wiping her forehead in the kitchen. Behind her blazed the dismal kingdom of the countertops, the cracked surface strewn with cut-up ingredients, fossilized dhania, and powder. "I was reading in the *Hindu*," she said, "that one of the boys they picked up was sixteen and he had come from Kashmir for the summer holidays, to stay with his brother, who sells papier-mâché things at Dilli Haat."

The Khuranas were cut-and-dried secularists and liberals. They took the left-wing position on everything. They read the *Hindu*, the *Asian Age*, and the *Hindustan Times*; subscribed to *Outlook* rather than the saffronized *India Today*; were among the special coterie of urbanites who counted the crusading P. Sainath as their favorite journalist; were partisans of DD-2's *The News To-night* under NDTV, which they felt had been better in its hour-long avatar as *The World This Week*; were opposed to globalization and the monstrous coming of McDonald's and KFC (why do you need McDonald's if there's a Wimpy? Vikas wondered); were against the BJP, which had sprung to power for thirteen days right before the boys had died, the government lasting only long enough to encompass the blast. And of course, they had a few token Muslim friends, like the Ahmeds, of whom they were inordinately proud—

whom they had cultivated partly (though not entirely) to give ballast to their secular credentials. Therefore, had they been on the other side of the blast, or rather not on any side, but outside its murderous circumference, they too would have doubted the speedy arrest of the terrorists, the conflicting but confident storylines offered by the police, the heartless manner in which the suspects had been held for a month before being produced for trial.

Of course, being victims, they'd had to suppress all that.

"What are they saying?" Vikas asked, buying time. In fact, he didn't care whether the terrorists were guilty or innocent. The four men standing in the court were like the obligatory impurities in a paperweight: They were just there. A thing to hold down time. One more new room for the Khuranas to pass through. And how did it matter if they were guilty or innocent, if his kids had already died? How could the suffering of these suspects, even if it was greatly exacerbated by being wrongly jailed, approach his own? On the way out of the court, he had seen a woman with reddish hair crying, her head bent low, hands gripping the sides of the plastic chair, two crooked front teeth visible at the top of the cave of her glistening, depthless, open mouth—he had seen this woman and his heart had tightened and he had assumed she was a nameless mother of the nameless dead in the blast. Now he wondered if she was the mother of one of the young terrorists and his heart leapt again—not for the terrorists, but for her, for how alone she must have been in that courtroom, surrounded by people who hated her and her son.

Deepa, in the drawing room, propped her head against him and cried.

Afterwards, she said, "I made a mistake. There's nothing we can do. We can never catch the people who did this. They're a thousand kilometers away."

"Deepu, darling, you can't believe just one newspaper report."

"But it's the *Hindu*."

"It's put together by people like me," he said. "Look at me. Of course it lies." As he said this, he cast his eye around the drawing room. What a decrepit room it was. A sideboard stood next to the dining table, full of generic award plates you see in doctors' offices—prizes from meaningless film associations, trophies won by the boys on sports day, medals from galas at the Friends Club. Closer, past the cheap, laminated fake wood surface of the dining table, wood the color of dark ale, eagerly foaming up any white impurity or dirt, lay the centerpiece of the shabby sofas pushed against the windows, windows that faced the adjacent building and were alive with dust, birds, chirping, the horrible guttural fever of sunlight. A maroon, moth-eaten, uneven carpet covered the floor. Somewhere, out of view, hiding behind a book on the sideboard, a clock ticked. Deepa was on her knees before Vikas now, crying. He had an erection—not from desire, but from a kind of excess vividness, the noises of the complex (the birds, the projecting hawkers, the grumbling servants, the hammering of new construction in the neighbor's plot), building symphonically around the central instrument of the crying woman: he wanted to fuck the house, to fuck every little particle he could see.

The house changed shape and color with passing clouds, like a woman angrily putting on and taking off clothes in a changing room. "Don't cry," he told his wife, inhaling the smell of cakes from her hair, and then he cried too.

The trucks came every day at eleven, emptying their bricks and cement pipes and the load of construction workers before the snazzy gates of the neighbor. Vikas watched it from the window, drinking tea, tending to a fire in his stomach. Since the day of the blast, he had eaten very little—had come to subsist, like so much of the starving subcontinent, on tea; he loved tea, loved caffeine, felt naked without a cup at the end of his long fingers, giving him a reason to drop from his height and drink; he felt there was no harm now in indulging his worst habits—what was the worst that could happen, you'd fall sick? Tear away your stomach lining like the great French writer Balzac, so that you'd have to snort lines of coffee, chew tobacco? Bad things were going to happen to you anyway. Humans, especially bourgeois humans, were not meant to handle this kind of stress.

He had not worked on his film project since the day of the bombing—
Scenes from a Marriage, a documentary about divorce in India, so named in

tribute to his favorite auteur, Ingmar Bergman (how would Bergman's sharp bourgeois melodramas hold up against a bomb? he wondered). He couldn't bring himself to do it, couldn't tear himself from this window, which was like a portal into heat, death, futility, irritation—and also a stage. What had happened to him was so real, he couldn't reenter the world of make-believe—yes, that was the work of a documentary film-maker too: make-believe. It was artificial as anything else. You found a location, staged a scene or an interview, blocked out your story before-hand (after months of pleasant research on the subject), and then edited and reshot for effect. But all this seemed now to Vikas like a kind of te-dium. He couldn't look at the footage from *Scenes from a Marriage*, listen to the complaints of married women, try to carve a meaningful narrative from their frayed individual stories. To make a documentary out of many stories was to make a family out of inmates in different cells of a jail. It wouldn't work. Or it would, but it would have the same sickly futile simul-taneity of jail.

"I just want to be here with you," he told his wife when she expressed concern about him. "And how will it matter if I don't work for one or two months? It's not like I make any money. You make a lot more money than me—in fact, I should be your assistant."

"You'll get more depressed being home," she said.

"I'll read," he said with a smile. "I'll catch up on various things." But there was something off and light and overly optimistic about his tone and he knew it too.

When Deepa started crying again, he said, "What's the matter, Deepu?"

Throughout their marriage, he had marveled at how little she cried, how she never used tears to blackmail him, and in the past few weeks, there had been something particularly awful about watching this lovely, tough woman reduced to a shivering mess. But now, strange as it was, he was getting tired of it. He only had enough space for his own grief.

"I've lost not just Tushar and Nakul but you too," she said.

Vikas hugged her and made a savage mental note that they shouldn't be left alone like this, that there should be a relative present at all times to diffuse their grief into politeness. But he couldn't argue with her. He was growing distant from *himself*, floating away above his body. Sometimes he felt, when he was in front of the window, that he wasn't standing there but was looking down at the entire city from a blimp in the stratosphere, seeing the blackened roofs and the water tanks and the trees and the roads as one sees them on architectural plans: not dirty and ruined, as in reality, but clean and serene, occupied by no one.

He started going again for his evening walk, his heart murmuring, his legs wobbly; it was his attempt to get back in touch with his body. But his mouth would be dry by the time he'd walked to the T-junction, and he'd turn back and go home. Each time he saw a neighbor, he bolted into the safety of his flat. He'd become a proper recluse. At the same time, since his wife had planted the seed, the idea of work was in his head. How to make a documentary about terror?

The thing was, he didn't want to make a film about the aftermath; he was living the aftermath. No—he wanted to make a film about the moment itself, when there was a hush as the bomb shut off humans and machines in the vicinity and then viciously rearranged everything. Yes, he wanted to film the moment itself, slow it down, open it up like a flower over time, like the ultraviolent bomb dreams that filled his nights.

The dreams had been growing. At first he had seen the eye, bloody and syncopated and concocted, opening. Then the visions had become stereoscopic, his mind racing out in many directions to places like Sadar Bazaar, Faridabad, Indranagar, Rohini, Gurgaon, Sabzi Mandi—places where the news of the bomb turned into muddy rumor, as if his mind wished to establish a circumference for his grieving, come back with all the places that didn't know about it, that certified its smallness.

And yet there was something these dreams couldn't approach. How to be present, he wondered, for the moment itself? How to know when a bomb was about to go off? A few years ago, during a lull between documentaries and commercials, he had become interested in the functioning of futures markets, and he wondered now: Was it possible to put together a futures market for bombs? Surely there were people with information about terrorism that a market would happily sponge up. No, Khurana, don't dream. He'd have to be more specific than that, more practical. Surely there were times of the year and markets (real markets, not the abstract entities of economics textbooks) in which blasts were concentrated. Crowds attracted bombs. So did festivals and political rallies. There were festivals almost every day in Delhi—festivals of life, death, birth, benediction, and general sorrow and repentance, staged by obscure sects of Hindus, Muslims, Jains, Christians.

At home, unlacing his shoes, dumping out the sand that collected on the soles, feeling his stubble like a proof of advancing life, he did not sit down to calculate the odds of walking into a bomb. He knew enough about mathematics to understand it would only disappoint him. "I suppose I could speak to the police and to journalists about where they think bombs might be set off," he thought, the old documentarian instinct asserting itself.

He saw Delhi as a city vibrant and roiling with possibility, with bombs as pockets of heat, geysers that sprayed up naturally.

He started visiting these markets at rush hour with his camera. There was the one limiting rule he set for himself, so that he not bore of the project, or simply go mad from the heat: he would film only at or around the time the boys had been killed in Lajpat Nagar. If this foreshortened the odds, so be it. As for filming, the act itself, he made sure he was inconspicuous; he did not want to scare away potential terrorists with his equipment. (He did not think, in his half-cracked state, that this way of *thinking* was extremely odd.)

His first visit was to Lajpat Nagar. Armed with a Betacam, entering the square, he set up a tripod in the ruined park in the middle. Immediately urchins and shopkeepers came up to him, asking what he was doing—people wild-eyed with the rushed newfound suspicion of bomb victims. When he told them he was the father of two victims, they quieted down, but they were obviously not pleased. Having suffered so much, they did not want to be filmed within the broken cages of their shops, shacks with the distended lips of shutters and fragmented beams.

From the park, Vikas took in the market in cinematic gulps, saw people traipsing over rubble, over blasted loops of cloth, old shoes—signs of the bomb that hadn't been cleared away but were being compacted into the deep archaeology of the city. He thought of Tushar and Nakul, the parts of them that had been left behind here, merging with the earth.

After a while, he began to spread out. He went to GK, South Ex, Karol Bagh, Chandini Chowk, Sadar Bazaar, INA—places even denser than Lajpat Nagar, more eager to be blown up. He became a fixture in these markets, setting up his camera in the shacks of paanwallahs and tea sellers, buying their loyalty and canceling their grumbling with payments. He was making a movie about the bazaars of India, he explained. No, he was not with the police. To put them at ease, he described his other documentaries and exaggerated acquaintanceships with Bollywood stars.

"So why are you here if you know Raveena so well, sir?" one chaiwallah asked, referring to Raveena Tandon.

"Abe, what do you think, we can all sleep with her?" Vikas said.

There was a contradiction within Vikas, an open wound: though he was fascinated by the poor, good at joshing with them, he was afraid, thanks to his bourgeois background, of being perceived as poor. Poverty equaled failure.

And at these moments of light banter, it was possible to see a different Vikas emerge, one who had little do, at least externally, with the man who spent hours glued to his window as if it were a TV, looking for his boys out of powerful habit, his heart wrenched in place.

"It'll be a tribute to the children," he explained to his wife one day. "And one thing no one mentions is how brave the shopkeepers were," he said. "After all, they have to go back to work right where the blast happened." Though the record, in the case of Lajpat Nagar, at least in terms of bravery, had been mixed. Some shopkeepers had immediately leapt after their burning cars or their things, ignoring their injured assistants. The owner of the framing shop, a young macho Punju fellow with a lippy twenty-five-year-old wife and two young kids, had actually escaped the initial explosion and rolled into the alley between shops; then, overcome by greed, he had climbed through the burning tarpaulin to retrieve the cash from his box, only to be crushed by the falling A/C he'd had installed the week before.

But there were also instances of out-and-out heroism in this capitalist scramble. One of the shopkeepers, half his face blown off, had picked up a megaphone and warned customers to keep away. The assistants risked their lives to pull other assistants from the rubble. Mansoor ran away in fright but someone, some kind person, never to be named or found out, had taken the boys to the hospital; auto drivers, god bless their souls, had lined up outside the market, transporting victims to Moolchand and AIIMS for free. "I should make a separate documentary about them," Vikas said.

He expected his wife to pick out holes but she said, "Don't get killed in a bomb yourself." Which, of course, was exactly what he wanted.

Deepa had not been idle during this period. Vikas came from a politically well-connected family—his grandfather had been an ICS officer and the chief commissioner of Chandigarh and a chacha had served as a cabinet secretary under Indira Gandhi; another cousin, Mukesh, was a friend of Venkaiah Naidu, the spokesperson of the BJP party.

Deepa, who had previously kept away from these family members on account of Vikas's distaste for them (he hated anyone who didn't flatter him about his art, who asked how he made money), now began approaching them for favors.

They were helpful. One of the more surprising moments at the chautha had been the appearance of Venkaiah Naidu—present at Mukesh's behest—and now Mukesh said he would be happy to talk to Naidu again. "He's not in power but I'm sure he'll know the right person to talk to," he said. Then, putting his paw on Deepa's hand—he was a notorious groper of women, widely recognized as the colony's lecher—he said, "Are you sure you want to meet the terrorists?"

She nodded. "Who knows how many years the trial will go on? Just once, I want to talk to one of them, to understand why they did this."

"They wanted to disrupt the election in Kashmir," Mukesh said, his eyes sympathetically grazing her grief-shattered face. "Will you have some tea?"

They sat in his office—he ran a construction business from a building across the street from the family complex—and drank tea. He reflected that it was the first time they'd ever sat together like this.

He'd always thought Deepa an exceptionally attractive woman, her exoticism enhanced somewhat by the fact that she was Christian and from the South, with sweater-gray eyes that seemed only a few nicks of color removed from her grayish-brown skin, a peculiar color that didn't appear in Delhi, where the shades seemed to swing between black and white, Dravidian and Aryan (Mukesh himself was dark and hated the world for it).

Poor woman, he thought. Trapped in a doomed marriage with my depressed cousin (Vikas was ten years younger than Mukesh, but they were cousins)—a man who never knew how to handle women, who, with his nervous shifty mannerisms and sudden uncomfortable smiles, seemed to attract bad luck. You could see misfortune imprinted on people's faces years before it hit them. Mukesh had always known that Vikas, the academic star of the family, would be a failure. Which is why he'd been surprised when Vikas had come one day to the communal drawing room with this sexy item at his side. Women work in mysterious ways; men do too. "Will you have biscuits with your chai?" he asked.

"No, no," she said. "You have a nice office. Tushar and Nakul always wanted to see your construction machines and excavators."

"You should have brought them."

I thought you didn't even own the machines, she wanted to say—you're only a middleman—but she kept quiet. Mentioning the boys had opened up a door of mania and sickness right in the very center of her chest. She put down the tea.

Mukesh watched her sympathetically, his head slightly askance, as if looking at something around a curtain. His brows were distended with worry; he drummed the table in a way that suggested he was watching but that she was free to continue; that what she was going through was natural; he wasn't going to draw attention to it, not until she wanted him to.

Deepa had always disliked Mukesh but she saw now that he had a certain natural comfort with women, surprising for such a bearish, hairy fellow, one who always barked at servants and saluted everyone as he passed them on the street. "It's been very difficult," she said.

He remained quiet; she saw that the whites of his eyes were filigreed at the sides with red capillaries.

"We'll make sure you meet the terrorists," he said, standing up and coming around to her. He was behind her now, with his hands on her shoulders. "You don't even worry for one second."

Why did she want to meet the terrorists? She suspected it was because she was on the verge of parting from life, and she wanted all the loose ends tied up before she went, joining her boys wherever they were. So there was a galloping excitement within her: the thrill of meeting the men who had killed her sons; also, the thrill of her own death.

"Naidu won't be able to help you," Jagdish Chacha, the former cabinet secretary, said when she went to see him at his flat in the complex. "Mukesh likes talking. The person who can help you is Jagmohan or Kiran Bedi. I'll phone them. But tell me: How is Vikas?"

"He's OK, uncle. Busy with work."

"Good. He has another film project these days?"

"Yes, uncle. A documentary."

"It's good that he's outside," Jagdish said. "Being outside I've found is crucial. Inside, one's soul starts to get poisoned. When Indira-ji died," he said, referring to Indira Gandhi, "I went and exercised every day. Now, tell me, what kind of meeting do you want?"

"Whatever is possible, uncle," Deepa replied.

"You can meet them as people do in prisons—through a window in the meeting room. You go, queue up all day, and then you get to meet the person for five, ten minutes. If you go, you'll see everyone has come there with tiffin boxes. Of course you won't have to stand in the queue.

"But you can also meet them, or one of them, face-to-face in a room. Technically this is not allowed, but a jail is like a school—if you know the principal you can do anything. It might be that we'll have to say you're a journalist—can Vikas bring his press ID?—otherwise they, the terrorists, won't want to meet you. Just to warn you, I'm not sure how much you'll gain. When the militancy was happening in Punjab, I remember, many politicians wanted to meet the militants in jail, to shout at them. But the meetings were never satisfactory. They always found that the militants were reasonable men, which was even more difficult than finding out the opposite." He was lost now in the halls of his past power, traversing them for impressive tidbits—Deepa had seen this before with Jagdish Chacha. She wasn't friendly with him but knew his wife well and so had an idea of his idiosyncrasies.

When he was done, he said, "Now, you go rest. The family is behind you. All his life Papa-ji fought against this kind of fundamentalism from the Muslims. We'll make sure you get everything you want."

Funny, Deepa thought—how this kind of tragedy unites and energizes a family. I've not just asked these old men for favors; I've reinvigorated their lives with purpose.

A few days before the blast, Tushar had come into the kitchen in the morning to watch her at work. An earnest boy, he loved the hectic action of the kitchen. "And how much frosting do you have to make for the order, Mama?" he asked.

"Two or three kilos since it's a bulk order," she said. "And we'll let it cool in the afternoon. Hopefully we'll have electricity so it won't turn green from mold. You want to mix it?"

He did. With the whisk tight in his hand, he churned the butter and the sugar. He was not as effeminate as his father made him out to be. It was a matter of context. In the context of the kitchen he was an expert. As he mixed the frosting, Deepa hugged his small frame from behind.

Later that evening Nakul played "Edelweiss" for her on the small guitar they had bought him. "Edel Vyes, Edel Vais, every morning you greet me," he sang.

Now, back home from visiting Mukesh, Deepa reflected on the tragic oddness of her own life, how she'd grown up in a tiny family in Bangalore, the only daughter of a reclusive man who ran a famous bookstore and could talk about nothing but sixties rock 'n' roll (he had not been a recluse before his wife died, though she could barely remember that); how she'd been a shy and frightened but persevering creature, doing well in school and ending up in Delhi and working for Arthur Andersen, the CA firm, thanks to a family connection—Delhi, that odd world, so much more spacious and rude than Bangalore; Delhi, a place where no one was firmly rooted and there was a sense that if a better city presented itself just fifty kilometers away, the opportunistic inhabitants would immediately quit the city, caring not a jot for the earth that had nurtured them. And, of course, out of all these Delhiites, these savage North Indians, she'd picked Vikas. Or Vikas had picked her. She'd liked him because, in the middle of the rude crush, he had the disarming gentleness of a South Indian—he was a Punjabi but he could have been sprung from St. Joseph's. Calm, sympathetic, patient, he was a good listener, marked with none of the prejudices she imagined North Indians carried toward South Indian Christians (and she wasn't wrong about these prejudices: years later, when she became a de facto Punjabi as well, she learned that most North Indians thought all Christian women were maids); and their courtship had an easy, light quality; they'd melted like two shy creatures into one another.

Tears came to her eyes remembering those early days—days of infatuation. After that everything had gone to ruin. Vikas slipped into a depression about his career as a documentary filmmaker from which he never recovered—angry first at his family for not understanding why he wished to be an artist rather than a CA ("There's only one artist in the whole bloody family and they can't even handle that!") and then at himself for having chosen such a nugatory, ascetic path at a time when India was booming with money and rupees fell from the trees like soft petals, enriching even the fools of his family, whose property values shot up. How many times had she told him to quit? To go back to being a CA? To do something else? To sell his inherited lands in Patiala? But he refused. Descending into bitterness, surrounded by the braying, pointing, mocking audience of his family, he had become attached to his own pain. He did not want to make changes because that would mean losing his precious exchequer of bitterness.

And then there were the kids. He had, in his bitter, depressive way, been opposed to having any, but she had pushed him and pressured him, sending subtle messages through family members, thinking that children would rouse him from his emotional torpor, give him a reason to *act*. And, in fact, there was a change in him after Tushar was born. Vikas loved the boy in the obsessive, cuddly way he loved animals—constantly nuzzling against him, singing wicked, demented songs; he was energized (as many artists are) by his own creation.

But soon he lost interest in Tushar and Nakul and returned to his depressive state—in fact, he blamed the boys for exacerbating his depression. "We should never have brought them up here, with the influence of this family. They've also turned out to be Punjabi brutes with no understanding of art."

"I've told you many times we could move to Bangalore or Bombay," she said. "And the boys are much more like you than anyone else."

"And who's going to pay the rent, my dear? The fees for their school? This property is my curse. I'm stuck here. The property is probably my *subject*, though I'm not sure how to make a documentary about all these oafs."

Such self-pity! She wouldn't stand for it. "You have more than enough money locked up in lands. Why don't you sell it?"

But Vikas was incorrigible. "Do you realize how complex it is? I'll have to deal with Mukesh, Jagdish, Rajat, Bhim. It's not worth it. Better to let a few of them die off," he said viciously.

How had he become like this? Where had her husband—the sweet man she'd known the first few years—gone? She began despairing that this was his true self, that she'd been fooled those first few years. Such bitterness could not be minted overnight; it had to be implanted at a young age. Maybe he wasn't so different from the bad-tempered, cynical people in the complex that he despised—but whereas those people pinned their cynicism on the decline of the family's reputation, he pinned it on the decline of his career. It was all the same, in the end; it produced the same results. It occurred to her that she could have been married to any one of the shrieking, sniggering fools on the family campus. That she was like Draupadi, wedded to the *family*, not to a person. "You used to be different," she had said at the end of that conversation about selling the lands, trying to keep herself from cracking.

"No," he'd said. "I was just on a break from being myself."

Then, one day, in October, five months after the boys' deaths, they went to Tihar Jail to meet a man named Malik Aziz. Malik, it was said, was the ideologue of the JKIF, the man behind its violent philosophy. A bookish student of chemistry at the University of Kashmir, he had turned out to be a dangerous, charismatic figure in the student protest movements, egging his fellow students on from stone throwing to kidnapping a vice chancellor of the university to assassinations and finally terrorism. "According to RAW, he's one of the most dangerous terrorists in the country," the police escort whispered as he walked beside Deepa through the winding inner roads of Tihar, small paths canyoned on either side with high dirty yellow plaster walls, the walls overlaid with snaps of shattered glass and barbed wire.

A lot—too much—of family was present. Jagdish, who had organized the meeting, was in his small specs and crinkled face, looking short and wide in a safari suit as he walked with his hands behind his back. Mukesh: sticking out his chest, smoothing his mustache, constantly asking the police escort questions, as if to flatter him and overpower him at once. And Vikas, of course: slinking behind the two men and Deepa, acting even more distraught than he probably was, showing his displeasure about these men's presence by not standing next to his wife. "Come in the front, yaar," Mukesh said, grabbing him by the shoulder.

"No, no. I'll keep watch of the back," Vikas said, as if there was a chance they'd be attacked by escaping prisoners in these narrow Benares-back-lane-like channels.

————————

"Why are they coming with us?" he had asked Deepa a few days before, when she told him that the meeting in the jail was confirmed.

"They organized it, yaa." The South Indian *yaa*. These old tics were returning.

"They didn't even know the boys. In all these years, tell me one time they took interest in them. All Jagdish would do is go up to them and make faces and say, 'Who is Kumbhkaran and who is Duryodhan?' And Mukesh—he'll act like a chaudhary and take over the whole thing, as if *his* kids have died." He flushed, as usual, at this phrase. He'd become a man whose kids had died. This was his chief distinction. It occurred to him now that people are defined much more by their association with death than by what they do in life. *Poor thing, she's a widow*, they say. *She lost her mother when she was ten to cancer*. I've been immune to all this, he thought.

His parents had not died early—nor had they died late. He was the third of five siblings; his parents were thirty-five and thirty-three when they'd had him. They'd both died in their early seventies. People lived for much longer now but he had not grieved too much for them—they'd led unhappy lives and they were especially unhappy in each other's presence. Mama's stroke of genius, he thought, was to die first. Her poor husband—angry, stingy, abusive, like all the men in this family—had been unmoored.

What a bitter man I am! he thought with some satisfaction. Can't feel anything for my parents and soon I won't feel anything for my dead children either. I care only about myself and there's the rub—I'm not even worth caring about. Self-pity welled in his chest. It was a familiar, even comforting sickness, like the pleasure that a bulimic must feel when the food first starts rising in the elevator of her gullet. He thought again of his failures, thought of his wasted promise, thought of the way in which even God—yes, God!—had confirmed his suspicions about himself by murdering his children. I'm not fit to live! Everything I touch turns to shit! Now look at this poor woman—this lovely woman who's thrown in her lot with mine (he looked at her as these thoughts swirled through his head, gathering together the threads of his life: only a second or two had passed in the drawing room, where they were having the conversation. She was icing a cake again, as on the day of the blast). What has she got? Nothing but years and years of heartbreak, of being pushed physically, I am sure, into the country of her mother's cancer. When she married me, with my encouraging smile and my famous family, she probably thought she was gaining security—exactly the thing she craved after that tiny lifeboat of a family in Bangalore. Instead she got the opposite. Or not the opposite—just a continuation of her childhood. Secretly we are all looking for ways to continue our childhoods—the hurt, the pain, the love, the fear, the shame. So just as I recognized in her someone who would let me carry on with my bitterness, she must have recognized in me someone who would let her down repeatedly. Lead her straight into the waltzing, frizzing arms of cancer.

He put his arms around her in the drawing room. Her small, perishable bones—light like aluminum. "We should get you to rest. I don't want you to fall sick," he said. It was this fear of sickness—which ticked inside her like a genetic bomb—that kept him from pushing things to their extremes, kept him back from the edge of terrible behavior. There was only so much you could hurt this lovely woman before she imploded.

Back in the jail, a door opened and they were led into a clean bureaucratic office. They had passed through a number of doors already—gates, really—unlocked by the guards and then padlocked behind them before they could pass through the next set of gates. It dizzied the mind. He tried to form an image of the prison in his head, and could come up with only an indeterminate squiggle and a respect for centuries of panoptical construction.

A woman was seated behind the desk. Thin, with healthy oiled hair emerging in a braid, her shirt spruced with epaulets, she got up to greet Jagdish Chacha. The man hadn't been a cabinet secretary for fifteen years now, but the trappings of power did not go away. While she spoke, he rocked back proudly on his heels and touched his spectacles to signal that he was listening.

Somehow Vikas and Deepa were holding hands again.

It was in this state—making physical contact—that they were best. He had never lost his fascination, never once in fifteen years (they had been married as long as his chacha had *not* been a cabinet secretary, he realized, with some satisfaction), for how light her bones were; his hands clawed through hers as if trying to break a spider's web. She opened up her hand and then clung to his tightly. If I had known it would come to this, he thought, I would never have married her. I would have let her go the very first minute we became acquainted at Arthur Andersen; I would have dived behind a desk as she passed.

The lady was the deputy head of the jail system. Now looking tougher to Vikas in her stiff uniform and military posture, she was telling them about protocol, the various things they could and could not do. He nodded, taking in nothing. Then, suddenly, there were too many bodies in the room—not just Mukesh and Jagdish and his wife and the escort but three or four assistants, men dressed like backup waiters at a restaurant or snack servers at a wedding—and the whole group was now led into what appeared to be a barbershop, a vast, sparse space with polished mirrors on one side and chairs that reclined.

"This is run by our inmates," she said. "They charge twenty rupees for a haircut. The idea is to give them vocational training so when they go out they can adjust to the world."

"I made a documentary about jails," Vikas said. "I saw this in the Arthur Road Jail addition in Bombay."

"Yes, yes, they have it there also," she said. "But it started here." She considered Vikas coldly now, with the suspicious look of someone quite unused to having her authority defied. "So you make films, is it?"

"Documentaries, mostly."

"He's won two National Film Awards," Jagdish said. "You must watch them. About social issues," he muttered. (Vikas had won two Film Society awards, a lesser honor, but he did not interrupt).

But the woman's attention, in the vast modern-looking white barbershop, had been snared. "A woman came here a while ago, a Mrs. Sujata Menon—you know her?"

"Ah, of course; she's a friend of mine," Vikas said, trying to ingratiate himself and also to be a little curt—he did not think this was a pertinent conversation to have seconds before a major meeting; it reminded him of the way surgeons bantered with excessive, rehearsed politeness before they plunged scalpels into you in the ICU. "She took a lot of footage and talked to a lot of my boys here," the woman said—this is how she referred to her inmates: as boys. "After that I never heard from her. Can you please tell her Mrs. Thapar was asking about her?"

"Of course."

"A very nice lady; I liked her," she said. "She really understood the type of reform I'm trying to introduce here."

Vikas smiled politely. He knew Sujata Menon well. She was a sharp and dangerous journalist—she was always gaining access to places with her upper-middle-class, convent-educated charm and then backstabbing her subjects. He was sure the documentary was about the horrors of these people who proposed "reforms." Not that he was opposed to such a documentary— that's what he'd been abortively working toward at Arthur Road Jail in Bombay—it was just that he didn't approve of misleading people.

The warder of the jail now seemed smaller to him. She was the supreme leader of this domain, of her "boys," but still wanted acclaim from the outside world; he realized that the server-like men were reformed prisoners. They took their place behind the barber seats. Two pathetic inmates, young malnourished boys, sat lost in the vast chairs before the mirrors. The wait-ers cut with teasing, pulling, staccato precision. A show for the Khuranas.

"Come," she said, leading them to another room.

Malik had learned about the meeting that morning; he had not had much time to prepare. He thought he was meeting a journalist who wished to hear his side of the story, and he had scrambled in his cell to put together a coherent narrative. Something about Gandhi, yes. Gandhi, Kashmir. Be-ing a student of chemistry. He flailed wildly for details about the other in-nocents who'd been arrested: artisan, student, summer holidays, framed.

For him too the walk through the chambers of the jail was a new thing— most prisoners did not get to see this part of the jail. It was for visitors only.

He marveled at the clean lines, the symmetric tiles, the photos on the wall—how did one gain admission here? What minor crimes did you have to commit? Of course, he dared not ask the guards. Getting to meet a sympathetic journalist was enough luck for a day. He was led into a room with tinted plastic windows on all sides and given a cup of tea. It was like being in one of those opaque government waiting rooms, complete with cheap plastic fittings. He slurped the tea slowly, amazed, savoring every last syrupy sip. Then there was a commotion and a few people walked in. As soon as he saw them, their mishmash of clothes, the white salwar kameez the woman was wearing, he knew something was wrong. The couple looked vaguely familiar: Had they been at the trial? Malik, with his photographic recall, tried to think back through the haze of heat and hunger to the dusty room in which he had been charged with the crime. Beyond his feet, in that room of his memory, people and faces foamed, indistinct in their seats.

Then a man said (this was Mukesh), "Do you recognize them?" and Malik fell silent.

"He's not saying anything," Mukesh said, shouting for a guard.

Vikas and Deepa were locked in a tight mutual silent stare with Malik, seated across from him. He looked back dumbly, limply. Vikas observed the smallness and narrowness of his wrists, that tell of malnutrition. He reminded Vikas of nothing more than the young, eager Kashmiri boys who had rowed his shikara on Dal Lake on his one visit to the state before the violence broke out. And yet, if you looked closely, through Mukesh's shouting, there was something guilty, even sullen, about his nonchalance and silence. Why choose to remain silent if you were innocent? Silence is the small man's only defense. "Now be a good boy and answer their questions," Jagdish said, going up to him and touching his shoulder. The man did not flinch. "It doesn't look like he's going to say anything."

"Give him some time," Vikas said. "We can also be quiet."

"Don't you people feel ashamed?" Mukesh said. "Oye, bhainchod."

"Maybe you should go out," Vikas said. He gestured at Deepa, who looked hurt and meditative. Mukesh went out.

Deepa too looked at the man. The gap between them was so small. Yet she didn't know what she could say. Her head burst with the boys' voices and gestures and shrill demands—somehow it was these demands and questions that stayed with her most. She saw the boys lying on their stomachs on the drawing room floor covering their school readers with plastic or brown paper. She saw them pausing in doorways, stretching. Smashing a sponge ball in their room with a tiny imitation cricket bat from a factory in Ludhiana. Making high-pitched sounds in imitation of their favorite cricket commentators. Nakul sitting on the sofa, with his brown thin arms, asking, "But what is a prostitute, Mama?" A teacher had called a girl with purple nail polish that. "And she called Madhur a gasbag!" he snorted, suddenly getting up at full tilt and going into his room, where, a few seconds later, you could hear a sponge ball tocked against the wall. Nakul's Chinese-looking eyes. His darkness, his innocence, his Olympian cuddling, his monkeyish way of nearly hanging off the bed while he slept. Tushar's perpetual mousy, frightened look. His habit of picking his nose, which irritated Vikas. "Where do you think he gets it from?" Deepa told him.

Together these voices created a viscid pressure in her brain. "Deepa? Do you want to ask him anything?" Vikas said.

She shook her head.

Vikas spoke now to Malik: "If you are guilty, if you've done this, remember there will be no peace for you or your families—not now or forever. You think you're saving Kashmir, but you're destroying it." A bubble of spit formed on his lips and he considered spitting, but held himself back. He pulled out a photograph from his pocket. "Recognize them? My boys. They were blown up by you. What did they have to do with this?"

The man looked at the photos but said nothing.

Vikas turned to Jagdish, who repeated, "He won't say anything."

Malik was taken to a cell and stripped and beaten; they watched across the room as he howled. "He hasn't said anything since we brought him in," Mrs. Thapar explained.

Why did you bring him to us, then? Vikas wanted to ask.

"The toughest ones are the ones who don't speak. Most just sign a confession and happily mention others; they say their own brothers have planted the bomb—they're such cowards. Not this one. If he saw *you*, I thought he might talk. I'd told him journalists were coming to speak to him. I knew from the paper he reads who his favorite journalist is, and I'd told him that he was coming and he was excited." She shook her head. "But nothing."

Of course—nothing was free in this world, Vikas thought. They were being used too—as bait. "But the whole point was to talk to someone," he said.

"I know, but there would have been no point talking to people who deny it."

And it occurred to him now that the others who had been arrested were either broken or innocent, and this silent one was the closest they had come to finding a man who was guilty.

CHAPTER 7

Within days of visiting Malik, Deepa began to disintegrate. Vikas came in from an excursion in a market and found her walking about and muttering in the drawing room with cake mix on her hands. The windows of the flat were open and birds came in and out, commuting, as at a railway station. When he asked her what the matter was, she said, "I'm looking for Nakul's crane." In addition to playing guitar, Nakul had a passion for origami, making delicate folds on small pieces of paper, twisting and pressing the paper on the floor like a person performing a ritual to keep something under the earth from exploding.

Vikas told her the cranes were in a shoe box under the bed—didn't she remember?

"Oh," she said, bringing her hand to her mouth and leaving a smear of batter there.

It didn't stop—the confusion, the disintegration. Deepa, characterized by her bright, chirpy alertness, was now inert. When they'd come back from meeting Malik Aziz, Vikas had feared she might kill herself, and for a few days he'd stayed home, keeping her under intense watch, with Rajat and his friends making repeated visits. But he saw now what had happened to her was *far* worse, the mind vacating itself before the body could even act.

They'd been sleeping on the floor next to the bed ever since the boys had died. This was because the boys, though they were eleven and thirteen, coming into their male sounds and snores, had shared the bed with them every night, the limbs of the four Khuranas tangled ferociously, like a sprig of roots, dreams and sleep patterns merging and helixing, so that on one particular night, when Nakul screamed in his sleep, so did the other three, and the family woke with a common hoarse throat, looking around for intruders and then laughing. "We're like tightly packed molecules," Tushar had said, invoking the words of his science teacher and squeezing his mother close. Here, the Khuranas, who were generally no-nonsense, were indulgent. They were physical people—Vikas vigorously petting one or the other boy, mussing his hair, pulling his cheeks; Deepa cuddling with them as she had liked to wrap herself up in Vikas when they were first married.

Bundled, snuggling, the family fell into tight sleep. For Vikas, those nights of togetherness were the happiest of his life.

So—afraid to revisit those memories, they'd been sleeping on a thin mattress on the floor.

Then, one night, Deepa started letting out a low moaning sound—not crying, but a steady sob, like that of a dog. "What happened, darling?" Vikas asked, sitting up, his face covered with sweat, the underside of the bed visible, a tundra of dust.

She wouldn't say. The moaning went on. He turned her over. "Deepa." The house, closed in by the multiple cells of the relatives' flats, was scary, lonely, dark. He shook her. Her eyes were open. She was not asleep. The sound was conscious. He was overcome, at that moment, by a panic he had never experienced before—the panic of a man alone in the world—and he put his hands on her small shoulders and shook her again. She wrapped her legs around his, still looking at the ceiling. Vikas pulled up her kurta and undid the drawstrings of her pajamas.

Soon, they were making love.

They did not discuss the lovemaking, but it continued every night for days and weeks. They had not been near each other's bodies this way in ages and they entered old patterns and rhythms. They returned to the bed. No longer drugged with pills, they moved swiftly.

During the day, they grew silent around one another, Deepa returning to work, standing angrily before the oven all day, absorbing its heat. Vikas worried she might pass out from dehydration and went into the kitchen and brought her glasses of ice water, which she always took a sip of and put aside. She lost weight. At night, her body was birdlike and small. Then one day, they learned she was pregnant.

CHAPTER 8

When the Khuranas received the news of the pregnancy at the office of their GP in East of Kailash, they fell silent. They'd known this was coming, had known what they were working toward, yet their actions had been suffused with denial, Vikas with his muddled commerce-student's understanding of science telling himself, "Well, she's forty; the chances of getting pregnant are lower," and adding mentally, "We can always get an abortion," imagining such a conversation would be easy to have given the higher risk of Down syndrome in a child born to an older mother. Deepa was in denial too, convinced they would kill themselves. She had thought that the lovemaking was simply a form of postponement. So it was a surprise to her when she was overcome by such raw, vivid emotion in the doctor's office.

"This is an interesting situation," Vikas said in the car on the way home, expecting Deepa to have a similar response. Instead she put her hand in his—cold, light fingers. Delhi even in December was dusty, lurid, sunlit, perplexingly dry, dug up on the megalomaniacal whims of urban planners and chief ministers, and it occurred to Vikas, as he drove, turning with the dips in the road, that Jagmohan, the politician, was the connective tissue between Vikas's life in Delhi and the violence in Kashmir. Jagmohan, the demolition artist of the Indian state. Working swiftly, tirelessly, without imagination—a true peon—he'd bulldozed the slums of Delhi during the Emergency and knocked the city's teeth out, what was termed at the time as "beautification."

Vikas remembered this period of history acutely, the way one can only recall one's college days. Twenty-one, he was commencing an MA in economics from DSE, already miserable, his future as a CA foaming at his feet while filmmaking was a distant flagless island beyond. His fellow students—especially of economics—knew better than to raise a fuss about politics and kept to themselves, huddled with exam guides and cups of tea. The situation appalled Vikas—who was already developing a social conscience in the apartheid halls of the university, where no two disciplines could debate each other—and one day, he followed the bread crumbs left by a newspaper to watch a demolition.

It led to his first short film. After seeing one demolition, he came back again, with a friend's camera, a Norelco. The demolition he filmed was somber by Indian standards. Slum dwellers, mostly Muslims, queued up alongside the bulldozer that would render them homeless, watching wide-eyed, intense, waving to the camera. Warned beforehand of the government's intentions, they'd dismantled their nests of tarpaulin and tin themselves; and now, as the bulldozer climbed upon and tossed aside layers of history—waddling over tarpaulin, crumpling tin, knocking out wooden supports—a surprising thing happened. Someone began to cheer. Party workers, maybe. A man came around dancing madly, his face painted and parodic with holi powders, distributing plastic whistles to the little slum kids that they then blew, cheering on their own demise.

Vikas caught it on camera, gratified by his luck. You always needed this kind of luck as a documentarian. He had told the government workers he was making a film commissioned by the state—and he had, in fact, received tacit permission from Jagdish Chacha, using the family connections he would later decry.

The demolition, of course, was Jagmohan's doing, and as a reward for his loyalty, Jagmohan would eventually be posted to Kashmir as governor, where, in response to an uprising, he ordered the military to open fire on protesters on a bridge over the Jhelum, inciting years of violence.

"What do you think we should do?" Vikas asked when they came home.

Deepa—walking about the kitchen, hunched, banging cabinet doors,

her behind prominent through the salwar—said nothing. She was letting
the news grow inside her. Was it possible that one of the boys would be . . .
reborn? When Vikas's mother had died, a puppy appeared at their door
every day for five days after the cremation and Vikas had tried to adopt it
and she'd mocked him.

"Let's think about it," she said. "I should have more tests."

His sensible wife! "Yes, of course," he said.

They were happy about the pregnancy, but also bewildered—had a sense
they were moving several pieces ahead in a game they were playing against
(or with?) God: on one hand, they were blessed—who knew how long it
might have taken Deepa to get pregnant; on the other, they were unsure if
they'd committed an injustice against their dead sons, having a child before
the joint pyre had even cooled.

The extended family, of course, was thrilled—thrilled to have news, also
relieved that Deepa and Vikas, the epicenter of silence in the crumbling
complex, had chosen life. Some of the evil and stillness that had settled over
the common areas, on the dusty bushes and trees and the tattered driveway,
lifted. The women went over with advice about how to handle the pregnancy. "Don't worry about your age," they counseled Deepa. "Dadi-ji was
fifty when she had Ashok. What matters is not age, but the amount of stress
one experiences." They brought her special paans, concoctions of halwa
and ayurvedic medicine, and recommended a midwife who was good at
giving oil massages that developed the brain of the baby in the womb.
"Papa-ji, when he and Dadi-ji lost children, always tried to have another
child immediately," Mala said. "It's the only way to get over this kind of a
thing."

Privately, of course, these relatives were worried. "Let's pray there isn't
a miscarriage," Bunty said.

"In my estimation, this is exactly the type of situation in which a miscarriage occurs," Rana prophesied, taking breaks to puff at his pipe.

There *were* frights. Deepa fainted three months into the pregnancy only
to be diagnosed with gestational diabetes. "Another blow," Vikas told a

friend. Suffering panic attacks, Deepa woke with the feeling of small hands at her throat. She barely slept, except with sleeping pills, which didn't count as sleep but as a sieve through which anxiety filtered, so that when she woke, she was even more panicked and sweat soaked than before.

Vikas, meanwhile, sank, rose up, lived, sank again—fighting off bomb dreams at all hours. They were not dreams, but upwellings of pain, moments when the fire of recollection and repression got so fervid he felt he might actually explode, which he did, suffering searing headaches, and shouting at Hari the servant (who had also become absent and bereaved) and at drivers who had the nerve to overtake him on the road.

To distract himself from pain, he played tennis at the club with his friend Prabhat, smashing the ball so ferociously that the fibers inside constricted with hurt, like a small heart.

The Ahmeds, when they heard about the pregnancy, were supportive. Afsheen, dabbing her wide-set eyes (set on either side of her face like the understanding eyes of a whale) with a hankie, told Deepa on the phone that this was the only way to preserve the memory of the boys. "And if it's a girl, who knows, maybe Mansoor can marry her," she said, becoming sentimental and hysterical.

Sharif, though, found the whole thing depressing. "It's a mess, horrible," he told his wife. "Do you think they'll just have another child and live happily ever after? Every child is a packet of disappointments, hurts, dangers. If something, heaven forbid, happens to this child—then? What will they do? We're assuming it's not a miscarriage, which could happen—remember how many Zaib had?"

"You men, because you don't go through it, are much more afraid of pregnancy," Afsheen said. "Women give birth through many kinds of stress. Your view is just negative."

"What *happened* is so negative." And again he thought of how close his wife and he had come to losing everything—their beloved son, her sanity, their marriage—and he shuddered with superstitious disgust about his own good fortune.

———————

The Khuranas had their baby in September, more than a year after the blast. Deepa gave birth to a daughter. It was a relief to everyone, again—to not have to make obligatory comparisons between the new baby and Tushar and Nakul, whose faces had grown distant, consigned to the scrap heap of children's faces, faces that were never watched closely in the first place because they were destined to be discarded, covered up with the eventual masks of adulthood.

The girl's name, Anusha, as more than one person noted, compounded the sounds in Tushar's and Nakul's names. But Deepa curiously denied this. Otherwise, everyone felt, the parents looked happy. "That's the thing about them, you know," Bunty said. "Deepa and Vikas are so mild and they never impose on anyone, but they're also very tough—Deepa once told me how much effort goes into making these documentaries, the amount of editing you have to do. You'll be shocked. We think when a thing is effortless, it must have been effortless to make. In fact, those things are the hardest."

"Quite right, quite right," said Rana, wheezing without his pipe.

In fact, the Khuranas *were* happy, but they were terrified about nearing the bend of that word. Deepa was gaunt and tired and exhausted and lightheaded from the delivery while Vikas became dreamy around the new diapers.

Then Vikas started having visions.

CHAPTER 9

It was a season of breakdowns. And it was Vikas's turn.

How far they'd come from the death of their boys! His life had leapt and swallowed itself up and rolled into a ball and split open. Now—as if it were necessary for him to be trapped to grieve properly—Vikas's true grieving began. He'd done what he always did, he realized: grabbed for the nearest middle-class solution to his problem. How could another child solve anything? How could they care for her, coddle her, bring her up—they were so old already! Depressed, destroyed!

When his wife received guests and held out Anusha to them, he imagined gunning them down.

"Can we go with you, Papa?" Tushar and Nakul asked.

Vikas stood in the drawing room on a summer day. It was hot and the air was shrieky with pressure cooker hoots and honks. He did not want to take them on the shoot. He had no desire to be a father, had always considered himself above these things, and yet there were now these two boys filling up his drawing room, issuing commands and requests, their sullen persistence reminding him of nothing more than the members of his extended family, those disappointed creeps who pressed on and surrounded him at all times.

"Why do you keep doing that to your wrist?" Vikas asked Nakul. Nakul had been flicking his wrist donnishly, an action he seemed to have picked up from his uncle, Mukesh. "Are you a sardar? Do you have a kara there?"

Nakul's handsome face hung.

"Yah, don't do that," Tushar chimed in.

"You take care of your brother, Tushar. I have to go."

Divide and rule. It wasn't just the British toward the Indians but all parents toward their children.

Vikas was awfully partial toward Tushar, though he would have never acknowledged it. Nakul was popular in school, good at sports, intense, competitive, moody—just like Vikas, in other words—whereas Tushar was lumpy, effeminate, eccentric, troubled, getting pushed around in school, and moseying up to his mother in the kitchen with the halting eyes of an abused animal, always eager to please, reading the newspaper and engaging his father in incessant chatter about politics, a pet topic for him, one he had honed through quiz competitions in school, the one area in which he shone.

Still, Vikas did not like the younger one. He found him entitled and bad-tempered. "All your good marks mean nothing if you don't have a good personality," he lectured Nakul, as if a good personality could be hammered into a child with hate.

"You're too hard on him," Deepa said at night. She lay next to him in the cabin of the bedroom, the walls pressed close with night, the TV on the side basting their bodies with light. They took some time to themselves before the boys jumped into bed with them.

He did not like being lectured by his wife. Whenever she told him he was being partial, he spent a few days ignoring both of the boys, and that's what he did now, closing his eyes and sulking into sleep before the boys climbed aboard.

He dreamed fantastically. He'd always been a dreamer. In the dreams, all the parts of his life came together. Film, family, mother, father, characters, children. Life is fragmentary but dreams are not. This is why, later, he would put so much stock in the bomb dreams.

A few months before the blast, Nakul stole a toy from a friend. Vikas heard about it from his schoolteacher, Sudha Ma'am, and then from Mrs. Aggarwal, the mother of the friend. "When he came over, he took Mayank's GI Joe," she complained with a lazy, lecherous indifference, as if pleased that this disease of immorality was spreading. "I found it in his pocket. It's not a problem—they're just boys—but I wanted to tell you." At home, Vikas confronted Nakul. "Haven't we given you everything?" Nakul reprised his morose expression. He fiddled with the imaginary kara on his wrist. At that moment, Vikas caught sight of the satellite dish rising up from the roof of the CEO's mansion across the street, noticed how it exaggerated the dilapidation of the Khurana complex, its hanging electric wires and busted driveway.

It was impossible to make any money as an independent filmmaker in Delhi. A tight-knit circle of friends supported each other in their endeavors—got together and discussed Scorsese and Fellini and Godard, hosted film festivals and also peopled them—but the audience just did not exist. Indians sometimes read literature but there was no appetite for serious movies. The filmmakers, all idealistic middle-class types, succumbed to alcoholism, depression, poverty. One couple moved into a slum to finance their film. Years later, the female half of this couple wrote *The God of Small Things*. A novelist became the biggest star of the independent film world in India.

Vikas was well placed when compared to his cohort. He had his flat in the heart of Punjabi Delhi (Maharani Bagh, at the time of independence, when it had been founded, had been at the very outskirts; now the city in its growth had smuggled it to the center). He had money saved up from his time as a CA. He made commercials and corporate videos for brands like Amul and Nirma and Weekender. He penned a film review column for the *Pioneer*. His wife, once an aspiring actress, was supportive. And yet, while the country boomed and erupted with money, he stayed steady or declined. He had an urge to blame his self-consciousness on his kids, who were constantly demanding things, but he knew his *own mind* was warped by money.

It was only when he was deep in a project—erased by filming and writing—that his anxieties subsided. For this reason he worked all the time, kept a low profile in the colony, hardly talked to his relatives.

He took loans, finally, from his brother. This was his ultimate moment of shame. Vikas had four siblings. They were all deeply estranged. Their father had disapproved of every marriage. The siblings had been, conse-

quently, wild. Rekha lived in Bombay; Raakhi, in Shillong. Arun practiced
dermatology in Dehra Dun. Only Rajat remained in Delhi. He too could
have claimed the property in Maharani Bagh, but he had gallantly declined. Vikas felt nervous around him. Artists, who are selfish people, become anxious around the self-sacrificing. Now he was approaching him for
money? Impossible. And yet he went one day with his kids to visit Rajat.
Rajat was hassled too, in his Friends Colony flat, drowning in in-laws, kids,
responsibilities—he could never say no to responsibilities. Quickly, with
eager, wobbling hands, he counted off the cash. Rajat was happy for this
connection with his unstable brother. If it takes money to bring us together,
so be it.

Vikas, now flush—Rajat had given him more than necessary—spent
generously on his sons, taking them to the markets: to Rio Grande in GK
Market, to Sehgal Brothers in South Ex, to Honey-Money Top Sports in
Lajpat Nagar. Some of it was done behind his wife's back. He wasn't honest with her about how much he'd got, and when she found out, she was
incensed. Her voluble nostrils flared. She believed she deserved the money
too. "How many years I've supported you and I've never asked that we take
a holiday once. They're spoiled enough already. Besides, they won't be
artists like you," she said. "They'll make money."

Why couldn't he let his wife spend? Because he had an urge to win love,
and his wife's, in a way, had been won and lost a long time ago.

One day, he was working from the bedroom, storyboarding in a scrapbook,
when Deepa came home fuming, having picked up the boys from school.
From the boys' swollen rigid faces he could tell that some kind of fight had
transpired in the car. Nakul's glycerin-perfect hair was ruffled. Tushar
stared out angrily from his girly face, clapping his chapped lips—a rare look
of defiance. Deepa sat the boys down at the dining table and then instructed Vikas to join them all.

"When I went to pick them up from school today," she said, "first they
refused to get off the bus. Then, when these two idiots got into the car, they
put their blazers on their faces so that the kids in the bus wouldn't see them.

Can you believe it?" She scooped back her hair with her palm, as she did when she was furious. "They're ashamed of the Fiat." (Vikas's old Fiat.) "They're ashamed of us." She looked at them, at their frightened faces— though only Nakul looked contrite, while Tushar had the smirking guiltless look of a victim who has just learned how to strike back. "Shame on you two. Is this what you're learning? Do you know how many people live in poverty?"

After they had retired to their room to sulk, she said to Vikas, "You spoil them too much. You make all these documentaries about social issues— can't you teach these idiots something?" She was literally spitting. Oh, how he loved it when Deepa, who was so kind and patient, got angry! How harmless her beautiful anger was!

That day, after she had busied herself in the kitchen, Vikas drove his brats to Lajpat Nagar to explain how footpath dwellers, about whom he was planning a documentary, had such difficult lives. But as soon as he got to the crowded market, with its glut of humans, heat, concrete, moving metal cars, elbows, he realized that there was something very strange about pointing out poor people in their natural habitat to children—like they were zoo animals. He had felt it when he had done his initial research, but it was somehow more pronounced now that he had two eager schoolboys with slick gelled pompadours and black shoes and shorts with him (as pun- ishment they'd had to bathe and dress up). Worse, when they approached one of the many tiny smelly canals in Lajpat Nagar, it was clear that the footpath dwellers were not going to put up a good show. Sitting deep in their tepees of blue crinkly tarpaulin, the men were smoking bidis and playing cards. A cobbler beat a shoe to death. The potbellied children were naked and dancing. Poverty wasn't so miserable in the winter. And Vikas realized with horror that poor people look nothing like the rich, or even the middle-class: they are a different species. To ask a child to feel sympathy for the poor is harder than getting him to feel sympathy for a chicken or a goat—at least you can see a goat being slaughtered. There is real revulsion in death. Whereas the poor keep living: dumb, insensate, nasty. They live among old newspapers, Saffola cans, Nirma bottles, Kohinoor rice sacks— brands you recognize so fiercely that you don't see them at all, that are as familiar as any other local building material: mica, quartz, sandstone. Why do the poor refuse to give an accurate picture of their suffering? Why aren't they frowning, or at least moaning? Vikas was almost upset at how much they were misrepresenting themselves. Then he felt bad for wanting them to be wretched—wasn't his job to humanize them? He also felt bad that he knew no statistics that he could rattle off to stupefy the boys.

They were looking at him, waiting. Finally, he took them to a shop in the Central Market, where they examined cricket bats together. The bats were as large as they were and smelled of linseed oil. Still, the boys looked grateful and were quiet, like two convicts on bail, and they were even quieter when Vikas paid for the bat. Outside, they made pretend cricket strokes with it. "He's hit a six out of the park and now Jonty's coming in to field . . . ," Nakul whispered, commentating under his breath. Vikas rested his back against the crumbling wall of the tiny park at the center of the market and looked at the name of the shop: Honey-Money Top Sports. What a crazy name! he thought. What a crazy world!

Later, this shop too would burn in the bombing.

Back in the present, Vikas's visions continued.

Why me? he wondered, sitting on his toilet and grabbing fistfuls of his hair. Was I Hitler in my past life? Did I massacre a million people and forget? Was I Stalin, General Dyer, Cortes, or Ashoka before his conversion? He looked into the mirror and saw his unshaved mouth and upper lip and felt deeply crazy, cracked. His mind was drawn repeatedly to the *texture* of the bomb—metal, nails, heat, fire, plastic, mud: Didn't that all correspond somehow with the texture of his *life*? The gooey plasticky smell of his shower curtain? The dirty gray terrazzo of the floor? The strange oil refinery of the Fiat's engine, into which he so often had to dunk his head just to get the thing to start? The orange magenta heat into which he so often ventured with his tripod? The poorer you are, the closer you are to machines in all their nakedness and grit. The suave decoration of consumer electronics falls away. Vikas felt he understood the bomb. It was part of his world.

One day, in a great confusion, not knowing where his wife was, he found himself walking around Connaught Place. It was October and everyone's face was red and inflamed with sickness. The office workers wiped their mouths with hankies or the backs of their hands—the end of lunch. He walked about in the dust and his black pants were painted white from the bottom up. Vikas had been many times to Connaught Place—his old Arthur Andersen office had been in the market—but in all those years, he had never bothered to look up, to lift his head above the ground floor, with its old, circular, white-plaster colonial British construction and cool corridors and robust colonnades. Looking up now, he saw a big, broad, deep-blue, hot, arid metal sign that read through the hard glitter of sunlight: **STATE BANK OF INDIA**. The words were repeated underneath in Hindi. There were numbers on the board—the pin code, a phone. An insignia that might have been a peacock.

Vikas began to weep. He couldn't stop.

What was it about this sign? Something about its familiarity, perhaps—he must have seen a sign for the State Bank of India a million times in his life, on endless crossings and in the tiniest marketplace. But the feeling went deeper as Vikas stood under the big board, looking up from the tarred earth, crying into his sleeve. It was the crying of a man who is not long for this world, and for whom the tiniest signs of belonging are enough to spur a great sense of loss. The government, with its stupid boards, its multilingual blandness, its boring acronyms, had been there for him since his childhood. It had seen him grow up. Through its boards it had told him: You are here. You are in India. You exist.

Do I exist? Vikas thought. Yes. Thanks to the State Bank of India.

I have started to love anything that exudes great power, he thought. To love anything that touches me from a great distance.

And why couldn't the State Bank of India be God? Who had proof that it wasn't God? What if the government of India *was* God?

He realized that, walking randomly, he had arrived at the Arthur Andersen office. He stood outside a small door in the curving edifice of the market; beyond it, steps fed into the second floor. What would have happened if he had kept his job as a chartered accountant? Vikas wondered now, imagining an alternative life for himself. Why was I so foolish? I must have been suffering from a fever when I resigned; that's the only thing that can explain it.

He couldn't remember in this depressed state that he had hated his job as a CA, that the work had been so dull that his body had developed phantom pains and a sinus problem to keep his overactive brain annexed while it ran helter-skelter over spreadsheets—no, what he remembered instead was the visual grandeur of the Arthur Andersen office, which annexed the entire second floor and bulged with views of the street—the windows so ancient, with such congealed glass, that you felt they were quietly weeping light. And of course the whip-smart cadet-like CAs who came every morning in their suits, looking very British and unfazed, some of them with combs still sticking out of their back pockets. The tables piled with fresh-smelling paper. Above all this, the enormous distant ceiling fans that shivered like the antennae of insects and patrolled the sprawling empire of paperwork with their breeze. . . .

In the afternoons Vikas would go down the corridor and lean against the cool, hard plaster wall, feeling dizzy. When people passed by he'd rakishly bunch up his hair with one hand, cock his head to the side, and nod—his way of waving stylishly, though every time he did it he felt fake: it was not an original gesture but one he had stolen from a friend who was something of a playboy. Does everyone steal gestures? Vikas wondered. The workers in the corridor were bright and vigorous, moving with the assurance of people who know that the great horror of their lives—the big exams, their private world wars—are behind them. Yet they too must have been the sum of small thefts. The years of your chartered accountancy exams were years of nervousness, where you were still a child. You had a constant sense of falling. You were in the trenches with your guidebooks but when you came out you were on your own, dodging multiple-choice bullets. Meanwhile your self-esteem fluctuated. Some of your friends who had done wiser things—engineering or family business, for example—might already be married, and when you came into the company of these people you naturally looked up to them. . . . Or no. This theory was flawed. If Vikas had to be honest with himself he had stolen gestures aspirationally, from the people he knew he would never be, like Prabhat the playboy. And more weirdly, he had stolen gestures from people whose hand motions or mannerisms he had initially found ugly, loud, objectionable, weird. Dilip Patrekar, for example. The man had a loud hyena laugh: not exactly infectious. Within a year Vikas was emitting the laugh as well. Same with his college friend Mahinder, the sardar: a short, stout character with unblinking psychopath eyes, but popular nevertheless and a great success with girls . . . he would often make a gesture while talking in which he held one hand out and rotated it endlessly, as if rubbing a cricket ball against the air—really, it was a way of giving artificial momentum to a story that may be boring, and you could track how far along you were in the story by how much the rotation had sped up: the faster it was, the further along you were, and when it stopped, the story stopped, and the net effect was quite satisfying. So Vikas had stolen this as well.

Some more people passed by; he bunched up his hair and nodded again.

You have to stop that, he scolded himself. You have to be original.

When the next woman passed by, he was no longer leaning rakishly against the wall but standing with his arms crossed looking straight ahead, like a cadet.

The woman passed. He felt a touch on his shoulder. "Are you OK?"

It was another woman, a thin, slight, dark girl, who was a secretary.

"Yes," he said, smiling. He tapped his head. "Just thinking."

The woman burst into a bright smile, revealing an endearing set of crooked teeth. "Sorry, you just looked like an Egyptian mummy. I wanted to make sure you weren't having a seizure."

"A seizure?" said Vikas. "Do people stand like this when they're having seizures?"

"I saw it in a movie." She grinned.

"In a movie! So of course it must be true!" He meant it to be wry, but it came out sounding cruel, and he was relieved when she played along and smiled.

"An American movie, no less!" she said, shaking her head.

"Ah, the Americans and their seizures," he said vaguely, feeling bad that he was such a bad flirt and so easily embarrassed by women. "What movie was it, actually?"

"This new movie; you probably haven't heard of it. It's called *Mean Streets*."

He paused. "Of course. *Mean Streets*. By Martin Scorsese. From 1973."

"I wasn't sure how to pronounce it," she said, looking surprised.

"I haven't seen it, actually—I've read about it. I heard it was very good. Did you see it at the Rivoli film festival last month? I wanted to see it."

"Yes," she said. "Rivoli."

Vikas looked at the girl more carefully. The first thing about her was that she was a little darker than the sort of girl that Vikas would have wanted to date or marry. The second thing was that she was pretty. She had a small strawberry-shaped face with high cheekbones, big, liquid eyes, and a crooked goofy smile—in some ways it was a cartoonish face. He had never noticed before how small and delicate this girl's face was, because, when he had spotted her occasionally across the office, what stood out was her cascading curly hair, so uncommon in North India, and the fact that, unlike the Punjabi secretaries, she wore skirts and loose shirts with big starched collars. "What's your name, remind me?"

"Deepa. Deepa Thomas."

So she was a Christian; that explained it. Vikas, who was a serious man, decided to cut off his flirtation. He crossed his arms again. "Very nice to meet you, Deepa."

When Vikas, standing outside the office in CP, thought back on this memory, with its innocence, its inarticulate posturing, its sudden movement toward the common love of cinema, it made him cry.

Maybe it was my destiny to suffer.

But I could have ignored her. Instead I sought her out.

A week after meeting Deepa, Vikas had become silently infatuated with her. It was not an uncommon development for him. He spoke to girls so infrequently and was generally such a shy character that a pretty face and a few flirtatious words were enough to make him tipsy with love. Often he would begin fantasizing deep into the future about women—courtship, sex, marriage, the works—and with Deepa it was the same: he must have written several imaginary novels' worth of conversation with her in his head in that first week of infatuation. He also rebuked himself for his silliness.

She might have a boyfriend, he told himself.

She might be married.

She's a Christian, for God's sake—you can't go steady with her!

What will Mummy and Daddy say when you tell them you're going to marry a South Indian?

And your friends, won't they judge you also?

He began to rail against his friends. *What a judgmental, bigoted bunch I've been blessed with. Not one intellectual or broad-minded fellow in the whole lot of them. They all watch movies and read pondy mags and fantasize about all sorts of women but when it comes to marriage they'll be marrying the usual fat Punjabi kuddis. . . .* He suddenly felt very brave, like he was an activist hired by the government to promote national integration in a stubbornly segregationist Indian subcontinent.

Then a week passed. She made no effort to talk to him and was busy walking around the office twirling her hair with a finger, her crisp skirts making a sound like grains being raked, and Vikas began to feel nervous. What if she was about to quit? What if one of these British-looking fellows had designs on her? In the office Vikas had calculated that about fifteen men were better-looking and more articulate than he, while the other seventy were not; of course, he believed himself to be the most brilliant, with the best taste. *Your taste won't matter if you do nothing with it. If you just sit.* He thought of his playboy friend Prabhat, who was just finishing his specialization in pediatrics, and from whom he had stolen so many gestures. *Prabhat flirts with everyone: girls, aunties, babies, men, children. He has no shame at all.* Prabhat's lack of shame was amusing and endearing. He was in a sense an ecumenical playboy. In college in Delhi he had dated a couple of fantastically ugly coconut–hair oil types from Haryana—fellow medical students

who, Vikas had said unkindly, should consider specializing in the medicine
of self–plastic surgery. But then Prabhat had also snagged an air hostess
and a TV newscaster, and in fact was now engaged to the latter. *Bloody lucky
fellow, with his good looks, his height, his hair which stands up on end . . .*

Vikas went one day to Deepa's desk doing a full medley of Prabhat gestures: tousling his hair into thick black twisting flames; stooping a little, as
if he were a tall man; and looking off to the side as he spoke, as if deeply
distracted by the galloping machinery of his intellect. "Deepa, hi. Oh—I
saw *Mean Streets*, by the way. It's bloody brilliant, man."

She looked up from her desk. "Isn't it? I love that scene in the billiards
place."

"Yeah, yeah, what amazing camerawork," he said, fumbling—he hadn't
seen it. "Only thing was—I had a bad print. I saw it on my cousin's VCR
and there was that normal PAL/NTSC problem." He continued, "Someone should bring new wave to India also."

"Indian men aren't handsome enough to pull off new wave stuff," she
laughed.

"Insult, yaar. Insult."

"I'm joking, yaar," she said. She picked up a piece of paper and began
signing it. "One minute," she said, and signed something else.

Vikas waited with his hands on his hips, wondering if the crowd of CAs
was surveying him. To distract himself, he dished out more of his hair from
his scalp and looked up at the ceiling. It occurred to him that there was
something brilliant about Prabhat's gestures: he'd taken a host of normal
nervous tics and transformed them into something sexy and unpredictable
and moody.

"You love touching your hair," Deepa said, interrupting.

"No, no," Vikas said. "It just distracts me."

"What happened to your thumbs?" she said.

"Oh this?" he said, feeling suddenly embarrassed. There were two
gashes, like mini eyes, on the sides of both his thumbs. "I scratch my
thumbs when I'm bored and sometimes they peel off." He had been doing
it a lot recently, thinking of Deepa.

"It's quite deep," she said, taking his hands in hers and turning them over, like he was a child being examined for dirt by his mother.

Vikas felt a wild electric charge shoot through him. *I wonder what the other CAs are thinking*, he thought. But he let her look at the thumbs. *These Christian girls*, he thought. *So fast. No wonder Mahinder the sardar was always going on about them.*

She let his hands go and seemed to nod in a deep, knowing way. "I have many nervous tics also," she said. "I bite my nails. I also pick at my face." She grinned crookedly. For the first time Vikas noticed how properly filed her nails were, though they were bloodless and devoid of nail polish. The fingers were fragile-looking and wiry and veined with bluish-green vessels, and when Vikas looked at her face again he could suddenly see the vessels crisscrossing her large forehead, throbbing things like the pressings of stems in a scrapbook, the skin of the forehead already crinkled. She was just a mesh of blood, he thought, with pity. A fragile biological creature.

Vikas said, "Have you seen any films by Bergman, by the way?"

"Bergman? Let's see. *Scenes from a Marriage. Persona. Virgin Spring. Through a Glass Darkly.* So yes. Four."

Vikas was truly amazed. "That's more than I've seen, man! I've just seen *Scenes from a Marriage* and *Persona.*" He said, "He's a total genius, no?"

"I agree."

He went on, "Sorry—I don't know why I brought him up. I just thought, given that you liked Scorsese, you might like Bergman." This was nonsense and he knew it. He had brought up Bergman because *Fanny and Alexander* was playing at a festival at Kamani, and he wanted to see if she was going, but he had lost his courage. "Anyway, I'm glad you like Bergman; it makes me happy someone else watches him also."

"I think he's quite famous, no?"

"Not here," he said, indicating the CAs.

She smiled at him with her eyes and nodded back. It took Vikas a second to realize that she was gesturing about her approaching boss. "Chalo," he said. "We'll talk later." But then he didn't move. He was past embarrassment. The boss came and went. Six months later, they were married.

MANSOOR AHMED'S RESPONSE TO TERROR

MAY 1996–MARCH 2003

CHAPTER 10

The bomb became the most significant thing that had happened to Mansoor, cleaving his life into before and after. His hearing got worse for a while, cleaned out by the violent finger of the bomb. He wore a cast on his right arm for two months.

Mansoor's pain came in enormous fuzzy waves in his arm, doubling him over in his bed. At other times it was a claw of lightning, rapacious and singular, turning his limbs wet from the inside as he walked about the house in his pajamas. When he lingered with his parents at the dining table, a constant drizzle of electricity shocked his arm, and in the mornings his muscles turned sluggish with cement, and wet sand filled the gap between tendons.

When he recalled the day of the bomb, his eyes filled with tears. He hadn't known till then how selfish he was, and when he felt bad for the boys, it was undercut by a feeling that he was performing for God. And because he felt God could see him he was doubly guilty.

It was lucky, his parents said, that the blast happened in the middle of the summer holidays, giving him time to heal. But maybe, Mansoor would think later, when he was older, his life in ruins, maybe it wasn't. Had he been forced back to school, forced to confront the mundane dribble of homework and unit tests and weekly exams, he might have recovered faster. Instead he stayed home that summer—disturbed, upset, coddled, winched by nightmares, remembering the bomb, the boys as they lay next to the twisted car door, dropped and broken, and of course their faces before, the moments before, when they'd all been trudging through the market like heroes, talking about the prices of trump cards and bats, and he'd felt irritated at Nakul for acting so certain and authoritative. *I know you're not rich,* he'd wanted to say. *Why do you act it?* But he'd said nothing. His mind whipped back to the bomb, the meaninglessness of it.

His parents took him everywhere that summer—mosques, dargahs, the Bahá'i temple. Before, they had believed in nothing; now they believed in everything. He was happy to be escorted to these places in the air-conditioned Esteem, but when he found himself in a crowd his heart thundered, his palms sweated, and he looked around at the swirling faces of the devotees. "Mama, please let's go home," he begged.

"Of course, beta," she said, shouting for the driver, who always appeared with a knowing smirk on his face, as if he did not respect his rich young master's problems.

After that, the holy men trooped home: fakirs, maulvis, sufis, vaids, and the like. Mansoor, his thin legs tucked beneath his knees, said prayers with all of them, letting them press their old-man hands to his head for benediction and drinking whatever potions they offered.

He liked staying home, in the ground-floor flat in South Ex with its emporium-like drawing room crowded with exotic teak furniture from Burma and Indonesia (Afsheen's father had been in the foreign service and she had grown up partly in Burma). He had no desire to venture out again into the misery of Delhi. When news of the blast welled in the papers, he avoided it, scrambling the pages in a nervous blur till he was at *Garfield* and *Beetle Bailey.*

Then, just like that, one day, school began. He was twelve and had places to be.

On the first day of school, he was driven from home in a car by the driver, his parents lapsed on either side of him, his father's head tilted back and fingers on his lips as he looked out the burning window, a man fulfilling his duty with seriousness and without ceremony, his mother more involved, upright and relaxed and cooing, bringing her cold and fragrant Nivea hands to his forehead. Mansoor smirked proudly as the car gathered the

familiar landmarks on the way to school: AIIMS, Bhikaji Cama Place, the
sandstone nub of the Hyatt Hotel. He assumed this was special treatment,
bound to be suspended in favor of the school bus the minute he was settled
into his routine, but when he got ready the next morning, the driver was
waiting for him again.

The bomb had killed his friends. But it had improved his life.

The children at Vasant Valley School had by now gone through several
phases with regard to the bomb, not so different from society itself. Nor
were they strangers to bombs, the idea of bombs. Every year some joker
called the principal's office, said a bomb was hidden in a classroom, and
everyone poured into the field till the threat had been neutralized. It was
always the most memorable day of the year.

So—the children, on summer holiday, had heard about Mansoor and
been shocked, or rather tried to act as shocked as their shocked parents;
had been bewildered or not based on their experiences with death; and
then had forgotten. When they got to school, many were convinced that the
deaths of the Khurana boys and Mansoor's injury were just rumors, like
those you sometimes heard about fast senior girls having sex with hoodlums
who had finished school. These children were soon proven wrong, giving
rise to another round of bewilderment: What could this small Muslim boy
have to do with the exploding market? How could he have survived?

"Bhainchod, did you set it off?" one senior with a bobbing Adam's apple
asked.

Mansoor looked at him with confused, cautious eyes.

Mansoor's panic attacks in public spaces did not go away—they got worse.
It was absurd, he told his mother, that there was no security in school to
protect against terrorists and miscreants, and he was constantly on the
lookout for suspicious bulging backpacks; he started violently if a football
smashed against the grilles on the churchy windows, grilles designed spe-
cially to repel such invasions. In the break period he showed the wound on
his right arm to his friends—a long smear of fibrous reddish skin hanging

over his veins with the glistening clarity of egg white. Classmates surrounded him at all hours in the brick buildings of the school. It didn't bring
popularity but rather a sort of bland notoriety. He felt like a freak. He was
still the only Muslim in school and he wanted to hide.

He got the chance with physiotherapy. In a clinic in Safdarjung Enclave,
he lay in a cube of curtains, tortured by tinny Hindustani classical music as
a slight woman in a lab coat lathered his wrists with cold goo and ran the
feeler of an ultrasonic machine over them. Adults with decomposing bodies moaned around him in adjacent cubes. In this house of pain, he too was
a grown-up. His physiotherapist was a South Indian lady named Jaya—his
first experience with South Indians apart from Deepa Khurana. "You're
Muslim?" she asked, clearly startled. "You don't look Muslim." But she
relaxed when he mentioned the blast. "It's very bad. These days one can't
live in this country." She was one of those people who are lost within themselves. She told him the same story over and over about how her brother
worked in information technology in Houston and how she had visited him
there. "There is a very high standard of living there," she said. She asked
the same questions every time, as if discovering anew that there was a patient there. "You also want to study IT, no? There's a big scope in it." He
lay impatiently in bed. Afterwards, he went with his mother for a walk
through Deer Park, happy among the vaguely caged animals—deer, pea-
cocks, rabbits, the moving rubbish of stray dogs and cats, the mynahs with
their minimal beauty.

When the terrorists were arrested, Mansoor asked, "But Papa, what if they
get out of jail?"

"There's a strict sentence for terrorism," Sharif reassured him. Though
he himself was wondering whether the right men had been captured; there
was already talk among the Muslim intellectuals he knew, professors at
Jamia, that the police had rounded up innocents as "terrorists"; that they
had planted a stepney, a spare tire, in the room of a couple of papier-
mâché artisans in Bhogal and arrested their fourteen-year-old cousin, who

had come for his summer vacation to Delhi from Srinagar; that the other arrested men had been in custody even before the blast.

"Look, the thing is, they didn't do any of the arrests with an independent witness present," Rizwan Ali, a professor at Jamia, told him. "Without that, the case falls apart. There's zero credibility. Now, Sharif-sahb, we also want that the people be brought to book—that's the goal. But I have a fear, having seen these cases before, that you'll find the same problem here."

"Bhaijaan, it's none of our business. We're just happy that our son survived."

But when Sharif went home from this gathering in the Zakir Bagh apartments and saw his son, he became fearful. He sat behind Mansoor on the floor as he played his Mega Drive (his wrist had healed just enough that he could click a controller) and parted his son's hair in the peculiar way his own mother had once parted *his* hair, closing his fingers together into a spoon and running them from the part to the ear over and over again.

"Can you scratch a little also, Papa?" Mansoor asked, not turning around.

"Of course!"

That night, Sharif told his wife, "Watch your spending—we should send him to America for college when he grows up."

CHAPTER 11

Years passed. In 2001, at the age of seventeen, Mansoor left Delhi for the US, excited to pursue a degree in computer science, which had become his main passion after years of confinement in his home. He was more intimate with his 486—and then his Pentium with Intel Inside—than with any person in Delhi. After all, to see other people meant you had to leave your house, and this made them accessories to danger.

He had also become a decent programmer and web designer, building a tennis website, Sampras Mania, with a friend, which, though it plagiarized its stats and player summaries from ATP and ESPN, presented them in a (he thought) more orderly fashion.

He won second-place trophies in class eleven in the computer quizzes at ACCESS and MODEM, where he was, he noted, the only Muslim in attendance, the Azim Premji of the gathering, if you will.

The fact of the bombing, the exceptionalism of his last name in Hindu Punjabi society—these things filled him with an odd pride.

He became aware of the oppression of Muslims as the BJP tenaciously clung to power all through the late nineties. His mother never stopped being alarmed. "They're still angry about something that happened fifty years ago," she'd say, thinking of partition, and returning again and again to the images of party workers swarming the domes of the Babri Masjid, gashing the onionskin of cement with hammers. Mansoor concurred. He believed, like his father, that the imprisoned men might be innocent. "Is there anything we can do as informed citizens?" he asked, parroting the vocabulary of his earnest civics textbooks.

"In this country they prefer deformed citizens to informed citizens," his father said drily. "And how will the Khuranas feel?"

"They also want justice."

"Who knows what they want?"

The families, in the years since Anusha's birth, had grown apart. The Khuranas had stopped calling the Ahmeds for social gatherings—which they still organized—and often didn't return Afsheen's monthly, inquiring, concerned calls.

"Ulta chor kotwal ko daante," Sharif said, bungling the context of the homily. *This is case of the thief scolding the watchman.* "They should be thankful to us and to Mansoor. If he hadn't been there, they wouldn't have known what happened."

Since the first few visits to the market, the Khuranas had recovered scraps of cloth they were sure came from the boys' shirts. They'd found the exact spot where the boys had died from Mansoor's memories.

"You can't get inside people's minds," Afsheen said. "But their situation also isn't good."

She had her own theory: their marriage was in trouble. She had heard it from a common friend. But she did not think it right to gossip about this with her husband.

When Mansoor was set to leave for the U.S., though, the Khuranas came over with Anusha and everyone was together again. An anxious serenity pervaded the air.

"Have a wonderful time abroad," Deepa Auntie said, rubbing her nose, as she did when she wanted to convey emotion, and presenting Mansoor with a fragrant envelope of rupees, rupees, which, of course, would be useless the minute he stepped on the plane.

"Thank you, auntie."

"You must visit the museum where they keep Eadweard Muybridge's first film." Vikas Uncle was full of advice about the U.S., though it wasn't clear he'd ever been there.

Anusha ran over and gave Mansoor a hug at the waist and then went back to deftly polluting a notebook on the ground with the unnatural jumping colors of sketch pens.

She was four now, the daughter of the bomb.

Mansoor arrived in August on a farmlike campus in Santa Clara that was wide open and safe and he settled into his dorm, getting to know Eddy and Chris, his roommates, one a Hispanic football player from San Antonio, the other an Armenian-American tennis player from Los Angeles, each creature alien to the other in build and form (Eddy massive, Chris tall, Mansoor slight but hairy), the alienness canceling into a common brotherly bonding.

"Dude!" "Dude!" "Dude!" they said, addressing each other, and Mansoor had never been happier. He developed a routine of working hard on his C++ assignments by day and then loitering in the cool California air by night as freshmen stormed the campus, singing their dorm chants.

He was like a person who, thinking his vision perfect, puts on glasses for the first time to discover he has been going blind.

Then one day he was brushing his teeth in his dorm sink when he heard a commotion—a rare sound for this time of the morning. Wiping his mouth, he went down to the main lounge, a wide rectangular room broken by driving asbestos-smeared pillars. Boys and girls were draped on the sofa in their athletic wear—shorts, sweatshirts, T-shirts—watching TV. They had smiles on their faces, which Mansoor quickly realized were the tight expressions that came before tears.

Planes had crashed into the World Trade Center.

"Shit," Mansoor said, though he couldn't really feel anything.

Things began to change immediately on the pristine campus with its clear fountains like lucid dreams of the earth. People discussed the hijackers, who were all Muslims (the hijackers had made no effort to hide their identities, which had been radioed back by the flight attendants, who knew their seat numbers); and talked about Islam and its connection to violence. Mansoor felt uncomfortable, felt he was being looked at in a new way, but also felt he ought to stay clear of the debate. When he said hello to acquaintances as they marched past in the dorm, they didn't wave back.

"Are you OK my laad? My son?" his mother asked on the phone.

"I'm in California, Mama, nothing's happening here."

"They're saying al-Qaeda wants to blow up the Golden Gate Bridge. Don't go there."

"No one walks on the bridge. It's very far from my campus. People drive on it." Like many immigrants, he too had felt let down by the bridge.

Still, back in the dorm, the little confidence he'd gained was gone—the wit wilted away from sentences and he was entrapped by his own thickening accent, which people suddenly found impossible to understand. He wanted to tell them about his own experiences with terror, but in those days after 9/11, when panic ruled the campus, and administrators warned students not to even accidentally drink water from a public faucet, since al-Qaeda was planning chemical warfare next, he did not get the opportunity.

Then one day, he was sitting in the dining hall with Alex, a polymathic Jewish boy from Boston who was interested in all the international students and also liked flooring them with his intimate knowledge of their countries, when he began speaking. Alex had been quizzing Mansoor about Sikh separatism. "It's strange for me to hear all this talk about terrorism," Mansoor said. "I was actually in a car bombing when I was young." Once he started, he couldn't stop. The story poured out. Telling it to a foreigner, in another language, having to put it in context—this made it small, exotic, alien, and terrifying. "The shop fronts had mirrors on them," he said, realizing how odd it had been. "It was a fashion. And the mirrors blew up and the shards cut up people's faces. I was very lucky. The worst thing that could have happened long term, apart from losing a limb, was damaging my ears. Your eardrums get blown out and you develop tinnitus, where you can hear a buzzing sound constantly. That didn't happen. But I did get a similar kind of pain in my wrist and arm. It was like a buzzing."

"Shit, Mansoor-mian," Alex said, spooning his hot pea soup. "Do you still have it?"

"No, thank God, though it took years to heal."

After that, Mansoor thought things would change for him, but nothing did. People did not care about a small bomb in a foreign country that had injured a Muslim, and why should they? They were grieving. Three thousand of their countrymen had perished. Why would they look outward? Mansoor stopped talking about it and concentrated on his work.

One night in the computer cluster in the basement of the dorm—a rank space that had clearly once been a boiler room; one wall was a jungle gym of gurgling pipes—a girl sitting next to him, a thin black-haired girl in an alluring tank top and shorts that had SANTA CLARA U stenciled on the buttocks (he had seen it when she got up to adjust the shorts), turned to him. She asked if he knew how to retrieve e-mails from the trash in Pine. Her manner was neutral and friendly and Mansoor was overjoyed. "Of course," he said, and leaned over the desk. "Just click here." She held back from the screen, blinking liquidly.

"Thank you so much," she said when he was done.

"Of course."

But when Mansoor went back to typing at his terminal, he heard her stirring again.

"Hi, I'm Emma," she was saying to the curly-haired white boy on the other side of her—a boy also in a tank top, playing *Quake* on the screen.

"Daniel."

That was all. The next day Mansoor complained to his friend Irfan at the campus Starbucks. "To them I'm either a computer programmer or a terrorist."

Irfan was a stocky boy with a limp that made him look oddly rakish and wise for his age. "American women are like that," Irfan said, twirling a wet Frappuccino bottle. "You have to fuck them first before they talk."

Irfan had a particular way of making his disaffection cool, and Mansoor hung out with him for a few weeks, before tiring of his misogyny and his habit of wanting to borrow Mansoor's problem sets. Soon after, Mansoor returned to programming with a vengeance.

He worked steadily for the next year. He had decided to become an exceptional programmer on par with Bill Joy and Steve Wozniak. Keeping a copy of *The Fountainhead* by his side, he rapped away at the keyboard into the night.

Then, one day, during his sophomore year, while programming Boggle for a Programming Methods class, his wrists started to ache.

His wrists had ached off and on ever since the Lajpat Nagar blast—Jaya, in her pedantic way, had warned him that such deep-seated pain, at the level of the tissues, where the cells and nerves themselves had been singed, did not go away easily, and he was supposed to keep up his wrist and arm exercises, lying on a yoga mat and lifting one-kilogram weights in contorted poses. Of course, he hadn't. Exercise bored him—why run if you weren't being chased?—and he'd been caught up in the ardor of college. Now the flaring pain sent vectors of electricity up and down his right arm. In the unintelligible void of his muscles danced a thousand pins and needles. "Don't panic," he told himself. But what scared him was that the left wrist, weak from all that typing, could barely continue on its journey along the valleys and plateaus of the keyboard. His neck ached.

After a few days of this (within three days, he was totally unable to type) he went to see the physiotherapist at the campus health center. Sitting among fragrant potted plants, amazed by how similar the place looked to the physiotherapy center in India, though the two countries were ten thousand kilometers and eons of income apart, he was careful to explain how it had happened, his history with the bomb—careful to separate himself from the other namby-pambies who came to see her. The physiotherapist, a bright and squat pregnant woman with blond hair and enormous overworked arms, put his arms one at a time in a hot bath of wax, so that a skin of hot wax hardened on them. It was like having another skin. "The heat will be good for you," she said. After a while, she cut the wax away softly with a butter knife—it was a pleasing sensation—and she gave him printouts showing exercises and different relaxation techniques and told him he would be totally OK.

But Mansoor's pain didn't get better. It got worse. A few weeks after his visit to the physiotherapist, he woke up in the middle of the night with his arms radiant and loud with electricity. The massive hunk of Eddy from San Antonio snored in the upper bunk. When he got up to go to the bathroom, sparks shot up his sciatic nerve and numbed his leg, and he stumbled.

"You've got tons of microtears in your wrists from typing," Laurie, the physiotherapist, concluded, when he went back to see her. "These things build up over years. You get injured, you develop a compensatory posture when you type, and bam!—years later you have herniated discs. When did you start using a computer?" she asked.

"Twelve," he said. He had got a 486 right after the blast—he had got so much after the blast!

"There you go—all those years of sitting still, hunched over, not taking breaks." She told him he had carpal tunnel, an incurable condition. "Though it *can* be controlled and improved," she assured him.

He was essentially crippled. Walking around the bright campus in a daze, he felt his right leg and right arm and left wrist go numb.

Free from India and still plagued by pain! After all these years! He'd changed his mind about the bomb so many times. Of course it was a curse to have witnessed that explosion, to have suffered so vividly—to have so many things opened to him at once: death, a woman's hanging breast, the cowardice of men and women who ran screaming from the market. At other times—the blast had improved his life, hadn't it? He'd eked a spectacular college essay out of it—the dean himself had congratulated him on it when he'd arrived. Now he played the essay back in his mind: those homilies and banalities he'd penned about terror, the death of his friends, communal harmony—bah! Maybe that was why he was suffering now: he'd tried to take advantage of a tragedy. His mind darkened. When it comes to cause and effect, he thought, I really do believe God exists; I really do think God is watching, drawing his conclusions, doling out consequences. Sometimes I don't even know I've committed a sin till a punishment comes along.

After all, he wouldn't have been typing so much if he hadn't been in the U.S., where everything ran on computers, where the Internet was available on tap and the electricity never went out. And he wouldn't have been in the U.S. without the essay. You have to stop thinking like that, he told himself. You *did* almost die. He saw again the small child with flaring red-hot fragments around him, the screams, the stampede, the cowardice of a whole society stripped bare. Most of the people who had learned these lessons about their country and city died seconds later, as if the bomb existed to prove to them, in their final moments, that they had lived a useless life in a useless place.

But the pain did not go away; it got worse. In the middle of his third semester in college, unable to function, he returned to India to recuperate.

CHAPTER 12

"How can it still be there?" his mother asked the doctor at the clinic in Safdarjung, blinking furiously.

The doctor was a stately Sikh who dressed in white shirts with matching white turbans; he worked with a lot of embassies. The great endorsement of anyone in Delhi: he works with embassies.

"Sometimes it takes years to heal," he said, clearly occupied by other problems: financial ones, maybe; he had an undoctor-like anxiety in his eyes.

"I don't understand why it's coming back now, at this moment. The last time we came, if you remember, the checkup said everything was OK."

Mama, Mansoor wanted to say, *it's not his fault.*

The patient sardar doctor gave a long explanation about pain and muscle growth and computer usage.

And so Mansoor was consigned again to the cube of curtains, back again with Jaya telling the same proud, unbelieving stories about her brother in Houston—only this time he was older and taller, five feet seven, the bed barely fitting under him. And he felt not comfort in the balmed air as he had in the past, but panic—panic that life was passing him by.

It was at this time that the Khuranas invited Mansoor over for tea.

"Why do they want to meet me now?" he asked, suspicious, in pain, churlish.

"They're curious about you," his mother said. "You're a grown-up now.

They want an individual equation with you." She became dreamy speaking about the Khuranas.

"Yaah but—" Mansoor was not convinced. He argued and debated the visit with his mother. Finally, on a windswept, befogged afternoon, the sort in which all of Delhi is wearing a sweater of atmospheric dirt, he went over with the driver to see the Khuranas.

The Khuranas still lived in the old flat in the Khurana complex, with the large windows looking out onto the mansions of Maharani Bagh, and the sofas rearranged to create an illusion of progress. The Khuranas welcomed him with a big tea—samosas, pakoras, granular chutneys. They hadn't aged much either—tragedy had given them an odd guilelessness, Vikas Uncle looking hyper as ever with his large buzzing forehead and thinning hair, the black pencil mustache imported from the Kissan Ketchup commercials, which, Mansoor now remembered, he had directed; and Deepa Auntie thin and shy and self-effacing, constantly wiping her upper lip with the end of her sheer dupatta, smiling, her crooked teeth showing through the cloud of cloth. As for Anusha, she must have been five now. Round-eyed, cute, a tiny black twist of a bun spilling out from her boyish hair, she walked about with her back excessively curved, slapping the ground hard as children do.

It was weird to be back here, accepting tea, flinching from the pain in his right wrist.

After asking him about his injury, the Khuranas, obviously glad to talk to someone who didn't need background, filled him in on the details of the trial, which was still going on—in its sixth year. The adjournments were ridiculous, they said. The government had let them down repeatedly. The prosecutor had been arrested for sexual assault. One session was called off because a stray dog wandered into the court and bit a policeman. Worst of all—"No word about the compensation."

"Still?" asked Mansoor, his teeth jumping from the overly sweetened tea, the dust of the city pouring into the drawing room from all sides in long mineral sunlit shafts. The glaring sunlight of Delhi—he had not missed this in the U.S., not one bit.

"Ask your papa," Vikas Uncle said, snorting. "Nothing. He and I've both gone many times to the thana. But the blast happened at such a strange time—the BJP had only been in power for a week and they were gone a week later—that no one took responsibility for it. That's also luck."

"But it's not that much, is it?" Mansoor said and immediately regretted it. They were not as well off as he was.

"It's a matter of principle," Vikas Uncle said.

Though he looked devastated.

"Yes, of course," Mansoor said, feeling bad. "I should look into it as well. I was so small then, I had no idea what was happening."

"They should be paying you for these wrist problems you're having," Deepa Auntie said, piping up from her large sofa chair. "We would get them to pay for Uncle's back problems but he wasn't present, so it doesn't count." Mansoor had heard about Vikas's back—how he suffered debilitating pain. But he didn't connect it with his own pain.

Mansoor sat shaking his tense head, ingratiating as always.

Suddenly, Deepa Auntie started crying.

"Auntie," he said.

"It's OK," she said, wiping her nose with the back of her hand.

He bent over his tea, his wrists aching. He knew he brought back memories of her boys—how could he not? His whole existence was a rebuke to the idea that their deaths were inevitable. Why them and not him? Why two of them and zero of him?

"You're wrong," his mother had said, when he'd said this to her before leaving. "They *want* to see people who remember the boys."

"Their classmates remember them too." The Khurana boys and he had been in different schools. This was one reason they were friends. Mansoor, when he saw them, was free from the baggage of reputation that attached itself to him in school, where he was taunted for being a Muslim, dubbed "mullah" and "Paki" and "mosquito."

"But you should go," his mother had said. "Do your duty. Don't worry about the outcome. When you lose someone, you think of them all the time anyway. You'll change nothing. You'll make them feel less alone, less crazy."

Mansoor remembered this now and yet felt uncomfortable. "Auntie, I should go home—Mummy likes eating dinner early," he said in the dusty drawing room, the walls shaking from renovation and construction happening elsewhere. Mansoor knew the sounds so well from years of living in Delhi that he could picture the machines—large cement mixers and pile drivers. Delhi has no bird-watchers, only machine-listeners.

"No, no, stay a little while more," she said. Now he'd made her feel guilty about crying. Fuck.

Pulling back her graying hair, she brought out a photo album with a dizzying fluorescent green and maroon cover. "Here are pictures of you and the boys at the Sports Day in Maharani Bagh," she said, opening to a plastic page with two photos jammed at sad angles inside it. But her eyes were blurry; she left the pictures open too long; she was lost.

When Mansoor was leaving, Vikas Uncle said, "I want to give you something." They went to the bathroom together. This was Vikas Uncle's studio, a space that had been converted after the boys' deaths—what was the use, after all, of two toilets? Above, water bled gauntly through the pipes, and notebooks lay in an abject circle on the floor around the toilet column. The bathing area was a chaos of equipment—black pieces of angled metal, tripods, cameras in their plastic hoods. From this pile Vikas Uncle fished out a bulky Minolta camera with a silver focus. "I'd kept it for the boys," he said. "But I want you to have it."

"No, uncle. Where will I use it?"

"Take it," he said. "I know digital is in fashion these days, but the quality you can get from this is unparalleled. I've photographed some very beautiful ladies with this camera, when I was doing shoots for *Cosmo*."

Mansoor had seen Vikas Uncle's movies before and had never cared for them. They were serious, stiff, shot in black-and-white, the characters speaking crisp English. Nothing good happened to anyone. People lived enclosed middle-class lives, taunting each other with petty memories, and women and men argued incessantly. "They're so joyless," he had told his mother, wondering at how tragic Vikas Uncle's sensibility had been even before the blast—it was as if he were sitting at a ceremonial fire, fanning a tragedy toward himself.

"But they are very acclaimed," his mother had said reverently.

"They gave you another thing?" his mother said when he came home. "They shouldn't have. Anyway, their finances aren't so good. Deepa was saying that these days, because there's a new distribution system, it's very difficult to get financing for art films."

"I'm so old now," Mansoor said, which was neither here nor there.

"Let me keep it," she said, taking the camera from him.

He knew what would happen—it would disappear, like all the things Vikas Uncle had given him over the years. His mother had immense empathy for the Khuranas, but like so many people, she was superstitious about death, cautious about not letting it sneak into her house.

CHAPTER 13

Now, for the first time as an adult, Mansoor became curious about the Lajpat Nagar case. Then one day, on the way back from physio, having read in the newspaper that a hearing was scheduled in Patiala House, he directed the driver to take him to the court.

Mansoor had never been to the courts before—those barracks of Indian life crammed behind the colonial facades of Lutyens's Delhi—but he had a chacha who was a lawyer and had heard a great deal about the institution. When his parents rang him on his mobile, he silenced it. He wanted time to himself.

He got out of the car and, after lightly acknowledging the guard at the entrance, walked through the open bricked corridors with their searching blind fingers of dead trees, their groggy supplicants in red and white sweaters. Through his swimming nervous vision he saw signs indicating the names of the courtrooms. Finally, he entered a courtroom the size of a classroom. At the front of the room, two lawyers in their penguinlike garb, their backs turned to the audience, were murmuring to the judge, who bent his head down from his high boatlike desk. When Mansoor sat down in the last row, his wrists almost spiritual with pain, one of the lawyers twisted around for a second and then went back to talking. A few moments later, several hassled-looking men with sweat-soaked shirts appeared at the door, carrying what seemed to be a Chinese changing screen, the type behind which naked women are always banished in old movies. Now the lawyers turned around completely. The men began to set up the screen near the front of the room.

"The proceeding is in camera," the judge said suddenly.

There was a commotion and throat-clearing in the aisles next to Mansoor.

"In camera," he repeated, irritated.

People began to rise.

"You have to get up," a woman in a smart pantsuit instructed Mansoor.

Perplexed, having exited, Mansoor lingered now by the tea stall outside the Sessions Court, watching the dhaba-wallah fry samosas in a deep wok. He was in a philosophical mood, thinking back to the stories the Khuranas had told about the adjournments.

"You good name?" a voice interrupted him.

Mansoor turned around to see himself facing a man with a squashed, eager look about him; a neckless fellow with crooked teeth bejeweling his gums. Mansoor recognized him from the courtroom.

Mansoor mumbled, "Hello."

"My name is Naushad," the man said quickly, placing a palm on his chest. "I work for an NGO, Peace For All." Peace For All, according to Naushad, focused on "communal harmony" and was looking to provide a just, speedy trial for the men arrested for the 1996 blast. "You're a journalist?" he asked Mansoor.

"No, no—just a visitor," Mansoor said, smiling slightly, now understanding the reason for his forwardness.

"You have a relative in the case?" Naushad asked in Hindi.

"No." Mansoor smiled again. He crushed the paper cup and chucked it into a bin, where it parachuted into a ridge between other crushed cups. "I just wanted to watch. Anyone can come. But I should go."

"But people don't really come just like that—that's why I was asking. But you're a Muslim, no?"

"Yes," Mansoor said, amazed at this religious clairvoyance. But he was gifted with it too; he had somehow known Naushad was a Muslim before he announced his name. "Actually I was a victim of the blast," Mansoor said. "But I don't have any connection with the case."

"*You* were injured in the blast?" Naushad said, pointing a finger down at the ground in surprise.

Mansoor nodded. "I was small. But I got shrapnel in my arm."

At that moment, Mansoor felt he had pulled out a trump card; that he had absolved himself of suspicion in the eyes of the dhaba-wallah, who had been listening to the exchange in an absent way; sopping up the conversation the way his samosas were sopping up oil.

"Don't take this the wrong way," Naushad said, clearly excited. "But you can really help us." He launched into an explanation. "We've been working for two or three years for people to give attention to the locked-up men. Everyone knows—even the judges—that the wrong men have been arrested. You can read it in the documents: there was no independent witness present when they were arrested. That's why they keep adjourning. But the issue is that after 9/11 and the Parliament attack, no one wants to help these people. 'They're bloody terrorists; let them rot,' they say. But, bhai, they haven't even been proven to be terrorists! One is a papier-mâché artisan. Another was a student in class eight when he came to Delhi to stay with his brothers. And the last one, he used to work with his family in a carpet shop in Kathmandu. These people's lives have been ruined, and now six years have passed without a trial. So we're making an effort to bring out the story in the press. And look, if someone like you, an educated person, a victim— if you say something, imagine how much more of a difference it'll make. Let me write my name and e-mail and phone on a chit"—he had already taken out a tattered lined paper and was pressing a pen into it against a timber column in the tea shop—"and if you want to help please phone us or e-mail us. Here you go." He handed Mansoor the chit. "As salaam aleikum," he said.

"Wa aliekum as salaam," Mansoor said.

Mansoor liked that the man did not press him, but it was also one of many encounters during a sullen winter and he did not make much of it. Instead, at home, Mansoor focused on coaxing his injured limbs to life, dipping his arms in alternating casseroles of hot and cold water and pulling up his sweater sleeves, his feet feeling cuffed to the marble floor. When he doused his arms in the water, his back ached; his body parts jostled and screamed

for attention. When one part improved, the other took on the mantle of
pain. Jaya explained that the computer, because of the intensity of attention it demanded, turned the muscles into hard microchips.

He was in the middle of this ritual when he got a call from his friend
Darius.

Darius had been a schoolmate of Mansoor's, but not someone he'd been
particularly close with—whom had he been close with?—and so when
Darius came on the phone, Mansoor was oddly excited.

"How are you, Mansoor?"

"Fit, yaar," he said, turning back into the anxious-to-please second-tier-
popular student he'd been in school.

They talked for a while about an elderly art teacher who had recently
died of a stroke—she was a chain-smoking radical leftist who had made
them paint antinuclear signs (INDIA: NO CLEAR POLICY) for half a year after
the Pokhran tests—and then Darius said, "So I'm calling because you met
my friend Naushad."

It turned out that after a year at St. Stephen's studying history, Darius had
become an activist. "Anyway," Darius went on, "he told me about his idea
of getting you involved and I think it would be excellent. In fact I had told
him about you at one point but I didn't know you had come back to Delhi."

Mansoor felt a dip in his mood. "Yaah, it's a health issue."

"Anyway," Darius said in his unhearing way, "it's a great group of people, very smart, and you'll like Tara, who runs it. A Dipsite but she's very
eloquent. Anyway, I think these people are making quite a bit of difference.
Wouldn't hurt to come for at least one meeting."

Mansoor didn't want to go, but he had never really learned to say no, even
after what had happened in the market with the Khurana boys, and so, on
a rainy afternoon, he went over to the nursing home in Defence Colony
where the group met—Tara's mother, a doctor, ran the hospital.

The nursing home was a wide dish of a building smarting of disinfec-
tant; the smell seemed to have struck dead the stunted palms in the front.
Shivering, Mansoor climbed the stairs past the rooms with their sounds of

conspiring patients and came to a bare room full of men and women sitting cross-legged in a circle. "You can sit down anywhere," a woman said, her sharp canines visible. She was attractive, in a fair vampirish way, and must have been Tara.

Darius and Naushad got up and introduced Mansoor, who put his palms together, like a politician.

There were twenty people in all, most of them his age, some wearing checked shirts and pants, the women in modest salwar kameezes, a few heads dotted with skullcaps, gol topis, the Muslim women identifiable by their coquettish pink head scarfs.

Tara, after a brief explanation of what the group did—she said it had first formed in response to the anti-Muslim riots in Gujarat earlier that year—asked Mansoor to speak. He suddenly became confused about why he was there. "I actually don't know that much about the blast. I was quite small when it happened."

"But you were hurt, right?"

"I was injured. And that's why I've come back, for treatment. The bigger issue was that my two friends died." The room hushed; Mansoor hadn't mentioned this to Naushad—nor, apparently, had Darius, who, like many people Mansoor knew, had forgotten the aching detail of the two dead boys. The bomb survived through the living, not the dead. "Tushar and Nakul Khurana," Mansoor said, savoring the Hindu names in this secular atmosphere. "I'd gone with them, and when the blast happened, near the framing shop, they died instantly. I had to run back all the way to my house in South Ex." Sensing that people were impressed, he went on. "I was in a lot of pain—even my fillings in my teeth had fallen out—and I also felt a lot of guilt, even though I think they died instantly. I was twelve. I'm not sure what I could have done."

"Poor boys," one woman said, shaking her head.

"Yaah, but what's more horrible is that other innocents are suffering," Mansoor said, suddenly finding the thread. "That's why I came."

The group filled him in on what, exactly, they'd achieved with regard to the 1996 blast. Through filing petitions and engaging public litigation lawyers, they'd managed to bring the case before a board that dealt with TADA and POTA cases. They were also selectively targeting corrupt policemen who arrested former informers and innocent Kashmiris whenever there was a terrorist event. "The police aren't happy about that, and they're going to come after us," a man named Ayub said, clearly looking forward to this drama. He seemed like one of the leaders of the group—a tall man with impervious dark skin, sandy hair, and an unplaceable class background, though Mansoor assumed he was lower class. "But the thing you can do for us," Ayub went on, "is write petitions and editorials. You know, the hardest thing in this media environment is getting a word in the papers or the press. But someone like you, eloquent, studying abroad, a nonthreatening Muslim—people will be interested to hear what you say."

Mansoor wasn't sure if he should be flattered by the word *nonthreatening*, but he straightened his posture and looked at Tara, who was picking at her bare feet, the heart-shaped frond of hair on the top of her head visible, crisscrossed by several partings.

Everyone but Mansoor was barefoot in the cold room, with its single bed pressed against the wall, suggesting it had once been a guest room. The shelves were empty except for weirdly out-of-place religious tomes in Sanskrit, bound in red. "I can consider that," Mansoor said, though he instantly tensed up, thinking of what the Khuranas and his parents would say.

At the end of the meeting, Tara and Ayub came up to him.

"So you're based in the U.S.?" Tara asked. Ayub stood a little behind her, smiling.

"Yeah."

Tara said she had studied abroad too, at Carnegie Mellon, where she'd majored in psychology. "What I loved about the U.S. was how open it was to the humanities. I would not have developed any consciousness had I not gone there."

He liked how unpretentious she was. "Me as well."

Ayub now stepped forward. "How long are you in Delhi?" he asked.

"A few months," Mansoor said, standing up on his toes; Ayub was taller than him.

"Then you should come with me tomorrow," Ayub said.

The wives and mothers of the accused had long since moved to Delhi from Kashmir to lobby for their husbands' or sons' release, and so the next day, setting off with his driver, Mohammed, Mansoor picked up Ayub from outside Tikona Park and they drove together to a small alley in Batla House overflowing with mud and gravel smeared on the ground from abandoned construction. At the far end of the alley, schoolboys, twelve- and thirteen-year-olds, poured out of an unfinished concrete building in their tired school uniforms, their socks drooping, their bags like the surreal burdens of soldiers. Their presence in the alley created an alertness, an impression of a herd of blind, ambling animals, of uncontrolled life, and for a second Mansoor was nostalgic for his school days. But looking at the boys again, their smallness, their jutting confidence, their scramble of limbs—restless, pumping, pointing, shooting everywhere, gesticulating for no reason, grabbing cones of chana from each other—their tense flowing energy, the symphony of gestures, all this filled him with fear and sadness: how ill equipped one was to deal with pain at that age! The ghosts of Tushar and Nakul flashed through the crowd: fat and thin, retiring, sharp. All crowds of a certain age contained them. Mansoor found himself praying for these poor Jamia schoolboys.

After leading him to another alley, Ayub ushered Mansoor into a small room that looked like the waiting area of a homeopath. When they'd been driving over, Ayub had told him he was taking him to the office of a friend's Islamic venture capitalist fund, which the friend allowed Ayub to use on weekends. "What does Islamic VC mean, exactly?" Mansoor had asked.

"It's a normal venture fund," Ayub said, "but you only invest in Sharia-approved companies. So, for example, if a company is involved in processing pork, you won't invest in it."

"What about a company that generates interest?"

"That too. You can only invest in Islamic banks."

"It's the way activists want the endowments of universities to be purified," Mansoor said, vaguely remembering a discussion he'd had with his friend Alex.

The women were sitting on a Rexine bench in the decrepit VC office, pressed together. One was young and pretty and wore all black and kept her head covered; another had a nose ring, with little fountains of hair visible under her dupatta; the third was toothless, gross featured, henna haired. But Mansoor could not see them, not really. As they spoke, holding their own wrists, as if permanently taking their pulses, they were swallowed up by their stories. One woman told Mansoor how her husband had been pumped with petrol in the anus. Another said her son had been hung from the ceiling of a police station till he lost all feeling in his hands. "He can't write anymore," she sniffled. The last one narrated an even bleaker story. Her son, Malik, a student from Kathmandu, where he had also worked in his uncle's carpet shop, had been shocked in the genitals and had had some of his tongue scraped off with a blunt knife. "They do it in such a way that you can still talk, but you sound like a stutterer," she said, displacing the cruelty she'd experienced onto the imaginary stutterer, whom she mentioned with contempt.

The cascade of horrors, the way they were narrated, with fiery intention but also deadness in the eyes, the eyes having turned into shields that guarded the inside rather than bringing light from the outside, reminded Mansoor of how he himself talked about the blast. After a certain point the violence in your life acquires unreality through repetition. What could he really recall of the day of the bombing? The heat, flying swords of metal, pools of blood, deafness, a watery distance from everything. But really what he recalled was getting up and running way, the walk home.

At the end of each story, Mansoor nodded his head—that's all.

After the meeting, Ayub asked, "What do you think?"

They were again in the alley, which was quiet now, evacuated of the schoolkids, broken only by the hiss of the illegal wires hanging overhead.

"It's terrible," Mansoor said.

CHAPTER 14

Mansoor became active in the group, going over to the room in Defence Colony two or three times a week for meetings, telling his parents that the NGO worked for "communal harmony."

His mother was happy that her son had found a source of distraction while he healed. His father, meanwhile, energized by Mansoor's presence, took him around to look at houses. "It's time to buy a new flat," he told Mansoor. "We need a bigger place and anyway South Ex is so noisy and polluted now." He had become fixated on this project, even though most of the flats they saw were out of their price range or in colonies like Neeti Bagh where the sellers would never deal with Muslims.

Mansoor was in pain still but felt oddly content. He was healing and would return to the U.S. for his spring semester, which began in January. It was November now.

Peace For All had serious intentions but was also a friendly group. The twenty-odd members knew each other well and were jokey and friendly and relaxed before and after meetings. There was Shahid, a tall man with enormous hands, plastered balding hair, and a goofy grin with gapped teeth, a second-year mass com student from Jamia. Jacob, the only Christian in the group, thin and nervous and colored with pimples, studied chemistry at St. Stephen's. Zeenat was working toward a diploma in computers from NIIT. Tariq had graduated from a forest management institute in Maharashtra but obviously hated forests—you could see it in the way he cursed whenever a mosquito buzzed near him. They were seekers. They had witnessed what Narendra Modi, the chief minister of Gujarat, had done in his state in March, how he and his administration had stood by, in localities like Naroda Patiya, Meghaninagar, and Bapunagar, as violent Hindu mobs, armed with swords, petrol bombs, tridents, and water pistols to spray fuel, had set upon Muslims, burning them alive, tearing infants from mothers and fetuses from wombs, raping women, killing a thousand. And they had realized that the Indian government wouldn't protect them, that in fact it had an incentive to demonize and exterminate them. The members of Peace For All were not radicals. They were eminently reasonable people, students engrossed in careers, people who wanted to be Indians but had discovered themselves instead to be Muslims and had started to embrace their identities. In their alienation, their desire to be included in the mainstream, Mansoor recognized himself.

"Do you think they'll let Muslims get away with that?" Zeenat might say, for example, when someone suggested a nonviolent protest.

"The police are the most corrupt. Just yesterday they stopped me and wanted to know where I was driving to at night."

"Your idea of doing communal harmony workshops is very idealistic, but we need something more extreme to awaken people."

Everyone had a story of being personally pegged for a Muslim too.

"Why do they always tell us to go back to Pakistan? You're a Hindu—go to Nepal! And why shouldn't I go to Malaysia?"

"The worst is when they say 'Oh, you don't *look* Muslim!'"

"I was once at my friend Akhil's house and I made the mistake of touching his father's Ramayan. That man, a baldie, started shouting, 'You've soiled it! Dharmbhrasht kar diya!' He made poor Akhil pour Ganga water on it from a Bisleri to purify it."

Mansoor sat cross-legged, bringing his bare feet together anxiously with his hands, pressing his soles together.

The voice of reason, of knowledge, during these raucous meetings was Ayub. Ayub was twenty-seven and from Azamgarh, but seemed older; it was as if he had digested recent history and sociology and philosophy, and could draw links between subjects without being the least bit pedantic. With his quick-fire noun-laden sentences, he made knowledge *attractive.* "The Brotherhood in Egypt is primarily a social organization. It only became politicized when they were persecuted, when their leaders were locked up in jail. I don't think Qutb was a great thinker as others do, but why martyr him?" People nodded their heads dreamily, not knowing much about Egypt or Qutb. But Ayub's style was inclusive, and Mansoor felt he could understand the problems of Muslims elsewhere too.

Then one Friday morning, after a meeting, as they all got up to leave, Ayub asked Mansoor, "Are you coming to the mosque with us?"

"I don't have my car here," Mansoor said.

"No problem, yaar, I can take you."

Mansoor had been hesitant to get involved with the religious aspects of the group; it wasn't that he disliked religion but that he felt it was outside his purview. When he heard the members talk about the rulings of the ulema, or what al-Tabari had written about the fitnah, or the corruption of Uthman, he instinctively zoned out, the way he did when his mother was overcome with piety two or three times a year, increasing the rakat in her prayers and promising a sadqa for the poor to express thanks to God for Mansoor's continued health.

Now, caught, unable to come up with an excuse, Mansoor walked with Ayub down the stairs and into the service lane before the main road, where leaves were coming unclipped from the dead trees and rattling down on the street, like the tail of a distant dragon. The roads were brightly bisected by newly painted white lines that stood out against the pervasive dustiness of winter. Mansoor inhaled the stink of racing petrol deeply. Growing up in Delhi, one gets addicted to pollution.

Ayub gestured to his motorcycle and Mansoor got on behind him. He was still racking his brain for an excuse when the motorcycle gunned to life. Mansoor clutched Ayub's waist, which was fleshier than he'd expected, and prayed. *Please.* He had never been on a motorcycle before and as it shot through the Delhi streets, the city close and vivid as it had been during that walk home after the bomb, he was sure he would die, and his heart raced crazily and he pressed his feet on the silver twigs of support jutting out from the chassis. Ayub wasn't wearing a helmet and kept turning around and talking and Mansoor nodded, terrified, his wrists filling with cold liquid. Why hadn't he said no? Because he was congenitally unable to. What would his mother and father think if Mansoor were found with his head smashed in, by a gutter? *Why were you so reckless? Didn't you learn your lesson?*

After a few minutes, the ride became exhilarating, the motorcycle making smooth crests against the road. He had always thought a motorcycle would be bumpy, but it felt instead like you were on a magic carpet. The pain in his wrists reached a sedative high.

When they got to the mosque, Shahid and Tariq were waiting at the entrance, by a row of carts selling sharifas, chatting with other plump young men, who kept their hands behind their backs as they listened. Mansoor was so relieved he embraced them all, and then, walked with them to the back of the mosque and washed and went inside. The mosque, a box of concrete, was simpler than the one his father and he had gone to a few times—usually during Eid—and the crowd was younger, pious, serious, a mixture of office-going people in white shirts and young men with beards wearing kurtas. The alien bubbles of motorcycle helmets broke the flow of bodies. The imam was giving a talk about something vague, like medicine and not betraying others, and after the azaan ended, they all began to pray. Mansoor, who hadn't been in the postures of prayer for years—who'd had to borrow a hankie to place on his head—was in pain, but also in a state of gratitude and relief. He hadn't forgotten how to pray. As he went through the motions, he relaxed as he had during the motorcycle ride.

Afterwards, when the prayers were over, everyone got up quickly and rushed out and Mansoor, Ayub, Shahid, and Tariq were pushed out onto the lawn.

"Oye!" Shahid shouted at a fat fellow who almost knocked him over on the lawn outside the mosque. They stood there and laughed together at the funny, quizzical expression on Shahid's round face.

CHAPTER 15

It was during this time that his father almost lost all his money on a property deal.

What happened was this: as the days went by, Sharif had become more and more involved in the property search. He found a duplex flat in Asiad Village and began negotiating with the sellers, a couple who lived in Palam Vihar, to buy it. The couple kept asking for Rs. 50 lakhs, whereas he wanted to pay 40. Finally, predictably, they settled on Rs. 45 lakhs, with some adjustment for black money, and the deal went ahead.

Sharif was happy about the property, relieved; but he also cautioned his family that they shouldn't get too excited. "I've only given a deposit. They might still withdraw."

"You'll love living there, beta," Afsheen told Mansoor. "It's right next to the Sports Complex and you can go to the driving range when your wrists get better."

Mansoor really couldn't imagine moving; he had lived in the same house in South Ex all his life; had grown up there, suffered there, grieved there, recovered from the bomb there. In fact, soon after the blast, the Ahmeds had discussed moving—Afsheen had said the house itself had brought them bad luck; there had been a spate of injuries in the family, culminating with Mansoor's—but they hadn't been able to find anything. Now, years later, this opening appeared.

The couple selling the property were acquaintances of Sharif's college

friend Mahinder; they were liberal and friendly and when they had met
Sharif, they had talked enthusiastically about their various Muslim friends.
"Do you know Arif Khan? He was the vice chancellor of AMU at one
point." These connections doubled Sharif's relief.

But as the day approached to meet and sign the actual deed and to
transfer the full amount, problems began to occur.

The Sahnis, who had been so warm and effusive when Sharif had met
them, became hard to pin down. One week they were on vacation in Goa.
Another week they were visiting their eldest son in Toronto, then the younger
one in Singapore. They returned Sharif's calls erratically, and finally, not at all.

"Do you think they're trying to cheat us?" Sharif asked Afsheen.

"I don't know," Afsheen said. "You should ask Mahinder."

"They gave you a chit—so you don't need to worry about the money,"
Mahinder said when Sharif called him. "You'll get that back. But the thing
we need to find out is if they've found someone else who's offering them a
higher price. People are greedy. She's a school principal but people who run
schools are no better than anyone else. In fact, sometimes they're even greed-
ier than others because they think they're being corrupt for a good cause."

"So what should we do?" Sharif asked.

"Let me investigate," Mahinder said.

During this time, Sharif kept phoning the Sahnis to set up a date. He
drove past the house in the Asiad like a despondent lover, wondering why
these perfect situations didn't work out for him. And he felt the loss of his
money—which he hadn't really lost, but was in limbo—keenly.

Then Mahinder confirmed what they'd both suspected: the Sahnis had
found another buyer willing to pay a higher price.

Sharif now sprang into action. His lawyer served the Sahnis a show-cause
notice for breach of contract. The Sahnis appeared in court, furious, no
longer the mild paternal Punjabis they'd pretended to be. But then the
Sahnis' lawyer, a young woman in a suit, muddled things and admitted
they'd taken money from two parties and the judge, snorting and shaking
his head, issued a stay order.

The Sahnis turned out to be horrible, unapologetic people.

"How dare you take us to court," Mrs. Sahni fumed at Sharif outside the court. "Is this any way to behave? You expect us to sell you our property now?"

Strange woman, thought Sharif—she acts like the property is some kind of business partnership between us. When in fact, as soon as she sells me the property, everything will be over in our relationship.

Sharif told the Sahnis that they had given him no choice. He had called about twenty times and been swatted away with excuses at every turn.

"You're too pushy," Mr. Sahni said. "We told you it would take time. When you saw the property I told you we didn't want the deposit till we came back from Canada. You only insisted."

But you accepted the money! Sharif wanted to say. Still, he kept quiet. He knew how to use silence; his goatee enhanced his impassivity.

For a few days, the Sahnis blustered—on the phone and through their lawyer. Sharif, advised by Mahinder and his lawyer, kept his nerve and refused to respond to these provocations. Finally Mrs. Sahni called and said she would like to meet the Ahmeds at the Golf Club.

"They're trying to show their classiness," Afsheen observed.

They had underpriced the place, Mrs. Sahni told them when they sat down for coffee and biscuits and fizzing lime soda at the overly slick, cracked Formica table that is the hallmark of all Indian clubs. It was their mistake, she admitted. They had not realized that the scooter garage that came with the place was also worth a good ten lakhs. It was an honest blunder, she said; hence the confusion.

Sharif was enraged. The cheek of these people! Caught red-handed trying to sell it to someone else, and now, instead of apologizing, they ask for more!

"I'm very firm," he said. "I've given the deposit."

But then Afsheen interjected. "We'll think about it," she said, putting her hand on Sharif's.

———————

"What do you mean—we'll think about it!" Sharif thundered at her in the car. "They're wrong."

"You do have a temper," she said. "And you put people off with your pushiness. What's ten lakhs in the long term? We like the property; we don't want to fight—might as well pay it and get it over with."

Mansoor, when he heard both sides of the argument, agreed with his mother.

But Sharif couldn't accept it. He raged against his wife and son, against the Sahnis, and consulted his lawyer. Finally he decided that it would be cheaper to pay this ransom than to pay lawyers' fees for decades.

The money was exchanged; the deal was completed in a urine-soaked registrar's office in Bijwasan on a cold December day.

It was only when it was all over that the lawyer noticed a problem in the paperwork.

The property came with a lien, a debt, on it. For Rs. 20 crores. Rs. 200 million.

Mr. Sahni, when Sharif had first met him, had said he was in the export business—had boasted about how well he was doing, how he had two sons settled abroad, one in Toronto, another in Singapore. But there had been something *off* about the Sahnis from the start, Sharif realized. They owned this duplex in Asiad, in the heart of the city, but lived in a strange farmhouse-cum-bunker in Palam Vihar, an incomplete colony on the outskirts of Delhi, a crisscross of plots overgrown with thorny scrub and grass and keekar trees. There was something provisional about the house too— the furniture heavy and Punjabi, with no carpets covering the terrazzo floor and no art on the walls and twenty balloons up against the ceiling of the drawing room, the detritus of their granddaughter's birthday, they'd said. But Sharif, who had been introduced to these people through Mahinder, was so grateful to have found a good house for himself, to find Hindus who would deal with Muslims, that he'd ignored all these signs and justified it to himself. And the Sahnis had justified it to Sharif too. "We want to give the money to our sons," Mrs. Sahni had said in her sweet convent-educated voice. "It's more useful to them, now that they're living abroad. As for us, we like living in this greenery, away from the rush of Delhi. The drive to my school is just twenty minutes from here."

Now, of course, Sharif saw it anew. A couple pushed into bankruptcy, pushed to the edge of Delhi, plotting an escape to Canada, seeking to off-load the huge debt they'd taken on when the man's export business went under. And they had found a sitting duck in Sharif but gotten greedy and tried to lure another duck. But Sharif in his pushy way had insisted that *he* be the victim. It didn't help that he had a shitty lawyer and bad instincts with property. And so he had landed himself in the biggest financial trouble of his life—sinking under a debt of twenty crores.

The lawyer told him he could win the case in court. Sharif fired the lawyer and hired another one and settled in for a long legal battle. But he knew even before it had started that he would lose one way or another. After all, he should have looked at the papers before he signed. He had clawed his way into this tragedy.

CHAPTER 16

"Why do we have such bad luck?" Afsheen cried at home.

"It's that lawyer's fault," Mansoor said. "It's his job to read the documents, to check them before signing. People in this country are incompetent."

"I told your father not to deal with such people, but he insisted."

Mansoor knew this wasn't the case, but said nothing.

"Don't worry," she said, catching herself. "We'll get out of this."

"How do they think they can get away with this?" Mansoor asked his father later that day.

"People get away with a lot more in this country," Sharif said. Again, he had the sense—the sense he'd had on the day of the blast, back in 1996—that this was punishment for staying on in an obviously hostile country. Many of his relatives had fled to Pakistan after the 1969 Gujarat riots; only he, bullheaded, had stayed on.

That evening, steeling himself, Sharif came up to Mansoor's bedroom. Mansoor was sitting on the side of his bed, bent over, reading *Deterring Democracy*, by Noam Chomsky. When Mansoor had first arrived in Delhi, Sharif remembered, his muscles had been so tender that he couldn't even lift a book, and Sharif had gone with him to a chemist in INA to purchase a reading stand—the sort apparently used by musicians—which held up books.

"Yaah, Papa?" Mansoor asked.

Sharif's heart plunged. "Beta, Mummy and I think it would be best if you stayed in Delhi longer. There's the financial issue and also it's good if you get some rest. There's no rush for college. We'd like you to be here with us. And Mahinder Uncle said he can get you an IT traineeship when you're ready to type." The words came out in a rehearsed flood.

Mansoor had known they were in trouble, but this much? That they'd suspend their son's education abroad? "Of course, Papa," he said, his voice reedy. "I was also going to say that. And I'm enjoying the NGO work. One semester here or there doesn't matter."

"Are you sure?"

"Yaah."

Father and son considered each other across a void of total comprehension. Mansoor thought he was about to see his father cry.

"Good," Sharif said, slapping his thigh. "It'll be nice to have you around."

After he left, Mansoor lay down on his bed and tried to not to cry himself.

CHAPTER 17

Why he should feel so bad, when he hadn't even loved his life in the U.S.—where he'd made as few friends as he'd made in school—confounded him. But he was torn about what he wanted. He didn't want to be in India *or* the U.S. He wanted to be in a place free of pain and tragedy.

The discussions about the property went on at home; the tragedy became one of suspension; and Mansoor, after a gap of a few days, returned to the Peace For All meetings.

But now, sitting among the group members on the floor with their lazily folded legs (as if they were sitting up in a bed, drinking hot tea) and listening to their earnest debates about the civil code, he was disoriented, distracted, felt he didn't have anything to do with this world or these people, that he'd stumbled into it by accident, during a period of boredom, and now that the period of boredom had been declared his life, he must return to serious things like programming.

"I'll be staying on longer," he told Tara and Ayub one day. "My health still hasn't improved and the doctor has said I should rest another month." This is the story the family had decided to share with strangers; they wanted to keep their suffering, their shame, private. "So I'll be able to help in the next few months." Though he felt and wanted the opposite: but the crucial thing, for Mansoor, was to get the announcement that he wasn't going back out of the way.

"I thought you were getting better," Ayub said.

"So it's continuing repetitive stress injury?" Tara asked, not blinking her eyes much beneath her steel-rimmed John Lennon–style glasses, glasses that were so clear that they seemed like dividers separating one world from the next, the world of wealth and good skin (she had radiant skin) from the world of activism. As the daughter of a doctor, she was fluent in the language of sickness.

"Yaah, I believe," Mansoor said. "Carpal tunnel, repetitive stress, whatever you want to call it."

It was only later, when the other members had come and gone and the meeting was over, that Ayub said, "Will you take a walk with me?"

"Of course." Mansoor lifted the Bittoo notebook he'd kept on the floor next to him. He hadn't even opened it once today and it was somehow glued to the floor and he had to pry it up. "Arre." He laughed.

Ayub, tall and hunched, bringing his palms together, laughed too, politely, eyes popping with delight a bit too late.

The brick complex near the hospital contained the Department of Tourism and also several shops—Flavors Restaurant, a toy shop, a kebab place; the normal assortment you find in a community center. Navigating the cool corridors, damp from mopping, alive with a potent lemony smell (one that must have been coming from a shop rather than the floor, since that was not the kind of mopping these places got) the air cold and making them shiver, Ayub asked, "So how long have you had these muscle problems?"

"Six years. Since the blast." He was hypnotized by the sound of Ayub's slippers thwacking the ground: that urban music.

"That's a long time," Ayub said. "What kind of treatment did you get?"

Mansoor told him: the physiotherapy, the exercises, the ultrasonic machine, the biosensitization, the alternating baths, the splints, the weights, the Volini gel, the words coming out like verses of some elegant, enigmatic poem.

"But what do the doctors say now?"

"That it's been a relapse. Basically, I was healing but I developed microtears in my wrists from typing too much." He was so fluent in this language too.

"I hope you don't mind my saying," Ayub said. "It shouldn't be there after so many years."

Mansoor looked at him.

"You see, I've been watching you since you came in," Ayub said. "You remind me of myself. You're sensitive to the pain of others but not so much to your own pain, isn't it? But here's the issue. Any pain that lasts this long—well, it can't. Pain is supposed to heal. When an injury doesn't go away at our age, it's psychological, no matter the cause." Standing tall in a striped blue Fabindia shirt—the stripes powerful and downward, red and green—wearing a gray woolen waistcoat over it, clapping his palms together, Ayub looked like both a politician and an abashed lover who has waited too long to make his declaration.

Ayub scooped back his combed hair. For the first time Mansoor saw that, at the age of twenty-seven, Ayub was balding already. The hair was carefully arranged, in powerful forward strands, to cover up the terra firma of the pate.

"I'm not saying your pain isn't real or the injury isn't real. I'm simply saying that the pain remains *after* the injury has healed." Ayub clapped his palms together again, as if it helped maintain his balance, as it were the steering wheel or joystick of the conversation. "When I was your age and I moved to Delhi, I had a bad scooter accident. I was riding pillion and my friend's scooter skidded—there was a motorcycle coming toward us in the wrong lane; it was Holi and the driver's eyes were red and he had clearly drunk bhang, because he was smiling as *he* skidded—and we went sliding on the road, like this"—he made a gesture with his palms that you may make to mimic the flight of a jet—"and I rolled off and only narrowly avoided being run over by a Tempo. We were young, so we laughed it off, but then I started developing horrible back pains." His eyes went dark as he remembered. "It was so bad, yaar. It used to keep me up at night. I couldn't walk, talk, read—anything. And I tried everything: Reiki, yoga, yunani, ayurveda, homeopathy. You think of it and I tried it." He paused. "It was only after some years when I realized that my pain was psychological and that I was holding on to it because I was addicted to it that it went away. It was only when I started praying and not thinking of myself that it went away. When I gave myself to Allah." Ayub had rich, long lashes that throbbed oddly when he was excited. He was a bit like a bulb that hasn't quite learned to hoard all its electricity into light and so emits it through twitches—in Ayub's case, of the hands, eyes, feet; Ayub was always sitting on the floor of the NGO, on the white terrazzo broken into squares by black lines, rotating his feet like they were radars processing the conversation—only to suddenly burst into cogent argument.

Mansoor now considered Ayub, his advice, his well-meaning invitation to stroll in the market, his height, his stoop, his provincial sureness about whatever quackish solution he'd discovered, the power he must feel giving advice to people much richer than himself, the joy he must get out of pitying Mansoor, his expectant look, and said, "It could be true." He blinked deeply himself.

Now Ayub became excited. "In fact, the way I solved it was by reading Dr. Mari's book *The Religion of Pain*. He brings up the issue also and suggests you do visualization and don't focus on your body. Between that and prayer, five times a day, I healed. You will too. I'll bring you the book and we can go to the mosque together."

"Thank you," Mansoor said.

Instead, that day, enraged in a way he could not understand, he vowed not to return to the meetings at all.

CHAPTER 18

"Papa, I want to do the IT traineeship," Mansoor said the next evening.

His father was sitting on the bed, his buttocks slumped forward under him and his stomach jutting up and out. A pack of cards with an elegant red paisley design on their backs—the same design Mansoor had noticed in the jaali work of the mosque near the university in Jamia—was spread next to him in an arrangement of solitaire. Sharif, his spectacles low on his nose, kept a couple of cards on his stomach for consideration. The floppy pipes of his white pajamas revealed thin white hairy ankles. "If you feel like it is the right thing, sure."

"Yaah, I'm feeling a lot better and it's good if I start and get work experience," Mansoor started, but then stopped. His father, dipping a card into one of the simultaneous stubby rivers of the solitaire piles, wasn't listening.

"The only issue is—are your wrists OK?" Afsheen said, carrying a bowl of fatty chicken bits swiftly back and forth in the kitchen. Her bun was done up perfectly and her forehead looked unlined and she was wearing one of her elegant purple-gray caftans. Tragedy had made her erect and confident.

"They're fine, Mama," Mansoor said, in the artificial unintelligible rush of the kitchen. "I don't want to talk about them. And please don't use them as an excuse for . . . our problems."

"Yaar, Razia, I told you to put the onions here," Afsheen said to the maid.

"Ji, madam," Razia said.

"Where will you do it?" Afsheen asked Mansoor.

"Mahinder Uncle's friend is an executive at Xansa," Mansoor said, his back to a counter—the back suddenly aching, crossed by a vertical sting of pain and the horizontal hardness of the slab of counter.

"I see. You think you can sit in an office all day?"

"Yes, Mama," Mansoor said. "As long as I take breaks."

"We should get permission from the doctor first."

So Mansoor went over with the driver to the clinic in Safdarjung.

He had been avoiding this the past few months. The nerve conduction test was the only objective measure of how you were doing and healing; by hooking you up to sensors and sending currents through your nerves, the doctors could determine how badly damaged they were. Mansoor had had such a test before in the U.S. He'd been frightened by the name, by its electric inelegance, but was relieved by how minor the shocks were, the way they felt like subcutaneous pinches.

The doctor wasn't the stately sardar he usually dealt with but rather a lumpy Bengali man with gapped teeth and large moles under his eyes, wearing a lab coat, with a fixed smile.

"Hello, hello," he said when Mansoor entered the small consultation chamber with its laminated surfaces and shelves piled with prizes from medical associations.

When Mansoor told him why he was there, he got up from his seat and removed a device from behind a glass case that looked like an old type-writer, complete with the gray fuzzy plastic shell.

Mansoor, sitting on a steel stool, tensed up. What if this Soviet-looking device was defective and hurt his nerves? What if the electricity went in the middle of the test?

"Put your wrists forward," the doctor said and then tied the wires around his wrists like rakhis. Before Mansoor could speak, the current, warm and beery, started. He relaxed. It wasn't as bad as he'd thought. His system wouldn't be permanently rewired.

"What do you do?" the doctor asked after a while.

"I'm a student." It was odd for Mansoor to be talking to this man without his mother's mediation. "BTech," he continued. "I'm studying computers."

"Well, Mansoor-ji, you better find another profession."

Mansoor looked at him with the calm that comes to people when they receive the news they have been dreading—the calm of disbelief; also perverse, awful relief.

"Your nerves are badly damaged," the doctor continued. "You'll never be able to type. You should find a profession that doesn't require typing. Luckily, for your generation, there are many options. You could become a teacher or a professor."

Somehow Mansoor endured this lecture. Do something else? But there was nothing else for people of his generation to do! They were hooked to machines. Everywhere one turned one encountered screens, keyboards, wires. And once again Mansoor experienced the bitterness he'd felt when the physiotherapist in the U.S. had told him he was suffering the consequences not just of the bomb but of years of mishandling his computer—why hadn't anyone told him? Why was he allowed to throw his injured body at these boxes of signals? Even in the U.S., on his pristine Californian campus, there had been no instructions about how to protect his wrists from repetitive stress injuries—the keyboards in the computer cluster were far from ergonomic—and in any case most people had laptops and spent their days and nights hunched over them, writing papers, playing movies, sending e-mails, and downloading porn on the high-speed networks. And now, after I've destroyed everything, they tell me? That's the meaning of having survived the bomb. I didn't survive at all. I just spent longer dying, rendered crippled and obsolete like that old 486 on which I acquired my first repetitive injuries.

He walked out of the office with his hands in his pockets and the world wild and broken around him—dust in the air; haze against the eye; telephone and electric wires stretching around the colony like a noose; the rust visible on the chain-link fence of Deer Park, across the street; the rank odor of the gutter in his nose; the freshly tarred road like a living, breathing thing, a rising piece of bread, rolled flat by the cars' tires.

When he told his mother the news, she grimaced at first in a show of strength, and then burst into tears. "Why is this happening to us?" she said. "Two thousand three. It's a terrible year. We must get a second opinion."

"No," he said. He was done with doctors.

CHAPTER 19

At home, Mansoor found himself in the grip of a profound anger. He kept looking back at the day of the bombing and seeing Mr. and Mrs. Khurana skulking about and talking in their bright house, tall human adults in their forties, Mr. Khurana in a white shirt and khaki pants, Deepa Auntie in a red kameez dyed with purple mangoes running down the front in parallel rows (how vividly he remembered the details of that day, as if it had been stained by the wine of memory), full of domestic swagger and confidence, lost in their adult world, discussing bills and the latest gossip about a relative who had left her husband, the kids playing around and under them, kids they were eager to shoo out. Why had they been so irresponsible—with him in particular? But Indians were like that, happy to be puppets of fate. "Chalta hai." "It's in God's hands." "Everything goes."

When Mansoor had told Vikas Uncle he'd call his mother so she could pick him up, Vikas Uncle had perversely cajoled him into going with Tushar and Nakul to the market. "Don't worry, yaar," he'd said, sitting back lazily in the sofa chair, his arms forming a relaxed hammock behind his head. Mansoor hated him.

The Khuranas had never apologized to him.

Mansoor's thoughts flew in a circle of rage. His wrists hurt, his back throbbed, he sweated, his sciatica sparked. In his room, he turned the pages of ten odd books strewn on his bed—the Chomskys, Roys, Dalrymples. He wasn't reading them, but testing his pain; even turning a page hurt. He was a highly defective machine, sensitive to everything.

When he sat on the sofa in the drawing room, the same old drawing room with its chests from Korea and Indonesia, its frantic unreconstructed Orientalism, the Orientalism only allowed to people in the Orient, a sickly current, like that of a tube light about to die, vomiting the last of its milky light, filled the columns of his arms.

Surrounded by unfeeling objects, his parents off to the lawyers to discuss the case and to figure out how to keep the business running (Sharif ran a plastics consulting and supply company), he began to whimper. Nothing had changed for him since the day after the bomb, when he had come back home to this very pain.

During a moment of insanity, he imagined doing something different—becoming a full-time activist and teacher with the group, traveling around the country and educating people about communal violence and . . . carpal tunnel. What if he became a doctor or physiotherapist like that South Indian bore Jaya? Well, that would be amusing!

Eventually, out of loneliness and rage, Mansoor returned to volunteering for Peace For All.

CHAPTER 20

The group meetings were the same—the discussions about the 1996 inmates had been put on hold to develop strategies to protest Modi when he arrived in Delhi a few weeks from now—but Mansoor, sitting on the floor, a mute spectator to the verbal drama, haggard and uneasy, avoiding Ayub, began to notice something strange: his pain had become much worse after the nerve conduction test. Whereas before he'd experienced a snipping tension and tiredness and a subcutaneous wetness, now an elastic, electric current spread through his limbs, dizzying him with its dull throb, making him feel like an overly tightened string instrument.

He began to wonder if there was something to Ayub's notion that the pain was partly mental, seeing how it had jumped after the diagnosis from the doctor. At home, on his bed, enclosed by a life-size poster of Tendulkar on one side and of Michael Jackson on the other—old posters from the age of fourteen he had never taken down or replaced—he began to read the book Ayub had given him, *The Religion of Pain*.

The book said straightforward things. Pain was a response to injury. But when pain didn't go away it was because a deep-seated psychological pattern had been established; besides, back pain hadn't existed till fifty years before—before that, people got ulcers when they were depressed; where were ulcers now? Replaced by back pain. Mansoor skipped pages, his wrists singing with pain, his chin sunk into his neck, the back of his neck stiff. He was a mannequin of pain, controlled by it; he altered his posture every few seconds and kept the bloated tuber of the hot-water bottle pressed to his lumbar.

Then Mansoor got to the part where the author proposed a solution.

The solutions seemed laughably simple. One, the author wrote, exercise frequently but don't focus unduly, in your exercises, on the troubled part of the body; and two, visualize at night the body part that suffers from pain and imagine it getting better.

In normal circumstances, Mansoor would have shrugged these off, but he was so down and out that he decided to give them a try.

Miraculously, as the weeks wore on, he began to get better. Establishing a routine of Iyengar yoga poses, swimming a few turgid laps in the covered Gymkhana pool, and skidding forward on the treadmill in the gym, he felt his pain beginning to dissipate, clear out, the way a clogged sinus might suddenly give up the ghost of its liquid. The months and years of struggle were suddenly canceled by three weeks of exercise and some visualization and focus.

(Later, when it was all over, when his life was coming to an end, he would think that he had probably started to recover because months of therapy had paid off; that he had been misdiagnosed during the nerve test; and that his recovery had been an act of faith and belief, the sort that can only take hold of a person when he is at his lowest.

But then, in the middle of this storm of circumstances, with his father's fortune disappearing and the family in decline and his future uncertain and curtailed and the bomb still sitting vastly on the horizon of his past, like a furious private sun, always pulling him toward it—in the middle of this, this experiment with visualization, with accepting there might be other reasons for pain beside injury, had seemed like a paradigm shift.)

"Mine, when I started it, was gone in three months," Ayub said one day, in the room at the back of Holy Child Nursing Home. The two men had become friendly again when Mansoor had told him his advice had helped; they had arrived early, before the others, and were sitting on the floor and talking. Ayub was wearing a white kurta with Kolhapuri slippers. He clutched one foot with his hands. He had enormous toes with bright symmetrical toenails. "I too was skeptical when I was first told about this idea. We're slaves of science. We can't believe there can be an answer outside doctors. We believe whatever they tell us—you have microtears in your wrists, is it? Well, there might be an easier explanation for why you don't see them! I don't mean to be too philosophical here, but we're brought up within that system and are incapable of seeing what may be wrong with it. You've read Gandhi-ji? He said that the two worst classes of human beings were doctors and lawyers. Lawyers because they prolong fights and doctors because they cure the symptoms, not the cause. Doctors don't eliminate disease—they perpetuate the existence of doctors. This is all there, in *Hind Swaraj*. But our own problem is—and I'm talking about all of us—we swallow everything Western civilization gives us. We reject even the best parts of our own culture. All these things we now call faith healing—what were they? Just forms of this, visualization, holistic techniques. But modern men like you and me wouldn't be caught doing this so-called jhaad-phoonk. That's something our servants do. But our servants aren't idiots. This is a *country* of servants. And these people are living, right? Healthier than you would expect given the water they drink, the food they eat, the air they breathe. How?"

It was a mistake to tell him, Mansoor thought. He's getting all excited. "The tough thing for you," Ayub said, "will be what to do when the pain starts moving around."

"Yes, the book told me about that."

"Your body's not going to give up on pain so easily. It's been living with it for six years. And it's been validated by the doctor. The doctor who is like a priest marrying you to your pain. Anyway, what will be interesting is not even what you'll do when the pain moves around—you'll handle it if you can handle this—but what you'll do when it finally disappears."

Mansoor felt close to Ayub. His wisdom wasn't just for show; he wasn't a quack—in fact, he was the only person to have truly helped Mansoor since the blast. Mansoor despaired about the years he'd lost to pain, and wished he'd healed faster. "Don't regret things. Look at the present, and pray," Ayub said. "That's why I started praying. If you look backwards or forward, you stumble. But prayer keeps you focused on the eternal present."

They started going to the mosque together again, several days a week this time, Mansoor driving over in his car, no longer ashamed of his new religiosity. In the mosque he wore a skullcap and tried to be near the front and was fervent in his devotion.

He used his time praying to do what prayer must have been meant for in the first place, before it became ritual: visualization. Pressing his fingers behind his ears, he'd see himself playing cricket one winter day with Tushar and Nakul, smashing the ball. He could picture, in that hothouse of intoning bodies, the leaves on the trees, crisp and crumbling, above and beneath his feet, crunching; a discarded cricket glove, white and dirty and stiff around the thumbs, lying on the dusty earth; Nakul's flexible, rubbery body curled over to bat, the bat kicking impatiently at the crease, looking sometimes like the leg of a tied horse and other times like the stuck tine of a clock—those were the happiest days of his life.

In visualization—used by athletes as well as the injured—you were first supposed to conjure and concentrate on a moment of surpassing happiness, a scene to which you could bring scents, sounds, colors. When Mansoor had started at home, he'd been surprised by how few happy moments he could pull out from the quiver of his memory. Had he never been happy? Then, one day, at the mosque, he'd hit upon this image of Tushar and Nakul and him and the other colony boys playing cricket and he'd been floored by the details, and kneeling on the ground in the mosque, the fabric of hundreds of worshippers crinkling and rustling around him, he had been overwhelmed. How long he'd suppressed that image! That image of life before the bomb, when one's main concern was how not to be accidentally neutered by the hard cricket ball and how to avoid being brained when the ball spiraled down toward you from the air and you stood underneath with your small, smooth, rich-boy palms to catch it. Sometimes he got so lost in the memory that he forgot the most important part of the visualization exercise: picturing oneself doing the task one feared, in his case typing. Sometimes he just roamed the placid heat-struck diorama of the cricket field of his memory, interacting with Tushar—excitable, nervous Tushar—who loved Mansoor for unknown reasons, and sly Nakul with his excessively opposable thumbs, a boy who, like so many athletes, seemed happy to be led, thought of himself as a highly respected grunt capable of performing only one specialized task (speed bowling).

How strange to have these thoughts in the mosque, in that place where no experience was supposed to be private, where each person was consumed by the same God, the same words . . . though of course that wasn't true: for most people, as Mansoor had noticed, going to the mosque was rote, like changing the oil in the scooter, or paying the school fees, another task to be checked off the list. Sometimes, coming up after the twelve minutes of prayer, he felt he was the only person who'd had an ecstatic experience with God on the clammy floor.

His hands were much better now and his fear of typing gradually went away. In fact, whenever he felt fear, or pain—the manifestation of fear—he kept going.

The Internet, which had been closed to him for so long, now was thrown open again and he dashed off e-mails to friends and read Yahoo! News and *Rolling Stone* as he had in the past.

It was when he almost visited a porn website that he began to recall what had caused this trauma in the first place.

When he'd moved to the U.S., he'd been fully healed. The pain in his right arm and wrist were in the past; the bomb itself was in the past. But the bomb, churning the materials of the city, eking a war zone out of a regular market, had ruined Delhi for him. He spent his childhood doing homework and pecking brutally at the keyboard. He had no desire to leave the house, to risk another encounter with a bomb, and when he did try to leave, to visit friends, to hang out with them at PVR and Priya (where the boys often got into A movies by showing the bemused lads in the ticket booths the hair on their legs as proof of age), his parents encouraged him to stay home.

"Watch a movie *here*," they said. "Invite your friends. Lamhe has such a good selection of LDs." So he never left.

When he went to the U.S. and found himself suddenly alive, free of fear, he'd been enraged about all the time he'd wasted; angry at his parents in conspiring with the bomb to keep him indoors.

Encountering freedom for the first time, he threw himself into everything: he drank, smoked, partied, smoked up, even kissed a girl in the corner of a room during a party. He was amazed at how quickly the inhibitions he'd rehearsed over a lifetime—the belief, for example, that one shouldn't have sex before marriage—fell away. He was like a snake overdue for shedding its skin. And with every inhibition he shed, he was angrier at his parents—parents who had first exposed him to the bomb instead of protecting him and had then punished him by keeping him indoors, where he learned and experienced nothing (in this new atmosphere of freedom, he forgot that much of his imprisonment was self-imposed, brought on by fear and panic attacks—he had been afraid of Delhi the way he later became afraid of typing, thinking that, just as Delhi might rip off his face in a sudden upwelling of fire, the machine might cripple him for life). He briefly stopped communicating with his parents. He led what he would later call a "dissipated life." It was after a weekend of drinking that his wrists gave way.

He made no connection between his wrists and his new life; he seemed incapable of making connections of any kind on his own (another symptom of an overprotected childhood). But even then he knew that he was overusing the computer—if not to study, then to watch porn.

He had become addicted to porn. The obsession with porn was an aspect of an obsession with sex. When he arrived in the U.S., he'd only seen a few pictures—his dial-up Internet in Delhi wasn't fast enough to load videos. That changed quickly. His roommate Eddy, with his Cheshire cat grin, watched porn on his computer openly, obsessively, keeping the door ajar so that the moans of women wafted down the corridors of the dorm. Dealing with some problem of his own—Eddy had been a football player in school, but was possibly gay; he had the largest collection of shoes Mansoor had ever seen, and he cried easily—Eddy plastered the walls with posters of seminude women from *Maxim* magazine. In the day, with the sun beating against the windows, the room emitted a rank yellowish glow—the glow of an adult store. Mansoor had not known how to resist this assault on the walls. Perhaps he didn't want to resist—he wanted to buck stereotypes about Muslims, stereotypes that were flourishing after 9/11, and anyway he too liked porn. He talked with disgust to girls about Eddy's pitiful misogyny but watched days' worth of porn, on his own, in secret, when Eddy was gone or asleep. He felt guilty, felt watched by God, but it was overruled by the great pleasure of seeing blond naked bodies trapped in his laptop monitor, providing him a template in which to fit the unapproachable girls who roamed the hallways in their towels.

Around the same time he read *The Fountainhead* and became obsessed with becoming a great programmer at the expense of everything else.

But his body had been unable to take it, and he'd come reeling back to India, his wrists aflame. Now, in India, in the mosque, he saw his body was simply rejecting this selfish way of life; it was begging him to pause, reconsider. And he did. He thought about who he actually was: a mild person, brought up with firm good Muslim values, someone who thrived not on pursuing individual pleasures, but on being among people like himself, living a life of moderation: praying, exercising, thinking healthy thoughts. The more he realized the connection between the mind and the brain, the more he wished to keep his mind clean. If you had horrible thoughts, if you carried rage against your parents and sexual fury against women in your head, as he had—how could you be healthy, happy? Your body imploded. You became the bomb.

When he told Ayub this, shared these revelations, Ayub said, "Again, you're coming up against the Western belief in the individual." They were walking once more in the shopping complex near Holy Child Nursing Home. "There are no higher values, people in the West say. Live by your own instincts, for yourself, for your own pleasure. You know, I went once to New York. My brother works for a man in the diamond business in Dubai and I went along. I transported the diamonds in my pocket. That's how all diamonds are taken—they're too precious to put in a suitcase. You know what struck me about New York?"

"The women?" said Mansoor.

"No. Not the women, the graffiti, the buildings—nothing. I expected all these things. What I noticed was the things that were missing. Old people, for example. I realized you could go days without seeing an old person. Where are they? I asked my brother. Why aren't there old people in New York?" He looked at Mansoor. "They're all in retirement homes, of course. Hidden away from sight the way dead people are immediately put in a morgue or buried. In America, you see, you're not supposed to take care of the elderly. You're supposed to look after yourself, chase your dreams. But what happens when you grow old? Will your individualism save you? No— you'll be put away like the dead. In America, you see, you die twice—once when you grow old, and once when you actually die. But the illusion of youth must be preserved at all costs. This is what I felt about New York. It was a place you could waste your whole life without thinking once about others—until you too were put away and replaced by the young. I could suddenly see why al-Qaeda wanted to target New York. It's a place that prides itself on being the most awake, but it's asleep to reality."

"Everyone I met was struggling with depression," Mansoor said, agreeing. "It was almost fashionable to be depressed. I didn't think about it then, but it was because many of them were cut off from their families. They had no way of making meaning. That's what happened to me too: the wrist problem, it was a type of depression." He turned to Ayub. "I just remembered something you said when we first talked. That your pain only went away when you started thinking about others."

"Not just that," Ayub said. "But when I found God."

Mansoor's mind was aswirl. He was on the verge of something great, of something new, and his entire worldview had been blotted out. He saw now that his selfishness stretched all the way back to the bomb: how holding on to fear, not facing up to the panic attacks, was a form of selfishness, of thinking your fate was in *your* hands, when in fact it was all up to the Almighty. If

his family had believed in God, they would have continued as they had before the blast. Instead, they'd been visited by a string of holy men—gaunt,
bent men with silver stubble and bronze lockets and bright eyes and patrician faces who asked him to bend beside them as they offered prayers, who
greedily drank the cold coffee and mirchi toast his mother offered. . . . Yes,
the family had been eager to thank God, but not to trust Him. The bomb
had induced in the family a kind of hypochondria. They saw the bomb
everywhere they went. It was not God they worshipped, but the bomb.

As these revelations crowded him on his bed, Mansoor felt a tug of regret in his chest.

He paved over this feeling by attacking books on religion eagerly (the
same eagerness with which he'd devoured *The Fountainhead* on the steps of
the plaza at his university) and saw within them a template for how to live,
the point of obscure customs like keeping women modest and veiled—it
was not to oppress women, he saw, but to reduce the sum of lust in society.
Ever since he'd come back to Delhi from California, he'd thought of sex
less, because he saw less flesh on the street. Thus, if there were no lascivious
hoardings and cutouts of lingerie models in *Delhi Times* and on FTV, one
would think of sex even less.

As he made these observations, he felt the centuries between him and
Mohammed collapsing and had the distinct sense that the words and wisdom passed down through the Quran and the Hadiths and al-Tabari were
meant for someone of his disposition and body type. As for God himself,
He was a universal blank, a lack of ego, a way of accepting and admitting
that you were a small person, that your problems were small, that you
should care about things bigger than yourself.

Going deeper into learning about Islam, Mansoor could see how a crisis
of values was afoot not only in the Western world but in India, which had
become a lapdog of the West, eager to imbibe its worst ideas while ditching
its best ones. This crisis was most evident on TV, with its profusion of sex
(probably where his own sex obsession had started, he thought); in the
rapid construction of malls; in the increased incidence of divorce and sui-

cide and rape and depression; most of all, in the profusion of health problems and clinics catering to them.

I've embodied these problems, he thought. I came from a background without God. I had nothing to keep me from imbibing, without discrimination, everything that gave me pleasure. I fell for the false prophet Ayn Rand. But then I got lucky. At my lowest, when I could find no way to go on, I met Ayub and found God.

Then, one day, Mansoor found himself back at Lajpat Nagar. He was dazed to be back. He hadn't been to the market in years, had avoided it in that unself-aware way in which it is possible to sidestep any part of a city—that's what cities are, devices to sidestep things—and now here he was, standing in the crush of tin and tarpaulin, everything smaller than he remembered it, also more modern: How many years had passed! He came across the framing shop, a small cube of glass, and could remember exactly where he'd been standing when the bomb went off, the earth-shattering stillness that followed, partly because he'd gone deaf and partly because everyone was in shock. He scanned the ground outside the shop instinctively for scars, cyclonic ditches left by the explosion. But there was no sign of the bomb in the market. Like all other tragedies, it had been covered up; the market had gone into a huddle of concrete and commerce around the blast, paving over the scars like a jungle coming back over a burnt field. Even the fence of the park had been repaired, painted an unrusting golden yellow. The only thing that had really changed about the market, apart from the natural modern face-lifts to the shops, was that cars—those chariots of misery and fire—had been banished from the square. Which was why, even as the square seemed smaller to Mansoor, it felt less dangerous. Men in white shirts and women in colorful clothes streamed past, but there was no physical threat from smashing marauding vehicles. A cow with rock-black eyes munched something in a corner, its horns rubbed down to nubs.

This was where it had started. The whole saga of his youth. Of course there was no saying another bomb couldn't go off here—the official-looking security doorway at the entrance of the square was unmanned and people passed around it (the only people who went through were scrawny kids in shorts with nerdy haircuts, delighted, in the way of all kids, to pass through a cramped narrow space, so that life itself had the aspect of a game), and the crowds were as rude, random, and relaxed as before, everyone keeping track only of the space around him or her, no one carrying in his head the larger idea of the market or staying alert to the possibility that this whole theater of commerce might be ripped apart at any moment.

Mansoor's heart tightened and his pulse raced. What are the odds that another bomb will go off on the one day I venture back into the market after years? he thought. Almost zero—but stranger things have happened. And who's to say I'm not, in God's mind, some horrible gate completing the circuit? He looked at the whirling willful crowds. Hold your nerve, he told himself. Believe in God. His eyes fastened on a mustachioed man with fair skin and a kara standing on the steps of his shop, his forehead smeared with an oily tilak. The man considered him without a clear expression—he was possibly looking through Mansoor. He was the proprietor of the chemist shop. On the day of the bombing, Mansoor imagined, the shop had been smashed to bits, the ceiling caving in, the medicines ground to a dust that rose and stood steady over the debris, the chemist with his wide nostrils inhaling the toxic mix of antibiotics—and here the chemist was now, standing on the steps, his face and body intact, but his eyes lost, as if the bomb were replaying somewhere in the back of his head or as if the inhaled chemicals had undone him for good. But there was another story there, Mansoor realized, over and under the destruction and any fear and suspicion the chemist may have felt as he looked out at the crowds from the stairs. The chemist had gone to work every day. The day after the bomb he would have been back at his rubbled shop, swathed in bandages, directing mazdoors and policemen or whoever was sent to help the shocked shopkeepers; he would have pointed to where his money was kept and where he thought they might find uncrushed medicines and the body of the shop boy who'd gone missing.

And after this, after the ordeal was behind him and the compensation (if any) had been spent and the shop was returned to a workable state—the shelves back on the walls even as the walls were grainy with black concrete, unpainted, the place looking unfinished—after this, he would have returned to his business and his spot behind the counter and peered out at the inferno of the market from his glass door. Unlike Mansoor, he had no way to escape the market or the bombing; he had to confront it day after day. He had to go to bed every night knowing his world had been destroyed and wake up knowing he must feel the opposite and go on.

How did he process this? How did he start day after day in the middle of the war zone that had almost claimed him? Did he flinch when he saw a young man drive up, when he saw a skullcap, or anyone young and dressed in heroish clothes standing by himself doing nothing? Yet he went on. He did not have the luxury of depression and injury that Mansoor had. And maybe by being in this same spot year after year he had cured himself the way Mansoor had cured himself of the pain that started up when he put his hands to a keyboard. Maybe the chemist's eyes, vacant and distracted, were just the eyes of an ordinary shopkeeper taking a break from the commerce inside, his head still storming with sums and figures.

Mansoor thanked God and steadied himself and went home.

"The problem is no one listens," said Ayub as they sat together in Lodhi Garden, enjoying the last days before summer started, burning the roadsides with yellow laburnums.

"What do you mean?"

"We're uneducated people, activists—no one listens to what we say." He looked around the park, tearing dry grass from the tarmac. "Now—I don't want to single you out, Mansoor bhai—but when I told you about visualization, you were skeptical, no? Your attitude was: Why should I try this out? Even though it was so easy. Don't feel shy—that's the normal reaction. The environment in which you've been brought up is of simple cause and effect. Pain means something is wrong with the body. QED. When some fool at an NGO tells you it's related to your mind, why should you believe him, especially when the pain is real, when it seems to crush you? No—and now I'm not talking about you; I'm talking about myself—you're insulted. How dare someone say your pain is in your mind! You'll see—the more you tell people, the more they'll cling to their old systems. People like you and me, we're exceptions. We have flexible minds. We aren't irrationally wedded to anything. We actually want to solve our pain. But most people are married to it and will attack you for questioning it."

"We could write a book or start a site," Mansoor said.

"The book's been written—it's called the Quran."

There is an unnatural concentration that comes with being freed of pain after years, and Mansoor felt the world was finally clear to him. The NGO wanted the country to own up to what Modi had done in Gujarat: massacre scores of Muslims in public view, with the police standing by and watching, even helping, the rioters. But Indians couldn't see anything. They were in the grip of materialism and individualism (he remembered what his father had told him about the Khuranas, the way they had lied about the reason Tushar and Nakul and he had gone to the market; how, even at this purest moment of grief, they could not shed their materialism). What was needed, he felt, was a revolution of values in the country, a retreat from Western materialism. People needed to be shown what religion could do for them in a practical way—how it could save them from depression, pain, meaninglessness, how it could connect them to a family beyond their small selfish nuclear units.

"That's the type of site we need to start," Mansoor told Ayub. "Something that connects old values with new problems." He knew he sounded idealistic, but he suppressed his self-consciousness. "I know someone who can help with videos for the site," he told Ayub, thinking, in that circular way of his, of Vikas Uncle.

CHAPTER 21

Ayub felt close to Mansoor too. When Mansoor had opened up to him about sex, he had been surprised and touched. After that he had started considering him a close friend.

They began to go for walks together in the parks of Delhi—Lodhi Garden, the Mehrauli complex; they even drove out one day to Coronation Park. Then one evening, in the park of Khan-I-Khana, with its powerful pocked tomb and its aura of a thousand bats, Ayub told Mansoor. "Tara and I. We have something special between us." He felt shy and fumbled with a leaf in his hand. "We've been together for two years, before Peace For All."

"I knew about it," Mansoor said, smiling broadly.

"Oh, we were trying to hide it," Ayub said.

Mansoor had noticed the tension between Ayub and Tara. They assiduously avoided each other during meetings and looked away when the other spoke. Mansoor felt happy for Ayub. Tara was a tall, sensible, brilliant woman with a comical face like a touched-up, feminized version of the principal in *Archie* comics. But this made her beauty accessible. Her smile gave her away as a sincere person—not one driven to the icy, egotistical, inhumane extremes of activism. Mansoor often stared at her during meetings—she was the only Hindu girl there, and the most cheerful and confident. "You would be good together," he said.

For a while it seemed that Mansoor, with the newfound glow of religion, could be happy for anyone. Then negativity once again took his world hostage.

CHAPTER 22

Mansoor was sitting with Tara and Ayub at a dhaba in JNU, drinking cutting tea, when it started.

After Ayub had told him about Tara, the three of them had started going out together, eating pizza and burgers and lime ice at Nirula's, savoring tea from Tara's and Ayub's favorite dhabas, and discussing their dreams.

Tara wanted to start a communal harmony institute, one in which common values would be shared and discussed. "There's a big scope for that," she said. "You can see people have a hunger to discuss these issues when you go to schools. But there isn't any outlet for them."

Ayub wanted to get into politics. "People like me need to take some initiative," he said. "That's why I left engineering. My whole family was in shock. Every day they send me messages through relatives trying to see that I'm not on drugs. They can't fathom why someone like me would do something of this sort." He grinned and pressed his hand for a second onto Tara's palm, which was open limply on the table, as if this were an old joke between them. Tara, who was slumped forward on the table—she slumped when she was happy and at ease with people—smiled at him, a tiny candle of a smile, one that created intimacy in the crowded dhaba with its students debating Marxism and whatnot.

"So what do you want to do, Mansoor? Be an engineer?" Tara asked, looking across at him after that private moment.

"Me? Be an activist, I suppose," he said. But he was gulping now, for reasons he couldn't understand.

He noticed that Tara was pressing her other hand against Ayub's under the dhaba table.

That's when it started. It was as instantaneous as pain. It was jealousy.

He didn't know why or how it took hold—but there it was, lurking powerfully. This relationship, Mansoor thought, it's just Ayub's way out of poverty, out of being lower-class. That's why he's in this NGO—to attach himself to this rich, idealistic girl.

As for Tara, she likes having power over these desperate Muslim men.

But Mansoor was thinking of himself. As the three of them had ventured out together, he had become more and more attracted to Tara. His blood jumped in her presence. Her perfume, her mysterious unfashionable waft of coconut, even her sweat—all this turned him on. All the old sexual obsessions returned. But he had no way to exorcize these thoughts now—wasn't allowed to masturbate. At home, in his room, *not* masturbating took up all his time; it was almost as all-consuming as watching porn and masturbating.

He wanted to talk to Ayub about this struggle against sexual impulses but felt guilty that he was struggling over his girlfriend.

As the weeks went on, Mansoor's struggle became solitary. Thoughts and images about sex, about undressed women, shot like arrows of flesh through his brain. *Stop*, he shouted, at home, down on the marble floor, praying. When he visualized the happy round of cricket with Tushar and Nakul in the park, a naked Elizabeth Hurley stalked onto the pitch, interrupting the game.

Please, God, Mansoor prayed. *Are you testing me?*

Then one day he lost control and masturbated and was filled with disgust and cursed himself: May your wrists go black!

But in this way, slowly, he fell into a trap of masturbation and self-hate.

So when he met Ayub and Tara a few days after the encounter at JNU—they were at Flavors now—and they told him excitedly that they were organizing one of the largest mass protests in Delhi's history to interrupt Narendra Modi's visit to the city, that they had corralled activists from all over the city, Mansoor could only nod grimly. He was a miserable, poisonous person, he felt, unworthy of God.

"We want to bring the city to a standstill," Tara was saying. "If necessary, we want people to court arrest. You know what Gandhi said the Jews
of Europe should do when faced with Hitler?"

"No," Mansoor said, though he'd heard her say this a million times.

"Commit mass suicide," Tara said, savoring the words with the intensity
of someone who has obviously not considered it seriously. "Throw themselves from cliffs. Think of it. If the Jews were able to muster that kind of
courage, the Holocaust would have never happened. We want to get to that
level of nonviolence."

"But doesn't suicide count as violence?" Ayub asked rhetorically.

"You're right. It does. But you're allowed that kind of contradiction
when you're up against a completely unrepentant force."

"I see," Mansoor said, interrupting this public lovemaking of activists.
"And what about the 1996 blast accused?" There had been a lull on that
front. Mansoor and Ayub and Tara had written editorials together about
the accused and mailed them to the *Times of India*, the *Hindustan Times*, and
the *Pioneer* but had not heard back; the editors at these papers, it seemed,
were not interested in the unique slant of a victim asking for a terrorist's
release.

"We'll work on that after the rally," Tara said in her direct, no-nonsense
way.

"Everything OK with you, boss?" Ayub asked him when Tara had gone to
the toilet.

"Of course," he said, though he meant the opposite.

When Mansoor looked at himself in the mirror at home, he saw a dark,
small, pathetic person, an ugly person, a person who shouldn't have lived.
He saw that these feelings had nothing to do with the bomb. This was who
he was.

AYUB AZMI'S RESPONSE TO TERROR

MARCH 2003–OCTOBER 2003

CHAPTER 23

Ayub and Tara had been planning the rally for months, even before Mansoor had joined the NGO. To see it on the horizon excited them. Then, in March, it happened.

Ayub and Tara came to the roads near the India International Centre worked up and expectant—having not slept the previous night, having stayed up reading selections from Gandhi's *Autobiography*, Ambedkar's essays, the speeches of MLK and Malcolm X and Muhammad Ali. "It's so touching, the sense of empowerment Islam gave to all these colonial people, to slaves. America's attempt to crush Islam is an attempt to destroy the self-esteem of the rising, conquered people," Ayub had said. Tara had nodded her head in agreement.

Then, in the late morning, right before the rally began, Ayub faxed the police about the protest from the market near the site of the event; this was a loophole activists exploited. You were supposed to inform the police about any rally you held, but there was no statute on exactly when you told them, as long as it was before and in writing.

Doing it in person was too dangerous since the police would ask you to lead them to the rally.

Yet, when Ayub joined the crowd on the road—hundreds of men and women chanting and holding up signs—he found the police already there, battalions pouring forth from Gypsies and coming up to the protesters, asking them questions and gently herding them onto the sidewalk. "You can't do that," Ayub said. "It's a nonviolent protest."

"You shut up, you terrorist," a policeman—younger than Ayub, livid with youth—said.

Ayub was wearing his skullcap.

Ayub made to attack him but a couple of older policemen, blasé in their interaction with the disaffected, pushed him aside.

"Arrest me," Ayub said, holding out his wrists.

"You're not worth an arrest," a policeman with gray hair said, stepping out to shout at a pimply activist who started running at the bark from the policeman.

Then something terrible happened on that spring day. The crowd dispersed.

The next day when Tara and Ayub opened the paper, there wasn't even a mention of the protest.

Tara and Ayub debated what had happened with the members of the NGO—all of them, including Mansoor, had attended the disappointing protest—and fell privately into despair. Ayub began to believe that nonviolence didn't work. He'd had this feeling for a long time but had said nothing to Tara about it. In the NGO room, where they often met to kiss before meetings—they had still never made love—he scolded her. "I knew it wouldn't work."

"I didn't personally tell people not to come," she said bitterly.

"But we should have known."

"You prepared for it too!"

Ayub went on ranting for a while—frothing, gesticulating, blaming Tara for her naïveté, for her earnestness—till he finally stopped. "I'm sorry." He lived like this—in these explosions of passion. He was a passionate person.

Nevertheless, his loss of faith in nonviolence cut deep. He believed nonviolence suffered the fundamental problem of having no traffic with the media. The media reveled in sex and violence—how could nonviolence, with its graying temples and wise posture, match up?

Ayub tried to come up with alternatives—nonviolent spectacles, theater, protests—but all these needed participants and an audience.

He was not prepared when, a week later, Tara broke things off with him.

CHAPTER 24

Tara had become tired of Ayub, of his brilliance, his neediness, his delusions of grandeur; she felt she deserved more. In December of the previous year, in anticipation of an eventual breakup, she had secretly applied to Brandeis for a master's in social work. When she was admitted soon after the failure of the rally, she confronted Ayub and told him she wanted to break up.

Ayub, when he heard what she had to say, stood up from the bed in the NGO room, his eyes livid. "How dare you, you bitch!" he frothed, full of his normal uncontrolled anger.

"It's my life!" Tara said.

"How dare you!" He thought she was doing this because the rally had failed.

They calmed down after a while and made up, sitting on the bed together, cajoling each other, feverishly discussing whether Ayub could find a way to go to the U.S. too.

But then, suddenly, Tara said, "I don't like your smell."

Ayub looked on in cool shock. Tara's fairness, then, on the bed, was frightening to Ayub—like porcelain, speaking of centuries of superb breeding, of Aryan excitement.

"Brandeis, applying, going abroad—these are all excuses to get away from you," Tara said. "I like you, *admire* you, but—something isn't right. I don't like the smell of your breath," she repeated, as if shocked with the truth of this, formulating it for herself.

Ayub looked out of the window. From the room he could see an alley, and beyond, a backyard festooned with clotheslines. In the alley, a car had broken down between two flowing gutters. Beneath it, a runway of needles, discarded by the hospital, glistened in the sunshine, the garbage ponderously overflowing, everything protected by the rusty, aggressive fragrance of the air conditioner, in whose lungs the krill of pollution stuck.

Ayub's heart got mixed up with the freezing waves of the air conditioner. A few days later, he left Delhi and returned to his hometown, Azamgarh.

When Mansoor heard of Ayub's departure, he was shocked. "Where did you go?" he SMSed Ayub.

"Decided to start a job as an area salesman for Eveready," Ayub SMSed back. "KEEP THE FIGHT ALIVE."

Area salesman? For a battery company? What about Tara?

Tara was not helpful either. "Oh, that's what he said? I think he's gone to visit his father, who's ill." She threw her hair back and laughed her rich, upper-class tinkling laugh. "He's so eccentric."

CHAPTER 25

Ayub started working in his father's "organick" nursery in Azamgarh, digging up turnips and potatoes under the hot UP sun.

He'd come very far, in a sense. Starting from a lower-middle-class Muslim family in UP he'd made his way to Delhi and established himself with his wit and charm and intelligence. Like Mansoor, he'd dealt with pain—the pain of separation, of being out of one's depth, fearing one's mortality—but had cured himself. (Unlike Mansoor, he hadn't had the luxury of physiotherapy.) But he saw now that freedom from pain was a kind of sentence too—your mind, free to cast about in any direction, latched on to every outcome, every path, every regret. Whereas pain was focusing and drew you into yourself. It cut off options.

Sometimes, working on his father's farm, Ayub tightened his neck, wishing the pain would return. It didn't. He'd made himself too sturdy through religion and exercise. But his mind began to flower outward, became crowded with mirages. Tara stood knee-deep in a field of wheat, a few meters beyond him, hunched over and ready and sly, her eyes blinking and the soft, sensual braid tossed over her shoulder. A rumble in the distance made him glance up and he thought he saw an airplane flaming overhead, but it was just a trigger of sunlight. At night, in bed, he dreamed of school bullies and friends who had let him down out of jealousy when he'd had a little success in college as a festival organizer. A mild person, he'd always gone out of his way to put others at ease, to not threaten them with his intelligence. Now he regretted it.

He kept endlessly revising the day of the rally, his conversation with Tara, the swiftness with which everything had fallen apart.

Why hadn't he said more when she'd broken up with him? But there was a part of him that was addicted to defeat. Even as he'd received the stabbing message from Tara, that part of him had swelled with brilliance and promise and negative fulfillment.

Ayub dug holes and toiled under the sun.

"We can show you a girl," his mother said.

His mind was coming unmoored. The field, with its hideous infinity of dirt packed into a few acres, didn't help.

He could have boarded a train and gone back, but he had no money and no real way of making any; his work with the Muslim community had taught him how difficult it was for educated Muslims to get jobs or even housing and this paranoia infected every future he could imagine for himself in Delhi. And the more he thought about money, the more he regretted how things had turned out with Tara—not only had they got along, but she had paid him a salary. "To hear you talk," she'd once laughed. He was irritated by this comment, but once he began to speak, his self-consciousness fell away and he looked at her with unembarrassed frankness. "So what if I love to talk! I'm good at it."

But there was also anger in him about how well she knew him, and he would be turned on and would wish to make love to her.

Of course, this never happened. Tara always stopped him—for religious reasons—and he couldn't refuse. Nevertheless, it frustrated him. He had a tremendous sexual drive and he sometimes thought he should have been allowed, by God, to break the rules—for the sake of revolution, for India. Instead he proposed marriage.

"You know I'm engaged, right?" she told him.

"What?"

"I'm only joking," she said. And they held hands and she said nothing and this had been a kind of promise.

Months passed. The possibility of returning grew bleaker and bleaker. He saw that his life was over, his happiest moments were behind him, and that he had lived those moments unthinkingly, so consumed and fired by thoughts of the future he hadn't even been aware of how happy he was.

Then one day he heard from Mansoor that Tara had left for the U.S.

That day he went to meet Zunaid.

Zunaid was a local fixer and thug, known to have ties with gangs, and Ayub came up to him in an alley late at night. In the distance, a Maruti van lay twisted in an open sewer trying to rev itself out. Two men helped push the awkward cockroach of a vehicle.

"Ustad, how many years it's been!" Zunaid said. "Tell me, how can I help you?" He was a big man in an impeccable kurta.

"I want to buy a gun," Ayub told Zunaid after some preliminaries. "We have a big monkey problem in the field. They come and tear our plants every afternoon. We've tried to use a spade and a scarecrow, but nothing works. I thought using a pistol might help."

"A pistol, is it?" Zunaid gauged Ayub's face. Ayub had been one of the golden boys of the town, with a legendary academic record, and Zunaid was curious about this shift. "You sure you don't want me to do it for you?"

"Monkeys multiply very fast."

"I see." Zunaid paused. "Eight hundred rupees."

"Five hundred."

"Very good, boss."

A few days later, when Zunaid brought Ayub the pistol, Ayub said, "What is this nonsense? Are you sure this won't explode in my face? This is the sort of gun the student union leaders carry in Shibli. One lost his hand shooting this kind of gun." It looked like a tin imitation of a pistol, the metal corrupted by holes. It had a handle ripped from a cooking knife and a barrel fashioned from the steering shaft of a rickshaw. The nails on its sides were poking out.

Zunaid explained patiently, pedantically, why it worked well regardless.

"Come, let's go try it," Ayub said.

In a field, Ayub took a long lead bullet from Zunaid, slid it into a hole at the back of the pistol, rocked back on his heels, and took aim at an old family-planning advertisement up along the road that ran into the town. "Shit!" he shouted, dropping the overheated weapon.

Zunaid looked at Ayub and marveled at how gaunt he seemed, how ringed his eyes were. Then he sighed, took the gun back from Ayub, and, while explaining its qualities, shot within the inverted red triangle of the family-planning sign. "You just have to practice," he said. "Can you tell me what you need it for? If you're trying to kill someone it's better if you hire one of our sharpshooters. Doing it yourself will only lead to trouble." As he spoke he was proud that he might be spotted with Ayub, and he went on. "For you, bhai, because I respect and admire you, I'd even give you a special rate." When Ayub said nothing, strange tears came to Zunaid's eyes and he said, "We'd even do it for free."

Ayub—standing in the field, with this man, days from Delhi, the country vast and unbending around him, the bullet in the gun small, the heart of the man he wished to kill even smaller—was overcome with despair. It was the kind of despair he felt often in Azamgarh when he walked through the alleys at night or watched the burqa-clad women cower in their homes or when he fell out of step with the pleasant mood of manual labor.

He told the pesky gang member he didn't need his help, paid him five hundred rupees, and left with the pistol tucked rakishly into his trousers.

Ayub now began practicing—first with bottles and then with pieces of wood, dead plants, mongooses, stray dogs. His aim got better; he grasped the wayward path of the shotgun bullet. He often chewed tobacco when he shot the pistol and sometimes swallowed an entire wad in excitement, experiencing a deep, watery high, the bullet magically standing still in its cape of smoke and the bottle exploding into shards moments later. There was no shortage of things to shoot in Azamgarh. It was a town made of trash.

As his aim got better, he laughed his high-pitched laugh. His parents, who were going blind from diabetes, groped around in the single room of the hut, worrying, not saying anything.

But at night, when he lay on his bed with the pistol under his charpai, praying that no one would break into the house and force him to use it, he was fearful of what was in store for him if he actually went ahead with his

plan, of the torture he'd be subjected to, the years in prison, the electro-
cutions and head dunkings—also, the almost certain failure. But there
would be one difference. Whereas other people who had tried to assassinate political figures or planted bombs escaped after the deed was done,
leaving innocent Muslims to bear the brunt of the police's fury and oppression, he would turn himself in. This was the biggest incentive for
taking matters into his own hands. No matter what, then, prison lay in
store for him. (He could also kill himself after committing the crime, but
this would lead to the same outcome as escaping; no one trusts a suicide
note by a nobody.)

Funny, to be confronted with prison after years of working with inmates,
of learning the full horrors of the system—but wasn't this always the case
with things you got to know too well, even if you feared them? He knew the
power of visualization. Most people never go to prison because they never
think of it. Whereas he had thought so much about prison, about the state
of inmates, that his ending up there had a whiff of inevitability. Would Tara
come to visit him if he were behind bars? Would that reignite her interest
in him? Romances conducted from jail were common, and Tara had always romanticized inmates, people cast down into complete helplessness,
people so disenfranchised that they had a certain dignity and directness.

In his sleep, he imagined a long trial following his arrest, Tara getting
him out of jail; he imagined being vindicated for killing Modi when the
man was officially recognized as a war criminal by the International Court
at The Hague; he imagined books being written about his heroism, his
humble background, his idealism, the world he carried within him, the
dozen rooms he'd occupied in different parts of India, his photogenic
handsomeness, the dignity with which he endured the indignities of jail.

The distance between these dreams and his ambitions was revealed to
him when he shot his shoddy little gun and wiped it with a towel in the
evenings. To kill Modi, it was necessary to aim from within a crowd, with
people around you, and then through the phalanx of bodyguards that
spread on either side of him like the multiveined hood of a snake—he had
seen Modi's setup during his Gaurav Yatra rally in Delhi.

How could he—a small person, in a ruined place, with a gun fashioned from throwaway parts, the rusted infrastructure of the town—succeed?

In May, he took a train to Delhi on the pretext of finding a job. In the cramped compartment, as he bent his neck to read a copy of Turgenev's *Fathers and Sons*, a commotion started up. An old man with powerful jaws was demanding a magazine from a bearded student. When the student said, "Let me finish," the old man started swearing. "You pigs! Fucking Muslims!" The student finally gave up and handed the magazine to the old geezer. But when the old man flipped through it, he snapped again, "This is in English!" and threw it down. Ayub did not intervene. He was light-headed and tired and hungry, the pistol pressed against his hip like a piece of bone, and when he hopped off at Old Delhi Railway Station, he took a rickshaw and then a bus to a vast field full of people. Modi's rally. Holding his breath, swaggering, he swam through the dam-burst of people: office men, peasants, women covering their eyes with free posters handed out at the entrance. Modi twinkled in the distance behind a stage. You could barely hear him. Nevertheless, Ayub lifted his head and stared at him, and imagined Modi staring back, and he felt something pass between them. He put his small, neat hands in his pockets. He couldn't do it.

He had planned to meet Mansoor and his Peace For All friends if this mission failed, but he took the train back the next day in despair.

When he got to Azamgarh, he was trembling and twitching from his inaction, a wedge-shaped headache squeezing the top right corner of his skull. He wasn't sure he could control his face—felt it might split away from him in a series of twitches. Perhaps, he thought, he had brought himself to the point of such stress that he would suffer another physical collapse, implode, experience something much worse than back pain—an aneurysm, maybe, a blood clot, one of those deadly killers that gathered evidence from the rest of your stressed body before detonating the whole sorry scaffolding.

When he ate a meal with his mother and father, he told himself he was seeing them for the last time. He clutched the pistol in his pocket; his eyes felt weak.

This sort of thinking continued for a few days, till he realized he was as incapable of killing himself as he was of killing Modi. Besides, he still loved Tara. He wrote her another letter and posted it to a friend in Benares, who, in turn, typed it and e-mailed it to her (Azamgarh still didn't have an Internet cafe). Afterwards, he felt happy. Having Tara even once, for a short period, had been a great thing. He visited a prostitute, mastering his disgust by imagining he was making love to Tara, her sweet face turned up, the braid beside her like a watchful dangerous snake that he took in his mouth.

It was in this unstable, ecstatic, endorphin-soaked mood that he went to visit Zunaid.

Zunaid was playing cards in his house with friends when Ayub entered; he immediately put the cards down in embarrassment, treating Ayub with honor and respect. "Tell me, Ayub bhai, what brings you here?" Zunaid said, clearing space for him on the charpai, his lips wet with spittle, as usual.

"I wanted to talk to you alone," Ayub said. "But there's no rush; play your cards."

"We can go back and talk."

"I'd prefer if you all played," Ayub said. "I've brought a paper. I'll sit and read."

"No, no, that's too awkward, you just watching us," Zunaid protested.

"Abe, play," one of the men on the charpai said.

So they played and were soon lost in their cards. Whipping the newspaper to crispness (like women whipping clothes to open them out before hanging them on a clothesline), Ayub watched the faces and personalities of the four men in the room and admired their concentration, their ability to find peace, even happiness, in this tragic hellhole of a town. My mistake was to leave in the first place, he thought.

Later, Zunaid and he stood side by side taking a leisurely piss over the garbage dump behind the house. Ayub examined the brands of the wrappers in the garbage, their good fonts, the fine print—he thought of the craftsmanship that had gone into these wrappers and had a strong feeling that, despite all its problems, the country was progressing. The fact that Azamgarh received all the trash of the country was proof that it would someday receive other things as well, that it was not cut off. Someday the trash itself would be of such high value, so beautifully made, that this awful place wouldn't need an economy at all.

"Are you good at keeping secrets, Zunaid bhai?" Ayub asked, tucking his dick back into his pants.

Zunaid said yes, he could keep secrets.

"You asked me why I wanted the gun," Ayub said as they walked back. "It was a test. To see if you were trustworthy."

Zunaid smiled, clearly pleased.

"And you were," Ayub said. "I'm going to let you in on a secret." He told him that he had been sent by a political party to recruit people to kill Modi and that he was looking for a team to carry it out. The payment would come from a rich man in Bhopal.

Ayub was dismayed to discover that Zunaid had no idea who Modi was. "Arre, yaar, not the tire company," he said. "He killed thousands of Muslims in Gujarat." He proceeded to describe Modi's atrocities.

"We must take revenge on such a person," Zunaid said, tears in his eyes. "For our own self-respect."

"The problem is that he's well guarded," said Ayub.

"Don't worry," Zunaid said. "We have means."

The two men talked for a while and then Ayub went home. He was lightheaded from excitement, the heat, the wood fires at dusk, the mosquitoes, the angle at which the sunlight pushed dust motes into his room through a small window, making him think again of jail. Maybe the thing to do is to run away from Azamgarh right now, he thought. Before Zunaid tells the police. But the same strangling pleasant inertia, which had been his constant companion these past few months, took hold of him and the next day he returned to work at the farm. He was reminded, watching the farmers in the field, of the opening of his favorite novel, *Raag Darbari*, the first novel he'd read about *his* type of town, in which a man dressed in khadi hitches a ride on a truck on the way back to town and is mistaken for a CBI agent. Ayub felt that he too, with these conversations, had turned himself into an agent—an agent for an imaginary organization, yes, but one that, on the edge of this field, verging on madness, he could summon into existence just by thinking about it. And who was to say such an organization didn't exist? There were thousands of groups trying to kill Modi—yes, one reason he had acted so quickly was because he was afraid of being beaten to it. Yet the presence of these groups gave him the confidence that this work would be completed—if not by him, then by someone else. There would be justice eventually. He didn't feel alone. The field grew smaller. The branches of the trees seemed to reach out, brown and hard, carved with footholds. There are times in the day when every plant seems to breathe openly.

He had never hated anyone with the passion that he brought to his hatred of Modi. He'd often wondered why, tried to examine how this bearded fellow had infiltrated his imagination, and could only chalk it up to one thing: Modi's arrogance. There had been so many killers in Indian history but none as unrepentant or shameless as this capitalist politician pig. None had operated in public view. And none seemed so above the law, so beloved by Hindus of all kinds—yes, he hated the Chief Minister because he represented the worst in Hindus, a belief in their own invincibility that always sprang up when they were doing well, making money hand over first, a belief that you could get away with anything *if only* you had money. Forget Modi: he hated money too, money of all kinds, stripes, and currencies. He hated what the country had become, a capitalist stooge of America. In his mind he carried an image of India's pure precapitalist past: a water pump by a paddy field unreeling a stream of electrified water. Where this image had come from he didn't know—he'd never actually seen it; all he'd seen was the trash of Azamgarh and the crush of Delhi, where all the garbage was generated. Still, the image was powerful, and Tara and he had discussed ways in which it could be achieved, how India could shake off the shackles of Western capitalism. But the economy was a large, inexorable machine. There seemed to be no way to turn it back. "Not till lots of people are miserable and poor," she'd said.

"But the rich will never be miserable," he'd said. "And they rule the country."

Zunaid came and told Ayub that he had someone he wanted him to meet. It was Shockie.

CHAPTER 26

Shockie had been reluctant to meet Ayub; he had learned, from years of experience, that no one could be trusted when it came to the work of revolution.

So, when he met Ayub near Zunaid's house, he asked Ayub basic questions about himself: his age, his birth place, his work background.

When he heard that Ayub had worked with inmates, people wrongly jailed for terrorist attacks, including the blast in 1996, he fell silent. "And you were doing this for free? Who was paying you?" Did Ayub know his friend Malik?

Ayub, meanwhile, was confused by Shockie. He must have been in his mid- or late thirties, but looked older: there were prominent worry lines on his forehead and something permanent-seeming about his small, black, tough mustache, as if it had been there from the beginning of time to assert his avuncular place in the world. His questions too, these worried, careful questions about money, were the questions of an uncle. Still, Ayub, who was used to being interviewed, said, "Sir, I worked for an NGO—they paid me. The condition in the jails is very bad, as you can imagine. There are no human rights."

Shockie's resolve, in the warm evening air, diminished. He'd waited so many years for news of Malik, for access to him—had even considered disguising himself and visiting him in jail—and now here was someone who had not only met Malik but also worked with him.

How would this fellow feel if he knew I was behind the blast? How

would he respond? But this was the terrible thing about the profession—
you could take credit for nothing. When blasts were mentioned, Shockie
tried to clear his mind completely and respond with the mild shock of a
civilian. He saw that he was on dangerous turf. "You will have to leave your
family," he said suddenly.

"Yes, sir."

"No contact with your mother or father." (He himself had never followed this rule, but that had been a different, less brutal time. The interna-
tionalization of terror, the increased scrutiny in the press, had changed
everything.) "You can't even know if they die. For you, they are dead from
this moment."

"Yes, sir," Ayub said, surprised at how quickly the man's tone had shifted,
how he had gone from a harmless middle-aged uncle to a priest, delivering
well-worn mantras and cleaning his nose occasionally by squeezing his
nostrils with his fingers. He might have been stating the prayers for a marriage. There was something practical, nasal, and strict about it.

"You give up money, drinks, happiness. You give up everything. You're
ready for that?"

"Yes," Ayub said.

Shockie paused, still testing him out. What was that expression on his
face—that ready, watchful, but resigned expression?

"Why do you want to do this?" he asked him directly.

"To take revenge," Ayub said.

"On who?" asked Shockie.

"On Modi," said Ayub.

"For who?" said Shockie.

"For Muslims."

"Why do you hate him so much?" Shockie asked. "He's just a man."

"He's not a man; he's a symbol."

"There's something else," Shockie said. "A man like you doesn't turn to
revolution just like that. What do you want? Are you angry? You want to
show the world you're a hero?"

Ayub considered this. The reasons were murky in his head, all the more so because he had lived them out with such intensity. Death. I want to die. Some weeks ago, he had taken a drug in the field. The drug was mixed with milk and peddled by the local witch doctor. What had followed was a series of terrifying hallucinations. First the fields, bulging under the sodium lamp of the sun, had changed colors, parted, leapt about, danced with flames of murmuring wheat. He could touch and see everything for kilometers around. Then, as he'd walked, he'd had a strong sense that all the people around him—the men in their small square stalls, selling bidis and phone chargers; the auto drivers; the farmers whipping their skeletal bulls; the man selling pomegranates by the circuit house; the boy riding his bicycle to and from the shabby hotel; the frightened women in burqas clustered outside their homes, awaiting their husbands from the Gulf—were *monkeys*. Yes, *monkeys, animals*. That's what people were when you took away the basic veneer of civilization. And he'd had a vision then of Tara, a vision of love. What was Tara but a lost monkey from a powerful family of monkeys, who'd fallen down from her tree and randomly played with a poor monkey far from its own family? No, there was nothing to do but feel sad about Tara— what fault was it of hers? She had been pulled back into the thicket of her family and that was how it should be. As for him, he was a small, wounded, seeking animal, one who had strayed from the path a long time ago; he saw now that his time in Delhi, with Tara, had been a conference of the weak. They thought they were changing the world, but everyone except for him could see they were weak, damaged animals, clasping each other.

Why am I so wounded? he thought. But that is the fate of certain people. They lose themselves and never find themselves again.

He saw too, in this vision on drugs, that the world was dictated by power (he did not think, as he would later, that the reason he'd had such nihilistic visions was that he was depressed). What was Modi but a violent, scream- ing animal demanding the death and destruction of other clans? There were two ways to handle such a fat chest-beating monkey: to hide away forever in the forest or to attack him and *his* clan. In an instant, hallucinat- ing, the field leaping about, he grasped the swift logic of violence. The world existed in a state of battle between clans and races. Each clan rose at the expense of the other. Whenever one came up, it was important to cut it down to size with violence. . . . He thought of 9/11, a crime that had, for all its religious implications, always seemed opaque to him, and it was clear that, in world historical terms, if you thought of the world as a jungle, what had happened was simple, obvious: sensing the rising power of one group, Atta and company had attacked the temple of that group.

As for death? It did not matter. We are only animals, and if we give a complex name to our grief, it is because we like to pretend otherwise.

A clan is more important than the animal. In fact, it is in grief that we become most like animals, hiding, curling up, refusing to accept the truth of someone's goneness, acting as if the person gone is a part of ourselves.

It was during this hallucination that Ayub decided to give himself to revolution and violence. "I tried nonviolence," he told Shockie now. "I was a big believer in Gandhi. You could say I was a self-hating Muslim. I wanted equality between Hindus and Muslims, brotherhood. I thought the majority could be persuaded with such action. At one point, when the farmer suicides were happening in Andhra and Maharashtra, I even staged a protest where Muslims threatened to take the poison and kill themselves. It was nonviolence taken to its full extreme. But the press gave it no attention. Now I see it's a world where everything operates by force. If you sit and let people go on, then they will. I had always thought you had to educate others about your pain, show them how to solve it. Now I realize you have to make them *feel* it."

"That's a very good speech," Shockie said. "You should be a politician."

Ayub grew exasperated. Maybe this wasn't the best idea after all. The door he'd been about to walk through closed a little. He had an inkling of how life would look if he retreated—how he could rebuild it. The sounds of hammers and construction were at his back. All of India was under renovation. Why was he so eager to destroy it? "It looks like you won't be convinced," Ayub said, curling his lips. "So forget it."

"You see my problem," Shockie said. "It's a problem of trust. But there is a way. If you can get me to meet Malik Aziz, who is a friend of mine, I'll be convinced."

"You know Malik?" Ayub said. "It's not that easy."

"I just want to see him," Shockie said.

"For that you can go to the trial," Ayub said. "If you're confident and well dressed you can enter anywhere."

"How is he?" Shockie asked.

Confused by the direction of the conversation, Ayub said, "You know he hasn't spoken in six years, right? Some of the ideas of nonviolence I got from him. He's one of the major exemplars of such protest in the country. Even the foreign media has covered him."

Poor Malik! Shockie thought. Who loved to talk! "I know," Shockie lied.

But now an intimacy developed between them. Shockie suddenly decided to trust Ayub.

At a certain point all such work is risk. The question is when you are willing to take it. In any case, the danger existed regardless of where you hunted for it; often it came from the most unexpected source.

The group operated out of a series of safe houses in the countryside of Uttar Pradesh. For Ayub, everything connected to the group was new. His fellow revolutionaries, shady figures he might or might not have heard about in the news, were serene individuals. Wrapped in woodsmoke, they conversed quietly, surrounded by sacks of cement or grain inside small huts. Several of the men in the group were educated, young professional types who'd given up their careers in big towns. Tauqeer was a former software engineer; Rafiq had an MA in psychology and had worked for Coca-Cola in marketing; Mohammed was a renowned hacker. These men greeted Ayub with interest, suspicion, condescension. He'd forgotten what it meant to be the junior member of a group after having a free run with Peace For All.

Ayub had always railed against Muslims who turned to violence (though he had been sure, after working with inmates for years, that many of the bombs were planted by Hindus to frame Muslims), but now he found himself on the cutting edge of news events, on the verge of becoming a *news maker*. He marveled at how this group of men, gathered in a warm, dark room, could alter the political future of a country. "If we disrupt the economy," one was saying as he chewed a bit of bread, his legs dangling from a ledge in the hut, "then Modi automatically goes." Ayub had been introduced as a new member with no criminal record, who could infiltrate Modi's inner circle—he had boasted of his connection with Tara, whose parents were rich, well-connected BJP supporters.

The men, because they were educated, talked in economic terms. Plant enough bombs, Tauqeer said (he had a memorable face with gaunt cheekbones, a prayer callus on his forehead, and black whorls where the cheekbones jutted out of his face), and you create uncertainty in the economy and investment dries up. "This so-called economic boom is fragile," he said. "It's caused simply by a cost advantage on the Indian side. The investors arc like hawks. They'll move to another country or state the minute they feel it's dangerous. And Modi too will be voted out of power." He was arguing, in effect, that there was no need to kill Modi directly. Just taking aim at the economy of Gujarat, the apple on Modi's head (or was it vice versa?), was enough.

"And think about what happens if he's killed," Rafiq said.

Ayub had an image of riots, bloodshed, babies speared from the stomachs of pregnant mothers—real images; he'd seen them a thousand times when he'd screened the documentary about the Gujarat riots for schools.

"We shouldn't be afraid of such consequences," Tauqeer, obviously the leader, burst in. "We should welcome them. Unlike our friend Rafiq here," he said, turning to Ayub, "I don't share such a rosy view of our fellow Muslims. They're corrupt, cowardly, hypocritical, and busy fighting among themselves. There's no difference between them and Hindus, if you ask me. The Muslims in this country are Indians first and Muslims second." (It occurred to Ayub that just months earlier, he would have considered this a good thing.) "Having a few more riots will awaken them to the reality in this country." Ayub saw now that he was being addressed directly—that he was considered one of those Muslims who had woken up *after* the riots. But was he the only one? All these people are young. I suspect they too only took this extreme step after the riots, he thought.

How much blood will we have to shed to create a million versions of me?

Tauqeer produced an inhaler and sucked on it. So that wasn't just a rumor, that he was asthmatic. Taking a puff, he said, "You want?"

The five men in the room laughed.

"In the old days they had hookahs," Tauqeer said, laughing.

The men traveled to a forest outside the city of Hubli, in Karnataka—a dry, arid region famous for its sweets and reddish rotis. At this time Shockie's position in the group became clearer to Ayub. He was a handler, an uncle who watched his reckless wards with his hands behind his back and eyes slightly absent till danger presented itself. Always dressed in a sleeveless sweater, whatever the weather, he wore dusty black pants with astonishingly sharp pleats. Later, Ayub would learn that Shockie, the son of a presswali, took a dandy's pride, despite his thinning curly hair, in wearing ironed clothes. Shockie kept a distance as they practiced and conducted training drills in the forest. The practice, Ayub had imagined, would be easy, a way of killing time before the actual killing. But it was exhausting. He was made to run through the bramble and brush till he collapsed. He lay in a puddle of his own vomit. Screaming, he hung for an hour from a branch on a tree, a branch that refused to spare him by breaking off, despite his prayers. He was left in a forest with a compass and no Odomos or light and made to find his way back to the camp in the forest. How could such training be possibly useful in the jungles of urban India?

Later, when they were exhausted out of their skulls, sitting dead-eyed around a fire at night, the fire like a performer throwing its hands this way and that, someone would pass a packet of biscuits and the others would accept and a warm, happy communal feeling would engulf them. Shockie remained standing off to the side.

"What is his position?" Ayub asked one particular night after he'd proved himself during training, shooting straight while running. All that practice with his country pistol had paid off.

"That's Shaukat Guru. You've heard of him," Rafiq said.

Ayub was blank.

"Yaar, he's one of the most dangerous men in India. He's set off bombs in every Indian city."

"And now he is—?" asked Ayub.

"He's like a coach."

Yes—that's exactly what he looked like—a sports coach. He even had that bulky avuncular look under the sweater.

"He's stopped doing it himself?" said Ayub.

"He's sick," Rafiq said. "Has a bad heart. Afraid of going *phut* with the bombs. Said he didn't take care of himself when he was younger and that's why he's turned out this way. You know, back in the day, even for militants, they didn't believe in training physically. You were given your guns, your equipment, and you had to figure it out yourself. Given all that, he did very well. One of his bombs in Delhi killed hundreds, they say. Do you know Lajpat Nagar market?"

Ayub froze. He nodded without betraying anything.

Shockie stood in the distance, swaddled and sentry-like in the fulminating firelight. Was it possible that Malik Aziz, Shockie's friend in prison, was guilty? Ayub wondered. He had thought a lot about the silent inmate over the years and had come to the conclusion that, despite his brave silence, he must be suffering from a mental illness, that he had been arrested precisely *because* he was somewhat retarded. Talking to his relatives in Anantnag had confirmed this—though, being village people they were eager to agree with whatever Ayub said, and anyway they changed their minds on any subject a million times. Village people had no central conception of truth or time or even of other people's memories; they always just played dumb when he told them they'd changed their stories. What if Malik was a terrorist after all? Ayub was seized by rage. If he were a terrorist it would have been helpful if the behnchod had admitted it and let other innocents go. Ayub had even tried to reason with him on trips to the prison. "Just say something. If you *have* done it, you can save the lives of others." But nothing. Ayub really did think prison was the worst way to spend one's life. This made the sacrifice *he* was making all the more grand, of course. If he were

arrested, he would be able to help people inside, apply his leadership skills.
Unless he were kept in isolation.

Despite the fact that he had almost given himself up for arrest at the
rally, he had a total fear of solitary confinement, believed it would absolutely break him. He was a person who thrived on company, who desired
camaraderie, even in its lowest, most base form; he felt that just seeing
other people, no matter the circumstances, even if the people were ene-
mies, filled you with health, gave you a reason to live (we *are* monkeys).
Without other faces it would be over; he'd be thrown down the well of
madness.

In the forest now, he prayed. They were all delivering their evening
prayers—Tauqeer carried a stopwatch so they could pray at the exact time
every day for the exact duration. Please, God, spare me if I end up there,
Ayub muttered, pressing his forehead against the root of a tree. Give me
an infection. Gangrene. Put ice and bacteria in my chest. Let me go off, like
a switch. I know what I am doing is wrong, but know that this mistake was
made in the spirit of goodness, sacrificing short-term happiness for long-
term change, out of a desire to establish your empire on earth. (He had
never stated it like this before; it sounded too grandiose, but not when said
directly to God.) Most men think in years and days. Allow a few of us to
think in eons. Spare us.

Soon after, Ayub's talent for speaking was discovered. He lectured the other
revolutionaries on world history, American politics, Marxism, concurrent
events in Bosnia and Chechnya. But he could never grip them in quite the
way he had gripped the members of Peace For All. These were men of
action, impressed by action.

"What was Malik like before the blast?" Ayub asked Shockie one day,
during a break in the afternoon in the forest. "You know, he never spoke
once he went in. He was the only prisoner I dealt with who refused to
speak. A man even made a documentary about him. When this filmmaker

threatened to kill him, he shouted no. So it wasn't that he couldn't speak or hear."

"Don't tell me this," Shockie said.

Ayub saw there were tears streaming down his face even as he kept his hands behind his back.

Was Malik his brother? An innocent sacrificed at the altar of terror?

Then Shockie told him the story. How they'd been best friends. How he'd been tortured at a young age by Indian soldiers. How Malik was part of the group but had renounced violence just before he was taken in. "That's the sad part," he said. "He had given up that way of life when he was arrested."

"Why didn't he speak?"

"I don't know. He must have been trying to protect us. He used to love to talk."

Watching Shockie cry, Ayub thought, Something is not right about this man. You can't be a terrorist and be so emotional and unguarded.

"It's normal," Rafiq told him later. "He's always been an emotional person. Used to cry freely about his mother, his brother, Kashmir—he lost everything, you know. But don't underestimate how dangerous he is. When he's making bombs he's another person. He's possessed. His personality when he's making bombs has nothing to do with how he is normally. His speed changes too. He moves fast. It's almost as if by crying and being slow, he's saving up all his energies for the bomb."

"I thought maybe he had recently lost someone."

"Unlikely," Rafiq said. "He has no one."

"Who do you know in Delhi?" Tauqeer asked Ayub one night.

Tauqeer was sitting on his knees with the stopwatch open on his palm, watching the seconds go by till it was time to pray.

Ayub, on his knees next to him, gave him an informal list of people. "And there's Mansoor Ahmed," he said finally. "He was injured in the 1996 blast—the one that Shockie bhai carried out." Then quickly, "I know him because of that, actually. He's from a rich, well-known family; he came back from abroad and became very idealistic and wanted to help release the accused in that case. He's a good friend. I didn't want to tell Shockie bhai because I didn't know how he would feel." Now he realized there was something suspicious about protesting. "Generally, I never get to meet victims, especially Muslim ones."

Tauqeer didn't appear to notice the shifting registers of Ayub's tone. "Can he be trusted?" he asked, the digital numbers on the stopwatch dissolving.

"Hundred percent."

"Good. Might be good to stay with a victim." Tauqeer looked at Ayub with the full skeletal form of his gaunt face, all the straight lines and dark indentations revealing themselves the way the sides of an octagonal satellite might shimmer melancholically in moonlight. "Because you'll be going in five days." There was something about the way he said it, with his whole testing gaze fixed on Ayub's face, that made Ayub feel Tauqeer had reached the decision right then, that it was revenge for the crime of being handsome and eloquent.

Then they put their heads down and prayed.

CHAPTER 27

Ayub had been trained in warfare; in shooting while lying on his stomach, while running, while out of breath, while the target moved; he had learned how to wire bombs, to carry fertilizer in a sack, to explain himself if he were caught (seven years later, the organization was using Shockie's old technique of pretending its members were farmers, for the simple reason that most of the Indian bureaucracy is sentimental about farmers); but it had all happened fast and it was a jumble in his head. He did not feel that any of these things had entered into his muscle memory. Afraid to protest—he knew he was still on trial—he called up Mansoor from a freshly purchased mobile when he got back to Azamgarh.

"Who is this?" Mansoor said, his thick, croaky voice coming on.

When Ayub revealed himself, he said, "Ayub bhai! Where have you vanished?" The strange thing about Mansoor was that, though he often looked moody and stormy—possibly on account of his flaming eyebrows—when you got to know him, he could be quite goofy and funny.

Ayub told him he was coming to Delhi—could he stay with him?

Mansoor was a little stunned by the request—didn't Ayub have other friends? Besides, in the past few months, things had changed for him at home. His relationship with his parents had turned toxic. As he'd grown angrier with himself about sex, he'd also become more self-righteous, judging his parents for their greed, telling them they should abandon the case with the Sahnis. "We're religious in action," his father had said.

"That's nothing without actually taking time out for God," Mansoor rebuked him.

Mansoor himself prayed five times a day, sometimes adding on the optional prayer, and increasing the rakat in each prayer.

If he prayed just enough, he thought, he could blot himself out.

"Why not do programming instead of praying so much?" his father asked. "Prayer is for old fogies like me. Young chaps like you should be out and about, working hard."

"We shouldn't be so ashamed to be Muslims," Mansoor replied.

"Arre, where's the question of shame? We have our last name. We *are* Muslims. If we were ashamed wouldn't we have long ago left India? I'm only saying—do you need to pray five times a day to be a Muslim?"

"When Mohammed flew to Jerusalem on the Night Journey, God initially prescribed fifty prayers a day for all Muslims. It was Moses who told him to bargain it down to five. So five isn't that much. So it's a bargain, which you would appreciate as a businessman."

"But do you need to wear the gol topi?" his mother asked, pointing to his skullcap. "You'll get unwanted attention. Nowhere does it say you have to wear one." Mansoor had overheard his parents talking about how it was a trend that had started only in the past ten years, as the mosques were flooded with Gulf money. They also talked about how people now said "Allah Hafiz" instead of "Khuda Hafiz" and how the money exchangers all carried signage in Arabic.

"Actually I should have a beard too—I'm only wearing the gol topi because I don't want to grow a beard." (He was afraid he couldn't.)

"These days to call attention to yourself for being a Muslim—" his mother began.

"But it's exactly because of this kind of shame that I'm wearing it! We have to get over all this shame and fear!"

So—to introduce his most strident Muslim activist friend to the mix would only increase the turbulence. Besides, what would Ayub make of his house,

how rich he was? It's good, thought Mansoor. I'll tell him about our property loss now. He'll like hearing about it. "Definitely come," he told Ayub.
"Stay as long as you want."

When Mansoor told his parents that a friend would be staying, they did not
react either way. "Of course," his mother said, sadly, coldly.

Ayub had by now learned about his mission: he was to go to Delhi, stay
with Mansoor, check e-mail regularly, and await orders. "It will be a blast!"
Tauqeer said in English, joking.

"Is there a chance this will get my friend into trouble?" Ayub wanted to
ask, but he was fearful and resisted. His palms turned on like taps. Sweat
ran down his forehead. He developed an itch on his scalp under his soft,
sandy hair. He blinked hard, often, girlishly. His breath hung in an awful
cloud in front of him.

Delhi was sedate at this time, mid-October. There had been a fire in a
hospital and a train collision, but nothing major—the kind of clear news
weather you needed for a blast.

"I don't want to kill innocents," Ayub said. "I'm happy to kill people in
the BJP, RSS, even the police."

"We talked about this," Tauqeer said. "Casualties can't be avoided. If
anything, it's preferable. If you are worried about innocents, think about it
this way—the fewer that die, the lonelier the victims are. It's better for the
event to be big, to affect many. People say 9/11 was the worst terror attack of
all time—was it? I think the small bombs that we hear about all the time, that
go off in unknown markets, killing five or six, are worse. They concentrate the
pain on the lives of a few. Better to kill generously rather than stingily."

The way he said it, without irony, was frightening. But there was also
something idealistic about his flat exhortation—puffing his inhaler, he presented the image of a man who had thought things through and resigned
himself to all of them. He had the unaffected, unshowy confidence of a
young man who has dedicated himself to a difficult way of life. As a master

terrorist, he no longer saw the strangeness of what he did or how he talked about killing.

Ayub became despairing. After spending a few days in Azamgarh, pretending to normalcy, visiting his parents for the last time after all, he headed to Delhi—the second time in six months he was making a journey to kill. He passed the tired stations with their tired paint and oozing pumps and acres of newsprint sold in stands, passed the charging boards, where men of all sizes and shapes plugged in their mobiles and sank onto their haunches, passed it all and felt: It's up to God now. If God chooses to be absent from this hellish place, I understand. That's the tragedy of Tauqeer, Rafiq, even me—we're all fighting for a place long vacated by God, fighting to save hell.

What if I've died a long time ago and come here? he wondered. What if the defining characteristic of hell is that you're locked in an endless, blind battle to reform it? He touched the dirty windows of the train compartment, pawing the yellow, urine-colored tinting to see if this was real. Yes, all tangible.

And what did that mean? Inside him, in a broth of blood and water, organs bumped softly, organically into one another, like fish in an aquarium. The train swayed. Who was to say there was anything more to you than *this*? A computer, a system of organs bumping blindly within a sloshing pool, the attached head only doing the slavish bidding of the body, like a periscope emerging from the depths and mistaking itself for a living thing. Ayub closed his eyes and tried to hear his own heartbeat. But it was lost too deep in there and the train mercilessly drowned whatever was left.

Refusing Mansoor's offer to pick him up from Old Delhi Railway Station, he took an auto to South Ex. In the past he'd taken buses, but he had decided to treat himself. Dozing between the open sides of the auto, he took in the industrial drama of the city. Factories, gathered and arranged into smokestacks, sent frantic plumes into the air. The power plants by the dried riverbeds were frightening to think about—the monsoon water tugging at the roots of the wires. Ayub remembered how, in Azamgarh, his friends put the two ends of a broken transmission line into a pond to shock the fish to the surface. The slick, oily shaking creatures that emerged were like the long, cut-off, vanished fingers of people. . . . Back in Delhi, trains charged by in their armor of municipal soot, bestowing their warmth and whistles on the city. A shuttered flour mill made of dull unaging brick, gorgeously stenciled in some ancient serif, went by, curved and flattened by the arc of a flyover.

Azamgarh had had a flour mill once, the main source of employment, but it had closed down the year Ayub was born.

A guard at the gate of the fancy house in South Ex let him in. The house wasn't big; it was palatial. He didn't feel so bad anymore, putting these people through trouble.

After Ayub had formally met Mr. and Mrs. Ahmed, crossing his arms and bowing to them in a manner that made Mansoor embarrassed, the two friends ate lunch.

Ayub, trying his best to act normal, asked through the steaming dishes, the heat rising up and sitting in a haze over the table, his eyes watering from the spices, about Peace For All: How was it doing?

"Fine," Mansoor said, chewing down the rajma. "There was more focus and zest when you and Tara were running it." Actually, ever since Tara and Ayub had left, the group had devolved into the languorous gossip session it had always been destined to be, with toothy, smiling members with adolescent mustaches from Jamia and JNU meeting in Baristas and Café Coffee Days scattered all over the city, backslapping and regaling one another with stories and theories about the "real India." But anyway, Mansoor had other things on his mind. Since Ayub had vanished Mansoor had been in touch with Tara over e-mail under the guise of asking for advice about programs in the U.S. "If my visa comes through, that is," he'd written. "One of my friends who gained admission to Wharton was denied a visa because his birthday is the same as a terrorist's. And he's a Hindu!" She had responded to this as he'd hoped: bitterly, in lowercase. He was quite in love with her.

Mansoor asked Ayub if he had heard from Tara, holding his breath.

"No. But what happened between us was amicable. Did I tell you I'm engaged?"

"Wow, yaar," Mansoor said. "And who's the girl? Who knew you were such a chhupa rustam?" He was somewhat disoriented at these rapid changes in his friend's life.

"Her name is Zahara," Ayub said. "She's from my native place. Her parents know my parents. They're also syeds." He took a heaping of rice from the casserole. "I used to be opposed to such matches, but when the background is the same that makes all the difference."

"Where did she do her studies?" Mansoor asked, bringing his palms together in a nervous crisscross of fingers on the table.

"She has an MA in social service from BHU," Ayub said, taking quick bites between words. "And she did a BSc in biology through correspondence. But the parents are very liberal people. I like them."

"Hmm. Sounds like moving back was quite good for you, then," Mansoor said, his heart freeing up: he could contact Tara without shame now! But he also felt bad for his friend. "One day I'd like to visit—I've hardly seen the rest of India. Maybe for your wedding."

"Of course," Ayub smiled tiredly, which Mansoor interpreted as a sign.

"I'll show you the den where you'll be sleeping." Mansoor said.

The "den," air-conditioning, marble floors, servants—these were all pleasures Ayub had forgotten after those months of hardship in the hot infertile fields of Azamgarh and the forests of Hubli. He marveled at the room as he set down his bags and Mansoor switched on the light and fan and left him to unpack. So this might be the last room I sleep in, that I'll see, he thought. What a pity. What a pity to have to do the heavy work of revolution while such rooms *exist*—to be out changing the country while people luxuriate, unaware, in these marble oases. He had a weird sensation that he was in a tomb.

He had told Mansoor that he'd come—astonishingly—to shop for the wedding and to find a job, and he began to go out during the day for "interviews" and "discussions." He had not been happy working for Eveready, he told Mansoor; he felt the job of area salesman was beneath him—what he wanted was a job that made money and also did good for the world.

"I understand," Mansoor said. "That's hard to find."

They were sitting on the hot veranda of the house.

"You know my friends who run the Islamic VC fund?" Ayub said. "I may talk to them."

"You have experience in that area?" Mansoor asked.

"Don't mind my saying this—but that's the problem. People value experience over brains and ideas."

"I didn't mean it that way," Mansoor said.

"I know you didn't," Ayub said. "I'm just revealing an attitude. How about you? When are you returning to college?"

"Actually, I wanted to tell you," Mansoor said, and he finally admitted the whole saga with the family's property deal, the tricks played by the other side in court, how they were using psychological warfare to weaken his parents. But then he stopped. "The point is that it has increased my parents' stress a lot. Maybe they were glad for this reason that you, a guest, were coming: we can at least feel and behave a little normal. So," he said, in conclusion. "As you can see, this is a bad time for the family—therefore it isn't right for me to go to the U.S." This long story! And still he hadn't been able to admit that the financial stress was the reason he couldn't go. The roots of shame run deep.

Ayub considered Mansoor and his story with a distracted air. Basic interactions had become hard for him. Language, that fundamental unit of life, which had once escaped his mouth like helpless bubbles from creatures of the sea, which had filled his mouth when he couldn't afford food, which had always seemed as natural to him as another limb, like the instinctive act of putting one foot in front of the other—language had deserted him. All his fluency was gone. And without this fluency to oil his interactions with people, everyone seemed distant, alien, blocky, impossibly trapped in the amber of their own emotions. Finally, he said, with a hard blink and a gulp, "That's very tough, boss."

"Yaah," Mansoor said. "But God will show a way out." Suddenly embarrassed, he asked, "How was returning home for you in other respects?"

Ayub was disarmed by the question. "It was good. My father is trying to sell organic vegetables. He's ahead of his time, but it was good to spend time with him. It humbles you, to be with your parents, to realize you're not as original as you think. I had always thought I was being a big renegade by being an activist, but it's probably a bigger rebellion to sell organic goods in Azamgarh. Now he wants to provide updates to farmers through his mobile." He smiled. "The only problem is that both him and my mother are becoming blind. They both had diabetes but they got into this naturopathy business and didn't do any of the things the doctors told them. As I say this I realize their attitude isn't so different from mine. I too probably would have done something like that, with my suspicion of science. I guess what I'm saying is that I'm my parents' child."

"What about your brothers?" Mansoor asked.

"They're both in Dubai. They send money to my parents but they hardly come. I don't blame them. When you grow up in Azamgarh, all you want to do is escape it. People are confused why I came back."

Why did you? Mansoor wanted to ask, but said nothing.

Ayub put a hand on his forehead. "I feel feverish." But what he meant to say was, How did it happen? How did my gift for speech suddenly return?

Mansoor tried to bring Ayub along to the Peace For All meetings, but Ayub refused. Mansoor thought, "He'll come around; it's God's will." In the meantime, the two men prayed together, with Mansoor happily leading the way.

It was turning out to be a hideous October, an October of dengue and death, and the waiting grew longer and Ayub's days as a guest stretched on. He was only allowed to contact Tauqeer through a cybercafe using a new Hotmail account every time, but he was given no answer beyond: wait.

"How long is your friend staying?" Sharif asked Mansoor one day.

Mansoor snapped, "How does it matter?"

Ayub visited many parts of Delhi, did all the sightseeing he'd never bothered with before, and wondered if this waiting too was a kind of test—to see if he would give up and go to the police. Certainly he'd had a lot of time to consider what he was doing—and he'd come to the very reasonable conclusion it was indefensible, and that Delhi would respond to a bomb the way it responded to everything: with indifference. He saw the point now of a large attack like 9/11. It guaranteed you were taken seriously. It made sure death wasn't wasted, as Tauqeer had implied. But what would a big attack, a 9/11, look like in this city? As he contemplated these ideas in Mansoor's house in South Ex, he felt he was losing his mind, splitting in two, the difference between his polite exterior self and the violence inside growing too great. He felt an actual line passing through the center of his face, splitting it into left and right.

"My job search has still not yielded anything," he said for the millionth time after coming home from a day of sightseeing.

"Maybe I can help you," Sharif said one day over dinner, in a rare moment of relaxation. He had just put his fingers in his mouth to cleanse them of the last bits of food and was leaning back heavily in his chair. "What kind of job would you like?"

As Ayub answered, Sharif said, "Arre, Mansoor should have told me earlier—you should work for me." Sharif ran a consulting business out of an office in Zakir Nagar; he was a plastics engineer and helped companies set up manufacturing and packaging plants in the country.

Ayub had wondered, more than once, why he'd been embedded so conspicuously in an alien family, where his inertia and lack of direction would be instantly noticed, where he was, in a sense, already under trial, being studied by Mansoor's parents, not just as an individual but as a specimen of their son's interests—it is through the osmotic medium of their children's friends, after all, that parents accidentally learn the most about their own children. And now he'd been noticed to the point of awkwardness. Being offered a job was a kind of ultimatum. "No, no, uncle—you should get someone more qualified," he sputtered.

When he looked at Mansoor for help across the table, Mansoor smiled back encouragingly, his eyes kind under the dense eyebrows.

"It's this kind of attitude that's preventing you from finding a job,"

Sharif said, thumping him on his back and revealing his large hollow-looking teeth in a smile.

"Thank you, uncle," he said. But hadn't Mansoor told him the business was suffering?

"I have to leave," he thought later, when he was back in the den. Tauqeer and co. have sent me here, tricked me into staying for weeks with the promise of an attack, and now I'm going to jeopardize my friend and his family's position even further by becoming his father's employee.

That night, from the cybercafe in South Extension, he wrote another e-mail to his comrades—aware, as he typed, of the strangeness of sneaking out to write e-mails (he had told Mansoor he was going out to buy cigarettes) when he could easily write them from his friend's fancy Pentium, which Mansoor used mostly to surf Islamic message boards. "It's funny," Mansoor had said before he'd left. "It makes sense that Islam would benefit so much from the Internet. In a way, Islam was an early form of the Internet—egalitarian, allowing anyone of any class and race to connect to anyone else, breaking down traditional hierarchies."

"But what about the role of pornography?" Ayub had asked, unable, as usual, to put the full force of his mind into the conversation.

Mansoor continued. "I know that that's why the Internet was probably started and where all the technological leaps happened. I've read this book, *Reefer Madness*; it was written by the same chap who wrote *Fast Food Nation*—have you read it? I think you'd like it. Anyway, in this book, he talks about the porn industry, but the point is—" How the tables have turned! Mansoor thought. Just a few months ago *I* was being lectured by this confident, self-contained, self-possessed sandy-haired pink-lipped hero and now *I'm* lecturing *him*! Though he didn't see it that way; he felt only that Ayub was one of those people in his life who brought out the best in him, a rock around which conversation could smoothly bend and flow—a sympathetic ear. So he went on about porn, Islam, and the battle between the two for the pneumatic soul of the Internet.

"I don't feel right taking the job," Ayub said at the end of this conversation. "I've put your father in an awkward position. And also I know you're in financial duress."

"He needs a person he can trust," Mansoor said. "Actually he's been asking me to work with him, but he's too bad-tempered and I fight back. That's the only thing I would warn you about. Consider it short term. You should look for another job. When you mix friendship and business, sometimes both can go sour."

It was with these thoughts raging in his head that Ayub wrote Tauqeer an impassioned e-mail from the cybercafe.

Two more days passed. Nothing. No reply. Should I go to the police? Are they trying to frame me? he wondered. Finally, disobeying orders, refusing the job, he left the Ahmeds' residence in South Extension and went to stay in a cheap hotel in Daryaganj.

"He's a very nice boy, your friend Ayub, very well mannered, well brought up," Afsheen finally said—as if his niceness was more apparent when he was gone.

"Yaah, very decent chap," Sharif said.

"I told you, you shouldn't have offered him a job," Mansoor said. "He's too self-respecting."

"That's why he doesn't *have* a job," Sharif said. "This, let me tell you, is a problem with so many young Muslims. There's discrimination, yes; it's a fact of life—but at the same time there's a lot of arrogance. Sometimes it's better to start from a low place and then win trust and work your way up. Instead someone like your friend Ayub, he rejects things preemptively—" That word! Mansoor thought. How it had entered the lexicon! "Then he complains about this country." That was Sharif's proud side emerging—he was proud of having made it in a hostile environment.

"But it is very difficult to be constantly rejected," Mansoor said. "You build a wall around yourself. Sometimes it's a wall of arrogance."

"Maybe, maybe," Sharif said, not listening.

"Razia!" Afsheen said, calling the servant. "Bring the food."

Cast out from Delhi, fleeing Azamgarh, rejected from bourgeois society, severed from the terrorist group—this is how Ayub felt in his hotel room with rats running up and down the corridor and drunk men in lungis lying near the entrance and making fun of whoever passed. Why is this my fate? Or is this too a sort of test? It occurred to Ayub that he had never really been alone—he always ran from one thing to the next. To be alone meant being alone with your thoughts, your consequences, your actions—it meant letting danger wash against your feet and holding steady on the beach of time even as the waves sucked the sand from under your toes. In the sordid room, centuries away from the palatial "den," Ayub thought of that wonderful feeling of being on a beach, with the earth sliding and emptying beneath you, the soles of your feet caked with black cement-like sand. How he had loved the openness of the ocean the one time he had been to Bombay! It had rained the day before, so the ocean was overfull and boiling, but the sun came out and the beach, with its coconut and pav and chickpea vendors, steamed, and all of Bombay was ripe and bright as it sat around the ocean in a semicircle—he felt he could look through windows kilometers away. Such a shattering vista he'd never seen—the ocean bunched up and tilting and delivering boats toward the shore. He sweated profusely. He was a vain man and he was worried about whether his spray-on deodorant was working. Tara, at his side, made tracks on the beach with her clawlike feet. She had a waddling, confident way of walking. He loved putting his head in the cleft between her neck and shoulder and taking in her flat clean smell. They did touristy things—drinking sharifa milk shakes at the Haji Ali Juice Centre and then walking at low tide, past the curled-up medieval beggars, the touts selling religious books and trinkets, to the religious dome of Haji Ali. The path was slippery, beaten by waves. The shrine, like everything else, was under construction, wrapped in the fresh skeleton of a scaffolding, while behind it, on the low black wet rocks, people sat running their hands through the seawater.

His eyes were closed and he inhaled deeply on his hotel bed. He was lost in the movie of his past.

He read the papers the next day. No news of the "Indian Mujahideen,"

which is what the group was called in the press. No news of arrests—when
the police made even the slightest progress, they immediately gloated to
their sidekicks in the media, subpar individuals who were thrilled, like all
Indians, to be instructed and beloved by institutions, people who had lost
the ability to think for themselves. It was the media he hated even more
than the police, when he thought about it. The police the world over are
ruthless, corrupt, brutal. He had read the biographies of Malcolm X and
Martin Luther King. He knew what the blacks suffered in the U.S. But even
there, in that unequal country, with its million injustices papered over by
money, there had been a notable organ like the *New York Times* bearing
witness, journalists who had written about Martin Luther King. What
about here? How many times had Tara and he contacted some absent-
looking, dead-eyed, dead-souled, half-listening journalist at a major newspaper, one of those people who nodded and took no notes and then shook
his head and said, "But what's the story?"

What's the story? The story is that thousands of innocent Muslims are
being killed in plain sight, that innocent Muslims are being harassed in
America for a crime they didn't commit, that innocent Iraqis going about
their business now wake to hear American armored vehicles razing the
sonic towers of the muezzin with their sirens while gangs of disaffected
young men in office clothes shoot back from the alleys, reloading their
AK-47s—and here is a group that has found a nonviolent way to address
the problem of our times, that's throwing aside partisan concerns and in-
viting activists of all castes and colors and creeds to march alongside it, a
new movement on a par with the independence struggle.

What would Gandhi do if he were alive today? Ayub wondered. Would
the press even notice him or would it quickly slink on to stories of starlets
spreading their legs in hotels the minute a protest came to nothing? The
future of the country is in the hands of the media. But the media is blind
and thinks its future is in the hands of consumers, and so it gives them what
they want—sex and violence. And that's why, to punish all of them, to show
them the end result of this strategy, I've come to plant a bomb.

That day he received an e-mail from Tauqeer, outlining the plan. "I'm sorry we were so delayed," it went. "But we were solving logistics for the chocolate shipment. So it was best not to contact you." Was I under watch? Ayub wondered. Was the man selling corn outside the Ahmeds' house paid to see when I was coming and going? Did I pass their test?

Tauqeer went on to tell him how to call and what would be required.

Ayub read it all with a sense of wonder and excitement. "Allahu Akbar," he said for the first time in days, praying from the very bottom of his lonely heart that nothing would go wrong.

CHAPTER 28

A yub felt much better already when he met Shockie—he was relieved
to see him; it canceled days of headaches immediately. They met in
a park full of children playing cricket amid roving swarms of mosquitoes.
Shockie, paunchy and coachlike, in his trademark sleeveless sweater,
touched his curly sweat-soaked hair. His green eyes blurred and multiplied
the greenery around him.

They sat next to each other on a concrete bench—a cool surface for this
time of year.

"You didn't get too scared, I hope," Shockie said.

"No, sir, the question didn't arise. My main concern was that the people
I was staying with shouldn't get suspicious."

"They're people with money, no?" Shockie asked. "They should have no
problem with hosting one guest."

"Yes, sir, but the rich are the most stingy," Ayub said, trying to appear
(for an imaginary audience) as if he were looking at and talking about the
cricket match unfolding before them. "Howwazzaat!" a cricketer exploded.
"They're screaming more than playing," Ayub said. Shockie had been
smoking; Ayub could tell from the ash crumbling on his black pants.

"That's how it is with this country's sportsmen," Shockie answered, rubbing his hands together to get rid of the ash on his palms. "Also with the
politicians, leaders, wives—everyone." That was the other thing about his
hands, apart from the missing fingers, that Ayub noticed—they were
rounded and swollen; the heels of the hands were like hillocks.

"Sir, if you don't mind my asking, what was the logic of making me stay there?" he asked again. "You could have e-mailed and I would have moved."

"There was no logic."

Ayub went quiet, spreading his arms on the bench.

"You have to obey what you're told, that's all."

Illogic, Ayub thought. Yes, there was something deeply illogical about how the group functioned, how it was organized, how it held its meetings—it *prided* itself on irrationality. He was the one still stuck in the old system of rationality.

"Nothing contributes to being caught or saved," Shockie went on. "No precautions. Nothing. It all depends on loyalty between members. Most people—they notice nothing. You can assemble a bomb in front of them, set it afire, and they wouldn't realize what had happened till they're dead. Look at how openly I'm talking to you in this park. That's trust. If we trust each other, anything is possible.

"When I've set bombs in Delhi," Shockie continued, "I've come from every direction, wearing every sort of disguise. I've made big mistakes. Once the bomb didn't go off. I had to come back. A lot of people saw my two friends and me. In those days they used to do a lot more prosecution on circumstantial evidence—so we used to travel in groups. To be illogical. The more illogical you are, the better you are at this game. The shopkeepers even saw and noticed us—they told us to move—but later, no one could remember our faces."

This is why innocents are in jail, Ayub thought, his old self surfacing for a second.

"People get too wrapped up in themselves," Shockie said. "And you know what happens when a bomb goes off? The truth about people comes out. Men leave their children and run away. Shopkeepers push aside wives and try to save their cash. People come and loot the shops. A blast reveals the truth about places. Don't forget what you're doing is noble."

Ayub nodded. "You know, the friend I was staying with—did Tauqeer tell you? He was injured in a blast you set off in 1996."

"I didn't know," Shockie said, his green eyes suddenly flicking on.

Was there a power struggle in the group? Ayub wondered, scratching a nail into the concrete of the bench. Had Shockie been demoted to aging coach against his will?

"That's how I met him," Ayub continued. "He was in that group that gave legal aid to Muslim undertrials. I mention him because what you're saying is right—when the blast happened, he had gone with his friends. And instead of helping them he just walked off. He says he was in shock and doesn't remember why he did this. He didn't even phone home—he was only a boy then, twelve—but he kept walking. And if you look at him today, his entire personality can be extrapolated from that one incident. He likes to pretend nothing bad has happened. To date he's suffering pain in his wrists from your blast," he said, glossing over his own role in Mansoor's recovery.

"It is too bad a Muslim got injured."

"Don't worry too much. They're quite unreligious, the people in that family."

"Still. This is one thing we must avoid," Shockie said. "Where our illogic must not extend. We need the support of our people. Accidentally blowing them up won't help."

From his expression, it appeared he had done this a lot. How many people had this man killed over the course of his life? Ayub wondered. Had it achieved anything? Kashmir, where he started, was as ravaged by violence as before, with little shift in the needle of negotiation. And in this country Muslims were still killed, detained, fired, disappeared. How did this man justify his life to himself? Ayub looked again at the tipless fingers and thought, I supposed he has suffered too, having gone through immense pain—and that has hardened him.

With these preliminaries over, Shockie began to sketch out the plan.

The plan was to cause as much damage to the economy as possible—for this reason, the blast was to be set off in the week before the festival of Diwali, at the end of October. Ayub was to drop off a bag with a bomb in Sarojini Nagar, a crowded open-air market where people shopped for fake branded T-shirts and clothes. "This Logus T-shirt is from there," Ayub said, pointing to his chest.

Shockie smiled. "So it's a good target, then."

"Why not one of the malls?" Ayub asked.

"There's too much security," Shockie said, shaking his head and looking around with an intelligent alert scanning gaze, his arms thrown over the cement bench. Ayub noticed that a heart had been carved into the rough billion-peaked concrete. How did they do it? With knives? This mania for defacing things—he had never understood it.

"But the security at these malls isn't so good," Ayub said. "If you look upper-class, they let you through anywhere. The Ansal Plaza in Khel Gaon, especially." He would feel less guilty, he thought, killing the rich rather than the poor.

"It's your first time," Shockie said. "Next time we'll look at the malls. First do this. It sounds easy to you, but it's not. A million things can go wrong and they're never the things you expect." He put up his hands. "You see these fingers? I lost them in an explosion in Jaipur. As for the Lajpat Nagar blast, where your friend was hurt, the first time it didn't go off. We were so worried about being seen, spent so much time putting on disguises, that we didn't even think this could happen." His mouth curled; he had a lost, self-pleased look on his face. "Do this first and you'll learn yourself what your capabilities are."

Ayub withdrew a little from Shockie on the bench. Ahead, in the park, the game of cricket was ending. An argument had broken out between teams. How could I have worried they'd notice anything? They barely notice they're *playing*, they're so busy fighting.

"Fine, boss," Ayub said, nodding.

In the end, his role was so small, he felt foolish about the buildup, the training, the waiting—is this all it came to? Dropping off a bag at Sarojini Nagar, a market so crowded it was surprising no one had set off a bomb there? Some people will die, he thought, that's true. But they'll expand the market's security after the blast. The MCD will push the encroaching shops back from the road. And the crowds will be funneled through one of those security doorways you see at cinemas and airports. No—I'm only doing the inevitable. If not me, then someone else. I'm pointing out the flaws in the system. Terror is a form of urban planning.

Back in his hotel room, he remembered that Mohammed Atta, the famous World Trade Center hijacker, had been a student of urban planning in Hamburg, in Germany. Was there a connection between the two things—terror and planning? It was possible. Atta, in his religious way, had wanted to design the perfect Islamic city—his thesis was on Aleppo, in Syria. In the end, though, his urge to design took a different form—he brought down the twin monstrosities of the towers over Manhattan, and there, in a single day, he accomplished what no other planner could have, erasing the cold shadows of those vile boastful buildings from the sun-filled streets of the city. Did Atta think of his task this way? Did he realize he was doing in death what he could never do in life—putting his degree into practice?

As Ayub sat on the hotel bed, his hands became damp. He felt he was intimately connected, in that moment, to Atta—felt that he might even *be* him, the dead man's spirit somehow invading his. And what is the difference between him and me? he thought. Atta too had a gaunt, Tauqeer-like, Skeletor look about him. A young student abroad, alienated from German society, he had strong convictions and beliefs about his home, Cairo, but no way to implement them. So, growing from within, leaping angrily across the Atlantic, he smashed the high locks on the gates of the West—but for what, exactly? Ayub had thought about this often since joining the group. Earlier he'd felt the attack was just revenge against American imperialism, but now he'd come to see that the reasons for such aggression would have to be idiosyncratic, personal. Did Atta wish to make a name for himself in history? Did he think this was the only way to enter al-Qaeda's name into American consciousness? Or did he feel—as Tauqeer suggested about India—that America, in beginning two retaliatory wars, would end up ruining its economy and self-immolating? Was it *really* economic? As Ayub thought these things through in the hotel, with its softly thudding rats and the throttled, overused soap visible in the bathroom on its steel holder, he was convinced this could not be the case. There was too much blood involved—blood tossed against the mile-high windows of the WTC like a libation—for the reasons to not be emotional and hotheaded, even if it took the hijackers a year of training to accomplish their goals. Killing others and then yourself is the most visceral experience possible. Atta must have felt himself full of sexual hate for the people piled high in the towers, bodies in a vertical morgue. He saw the opening between the two towers as a vagina into which to shove the hard-nosed dick of the plane. Sitting at the controls, his curly hair tight on his skull, eyes rubbery, underslept, blackly circled, he must have seen someone appear at the window and look at him—a woman, maybe, a blond American woman. At that moment he got an erection. At that moment he slammed into her alarmed face.

On the day of the blast, Ayub went to the local mosque and prayed, worrying the entire time that he was being noticed. He wanted to phone his parents, but he'd been expressly forbidden from making contact. He was to play it safe, treat it like any other day, and for this reason, after he'd prayed and the sun was up and the day had begun in its thousand polluted particularities, he called Mansoor and told him that he had thought about it some more and he would like to talk to his father about the job after all.

"OK, boss," Mansoor said, his heart leaping at how far his friend had sunk. If Ayub worked for his father, then he was truly not competition anymore; he had been removed from the nervy world of activism. "Just remember, he's a little brusque sometimes. He shouts at people who work for him but he's well meaning. And because of the court case, I'm not sure how much he'll be able to pay you." Actually the case was beginning to go well. After a year of threatening and frothing and refusing to show up for hearings, the Sahnis had phoned Sharif the other day and asked if he would consider settling out of court. At first, Sharif, injured and doubly cautious, refused to engage with them. "How do we know it's not a trick?" he asked Afsheen. "Last time we trusted them you know what happened. And this must mean we're winning   that they're coming to us with their tails between their legs. No. I don't want to talk to them. Let them spend their money on the case."

"You're spending your money too," Afsheen said. "We should at least talk to them."

"What, so you can accuse me of being pushy? I don't want to. I want to follow the law of the land this time."

But he was only being petulant, both Afsheen and Mansoor knew. He would come around eventually. He was famous for always saying no and then coming around. So the family was in a good mood when Ayub called.

"Tell him to come today itself," Sharif said when Mansoor informed him about Ayub's request. Even he, Sharif, could barely suppress his good mood.

How guilty he'd felt in the past few months! Guilty about having made such a big mistake with the family savings and guilty about not letting Mansoor return to the U.S. Actually, the reasons for making Mansoor stay were not only financial. Had they wished to continue his education abroad, they would have found a way—Sharif had enough goodwill with his fellow Muslim businessmen to take loans—no, he'd kept Mansoor back for the sake of his wife. Though she had always been eager for her son to study in the U.S., she'd become distraught after his departure, and this despairing state had been exacerbated by the news that Muslims were being targeted and mistreated in the U.S. "But he's on the West Coast," he said. "And on a campus what can happen?" To which his wife had responded by finding a clipping in a newspaper of a Muslim student beaten up in Berkeley. "It's one incident," he said, though he knew he was losing the debate.

Over time, though, he had begun to regret sending Mansoor to the U.S. He had one son. He'd almost died at the age of twelve—suffered a trauma few people experience in their lifetimes. Why set out to lose him again? So, when Mansoor came back quite suddenly one winter, he thought of ways to broach the subject with him, considered (to use the language of consulting) presenting him with a package of incentives to stay. The unfolding of the property drama was propitious in at least one way, then: he could act as if he were leaning on his son, as if he needed his help in this difficult emotional and financial time—oh, it was underhanded, opportunistic; he knew that nothing came of such behavior, but what could he do? He didn't feel guilty except late at night when he feared he might be punished in some exceptional way for keeping his son home: Mansoor might die in a car crash, or some other tragedy more obviously native to India rather than the U.S. Twenty-five years of marriage and Afsheen and her hypochondria have rubbed off on me! And he banished the thought from his head and tried, in the way he knew best, to be close to his son, squeezing his shoulders, mussing his hair, hearing him talk. Unlike his wife, he had no desire to interfere in Mansoor's development; he felt only that he should be present for the stages his son was passing through.

He considered Mansoor's friendship with Ayub, a young intelligent boy from the provinces, another stage. "Send him over today itself," he told his son. "I'm in the office all day. My meetings with the PearlPET people got canceled."

When Ayub heard the news from Mansoor, he was overjoyed, and yawned with a weird, thrilling happiness. Which terrorist interviews for a job on the day he sets off a bomb? He left the hotel in a DTC bus, drowsing in the mottled sunlit look of the city. It was early afternoon and it appeared that afternoon might never end. Everyone dropped beneath trees or awnings, the bus was puffed full with people like a patila of rice, young men hung out of every opening, and God only knew how they were holding the hot metal—instinctively, Ayub remembered moments spent on swings as a child when he'd come to Delhi on visits to see relatives. These swings were among the most exotic things about Delhi—entire structures made for play! Nothing of the sort existed in Azamgarh, even in those days when the buildings outnumbered the mountains of trash and slush. And yet, when he remembered the swings and the playgrounds of Children's Park, with their rectangular rusted ladderlike fixtures, what he recalled was the feeling of burning metal against his skin and a lacerating jolt of static that sent him leaping off the jungle gym. The bus lurched like a person weighed down with bags. The muscles of the people in the vehicle were aligned, rippling in unison.

What if a bomb goes off now? he wondered. And I am finished here itself, never to have a chance to follow through? When the bus dropped him off in a puddle outside the Surya Sofitel hotel he felt an acute sense of loss.

Zakir Nagar, Jamia, Sarai Jullena, New Friends Colony, Community Center—these were parts of South Delhi he knew well; most of the Muslims from his group lived in these areas and he himself had lived in Batla House when he'd moved to Delhi. Being back home, or in the vicinity of home, set his nerves tingling. He was overwhelmed with sentiment for his youth here, the time he'd spent showing Tara around—Tara, who'd grown up in Delhi but admitted she knew nothing about Muslims; there had been no Muslims at the prestigious Delhi Public School where she'd studied—and he kept looking at the women in the fevered light of afternoon and thinking they were his former love. A city of a thousand Taras! That was Delhi. He passed through the door of a nondescript building and up some stairs artfully covered in paan spit and came to Sharif's office.

"You're early," Sharif said, surprised; he had not been expecting him. "Come, come. God, it's hot outside for October, no? Look at how you're sweating. Will you have water? Mohsin, *yaar*, bring water for sahib."

The office wasn't much to look at—one of those seedy low-roofed places where every piece of furniture is covered in a layer of dirt or a plastic sheet and the computers and printers have long turned a milky brown or gray.

As Sharif spoke, Ayub smiled and held his chin in his hand and pretended hard to listen. Then, suddenly, Sharif was pointing at him. "You're OK? Your eyes are very red. Do you have a fever? You look very tired—you have dark circles under your eyes."

Not just that—Ayub was out of breath. "I'm OK, uncle—it's very hot outside," he managed.

"Where are you staying now?"

"With a relative," he lied. "Nearby only, in Jamia. Batla House."

"They're giving you enough to eat, I hope." He smiled, his large, hollow teeth visible through his graying beard.

"Yes, uncle," he said, trying to smile, but failing to fall back into the natural stream of conversation.

"You brought your biodata?"

Ayub stiffened.

"It's not that important," Sharif said. "You're the friend of my son and that's the most important thing. There's nothing in plastics that can't be taught. You're from Lucknow, right?"

They'd had this conversation many times at dinner and Ayub had long since learned that Sharif was not a good listener. "Actually, Azamgarh, uncle."

Sharif nodded. "Yes, yes, Azamgarh. Named after Azmi—the father of your Shabana Azmi, no?"

This wasn't quite right, but Ayub did not disagree. "Yes, uncle—actually we're very distantly related to them. Even the train to Azamgarh was named after him. My great-grandfather was his cousin and a freedom fighter. He was quite a famous poet. But after him, the family went into decline. I have many cousins—the smart ones are in the Gulf, but most are uneducated. I don't know how such a rapid decline happened in two generations. Now there's just the name, nothing else. The whole town lives off the name." Ayub was surprised at his own confession. The A/C made the place excessively cold. Maybe he did have a fever.

But Sharif was not thinking about Ayub or his family. He was thinking, rather—after a long time—of the Khuranas, of how similar Ayub's story was to that of Vikas's family, how so many great families had come crashing down after independence, as if the end of the revolution had robbed them of their raison d'être and they were condemned to forever looking back at towering figures from the previous era. Had these figures even been that great? Or was independence like any industry in India in which a bunch of mediocre entities with money cornered the market and congratulated themselves endlessly? Sometimes, in his darker moods, Sharif felt there had been no great figure in this country ever, that it had always just rolled along, a moody rock, a sticky mess of fictions and chaos and egos—like this fellow: Was his grandfather really great? Or had the mediocrity of the present made him think so?

"I see, I see," Sharif said, smiling. Then he began to describe the job. Midway through, he stopped. "You should go home, beta. You seem very sick. This is a formality anyway. The job is yours if you want it."

"Thank you, uncle."

"Don't thank. Any friend of my son is a friend of mine." Then he said, "It's up to you to raise your family name." He said it cheerfully.

Ayub, his heart crinkling like a tissue, nodded desperately and went out.

His heart was thundering; it wouldn't stop. Forget it, he told himself. There's no way to fight it off. Accept this excess energy. He took a bus back to his room and spent the last scraps of the afternoon masturbating, crying, moaning, alternatively hot and cold, joyful and ready and alone and sick. Then it was time. He went to the designated shop in Paharganj, picked up the backpack with the bomb, and took an auto to Sarojini Nagar. The bomb was made of ammonium nitrate and charcoal tied with a thread—it was shaped like a coconut. A mobile phone was attached to a mass of materials and covered up with a gauzy cloth, so that if someone were to open his backpack, it would look like he was carrying a coconut for a ceremony.

An odd calm overcame him—the calm of living in cinematic time. He had spent the past few weeks using up his drama and tension—he saw the point of being sent early and remembered too what Rafiq had said about Shockie's emotional behavior, how it drained him so he could focus coldly on action.

Sarojini Nagar is a horrible market in a nice part of South Delhi—an area characterized, in general, by wide roads, stately flyovers, government and private houses spaced decently apart, and well-demarcated lanes and street signs. He passed through the colonies the way a helpless person may topple down a waterfall, drawn along but also happy about every beautiful sight he encounters as he discovers he is not dying after all. With the evening had come an iota of relief and cool and he didn't even mind the traffic or the slightly circuitous route the plump auto guy—wearing a thousand old rakhis on his wrist, rakhis like a fungus or infection—took to bump up his meter. It's already happened, he told himself. It's long over. When I get to the market, I'll discover it's on fire and it'll be as if I wasn't even present for what I did.

He had a sense, suddenly, of why Mansoor might have walked away from the blast without understanding or comprehending why. He hadn't even set off *his* blast and time was compressing and skipping beats. He sucked on a Vicks; his throat flooded with cold.

When he paid the auto driver, he savored the texture of the notes, how difficult it was to uncurl them, how each one was crumpled in an individual way, how some had turned as soft as cloth from overuse. And that old-money smell—the smell of old keys.

The auto dropped him off at the mouth of the bazaar—near the square where the pukka market was based. He smelled ripe fruit. Elbowing rude unaware people, people passing quickly, people energized with purpose and conversation, pulling up their sleeves and smiling at the setting sun the way one may pose for a large camera, he went in deeper, into the warren, into this aquarium of fake brands. On either side, in a long row, shops churned with shoppers and shopkeepers, curling branches of incense, shiny baskets on sale for Diwali. A woman called her son close after he wandered off to a shop. A fat man stood talking loudly on his mobile, his hand pleasurably plucking the worry lines on his forehead and closing over his face like a crab, his eyes shut in happy concentration, his mouth open, his tongue moving about inside as mysterious roars came out. "Arre, bhai. No. No. No." He kept shaking his head. It was the most joyful *no* Ayub had ever heard in his life. Another man sat on a bench, crouching over, washing his hands with water from a used plastic bottle, its brand sticker torn off, leaving behind a patchy residue, the ribs of the bottle pressed and distended. The man had alert eyebrows and curly hair with streaks of baldness—something was wrong with his hair; he was too young to be balding—and as Ayub looked at him, he looked back and a question passed between them and Ayub kept going, conscious of being watched. He could imagine the man's head turning toward him, taking in his backpack. For that reason he went off for as long as he could. When he turned, the man was gone.

These looks were exchanged daily between men of a certain class. They said: I know you. I wonder how you made it.

There had been a moment—when he had seen the woman and the child—that he'd lost focus, become a shopper himself, but now he was worked up to full alertness. Standing before a shop, he took the bag off his back and held it at his side as if freeing himself to gaze.

The people in the shop did not notice him. The bespectacled owner, sitting behind a desk, was shouting at one of his assistants. The assistant was jammed halfway up a wall of clothes, his feet bare and his hands plunged into the layers of plastic. Ayub put the bag down on the road, turned, and walked.

A few seconds later, the bomb opened with a seismic roar.

Hundreds of people lay on the ground. From the shop came only silence. Ayub—thrown to the ground, rolling, sliding—thought: Tara will hear me now.

THE ASSOCIATION OF
SMALL BOMBS

OCTOBER 2003–

CHAPTER 29

When Vikas saw news of the bombing on TV, he called his wife to come over and watch. Deepa, who had been reading the paper in the drawing room, creased it into a tight square.

"How many dead?" she asked, peering into the cabin of the bedroom and then sitting on the edge of the bed and adjusting her spectacles.

The Khuranas, in the past few years, had started taking a morbid interest in blasts in all parts of the country, especially Delhi—they were excited by these bombings in a way that only victims of esoteric, infrequent tragedies are motivated by horrors. They knew instinctively what the victims and families would go through: how the government would promise help but the Municipal Corporation of Delhi would harass the shopkeepers, advising them to lower their estimated losses; how compensation would be announced in the papers, never to be paid out; and how the injured and dying would linger for hours in the market and the hospital before being treated.

"Are they saying who did it?" Deepa asked.

"No one's taken credit for it. The news came in only ten minutes ago. It's too bad. Sarojini Nagar is such a crowded market, especially at Diwali, and there aren't any solid structures to absorb the blast."

"They know this risk exists," Deepa said, scowling a little. "Why they don't improve security, I don't know."

"In this kind of market, how can you have security? I'm sure the shopkeepers would be against it."

Vikas, especially, had turned himself into a student of terror. He had come to see that people were blind to tragedy till they experienced it first-hand, and that they were willing to risk the unknown if it meant they could make money in the interim. This was the case not just with small Indian markets, with their reluctance to secure themselves, but with the U.S. as well: Airlines had known for years about the danger of hijackings, but had lobbied against security because it cost time and money to process passengers. Better to let a plane be occasionally hurled off track, the heads of the airlines reasoned, than to hemorrhage money in the terminals.

It didn't occur to them that a hijacker might wish to plough a plane back into the country, invest the blown and fluted metal into the mineral-rich earth.

"When should we go meet them?" Deepa asked.

"Tomorrow, maybe," Vikas said, putting his hand in hers.

In 2002, the Khuranas had founded the Association of Terror Victims. Over time, they'd come to realize that no one remembered the smaller blasts peppering the history of the country, blasts that vanished into a morgue of memories, overshadowed by bigger events. Therefore, the Khuranas reasoned, the thing to do was to corral the victims of these small blasts and create a group that could lobby for their rights and collectively remember the blasts in which they had lost their relatives or limbs. And why did the Khuranas want the blasts remembered?

Vikas grappled with this privately—was it just a zidd, the demand of a hurt child? Or was there substance to it? He decided it was important to remember in order to keep the past from repeating itself; the country was moving so fast, hurtling so enthusiastically into the future, that people had little idea of how easily everything could be undone. More important, a blast was a political tragedy, an act of war, in which people perished not because of their own mistakes but because of the mistakes of the government. Therefore it held that blast victims should be remembered the way dead soldiers are—Vikas always thought of the names of Indian soldiers who had fought in World War I inscribed in the sandstone biceps of India

Gate, a monument the boys had loved, and where he had often taken them for ice cream, the three of them standing on the reddish earth, the boys asking if it was true that the flame inside the gate had been burning for a hundred years and Vikas not knowing the answer—was it possible? Weren't all sorts of crazy things possible? The boys. How would they have been now, all these years later? Were they still alive somewhere else, being shown around monuments by another set of parents? Had they grown up in this alternative universe where they wore white office shirts and black pants and got ready for work, their adult heads emerging from sweat-stained collars, the shoes on their feet gleaming blackly, Tushar an earnest trainee in some firm, Nakul batting his handsome eyes at some girl who sat at the other end of the office, hiding herself in a giggling group of friends? Sometimes if he closed his eyes he could imagine them as adults and the vision would be so exact, his heart would stop and he would think they were alive or that, by thinking itself, they *could* be brought back to life and then he would chastise himself for admitting defeat so easily in 1996, for accepting the official cant that the boys were dead instead of brazenly imagining the opposite.

The bomb was so distant now that it did not quite seem real. When he went to Lajpat Nagar these days—and it was often—he tricked himself into believing nothing had happened, and in fact, it wasn't hard to do: the market had covered over every sign of damage.

Yes, it had never happened. He was forty-seven, successful, with a loving wife and two boys and a daughter. It was the thought of Anusha that jolted him to the present, pricked him with dread. She was the most solid recurring evidence that his life had changed. He hated his daughter. She was cute and round-eyed with flowing streamers of hair and an odd interest in learning how things were made—she was always hugging the walls, asking how they had been poured by workers—but he wondered if she were a little slow. He didn't want to be near her. Better to stay cramped in the markets of Delhi, among the throbbing crowds, shoulder-to-shoulder with death, with the city, the city that crammed you back into yourself.

Whereas his wife had grieved instantly, he only began to grieve after Anusha was born.

He didn't see it as grieving, of course. He thought he was taking an interest in the larger world, an interest brought on by the bomb; he thought
he was gathering material for a documentary. He filmed it all, became
known as the eccentric with the movie camera; people in the markets
learned to ignore him after a while.

He was making an encyclopedic film about Delhi, he told himself; cap-
turing the fluctuations in the moods of places. But he was always a little
vacant and bored when he carried out these explorations, just as he was
vacant at home, draped in his Bhutanese gown.

He was only happy when he was leaving his house, shedding the yoke of
this new life that had been thrust upon him.

His marriage fell apart. Deepa at first was patient, but then she became
shrill in her disappointment. "Not again!" she shouted, confronting his
cosmic sadness and anger.

She'd wasted too many years putting up with his depressions: depression
over art, his parents, his kids—now a depression over his daughter. As she
shouted at him to wake up from his grief, she became nauseated and started
burping and went to the sink and retched, but finally all that came were tears,
tears ransacking the dignity from her eyes. "Shame on you," she said, coming
back to the drawing room, where Vikas had not moved from the cloth embrace of the broad sofa chair as he read the *Hindustan Times*, the alpine slopes
of hair on his feet visible as they rested on the ground beside the leather
slippers. "You're not a real man."

Vikas appeared to listen earnestly, attentively, releasing one hand from
the paper, which sagged into his lap, the free hand massaging his chin.
Then he got up and walked out of the house.

Deepa's anger at her husband grew. She didn't know what to do. That's
when she visited Mukesh again.

Mukesh, sitting in his office, still dolefully managing construction sites
for a living, had been waiting. From behind his glass doors, he had been
following the distant eruptions in the Khuranas' marriage, noting the fre-

quency of Vikas's exits, his chancy drumming gait as he fled the house, his late returns in the evenings. He knew the marriage was at its end. He was an invigilator of grief—a realist. He knew, unlike the rest of the people in the complex, who confused optimism with high-mindedness, that no matter what Vikas and Deepa did, their marriage could not recover. Nothing did from a bomb.

He had seen the crater left by it when he had gone to the market soon after the blast. It had taken his breath away, given him vertigo, and his mind had circled the ditch with its lacing of trash blended in with the roots of a tree trying desperately to hold on to sinking soil.

When Deepa came to his office one morning, looking frighteningly thin and worked up, he was sympathetic and placid again; he listened to her talk about the construction the neighbors were doing, which disturbed Anusha.

It was in the anger that Mukesh saw the first shoots of life in Deepa.

Then, one day, when Vikas was out, Mukesh went over to the entrance to the house and rang the bell. The dour Nepali servant answered and led him up the cracked stairs into the drawing room. Deepa sat tense in a plain white salwar, clutching her own wrists.

She welcomed him in with a thin smile and offered him tea.

Mukesh was in there for an hour making faces at Anusha, who had come into the room, excited to see her chachu, who gave her dates and candies whenever he saw her. "What a little princess," he said to her in his disturbingly sexual manner.

"Show uncle your Ajooba dance," Deepa said.

Anusha was oddly obsessed with this Bachchan movie from the 1990s, and Mukesh, sitting there in his white pants, clapped. There was something perverse about how joyful this child was, he thought. It would have been better if she were morose. Her joy only outlined the tragic background. It brought out the sickness in the yellow walls, the groans emitted by every off-center painting and troubled spot of seepage on the walls.

Mukesh knew from Deepa's face that he was being watched too, carefully.

"How is the money situation?" he asked suddenly.

"Good," she said, but in a way that made it clear she had whispered a thousand *bad*s before it.

"So Vikas is finishing his film about markets?"

Another pause. "Yes."

"Good." Mukesh smiled, bending down from his chair to do a card trick for Anusha: he always carried a pack of cards with him, fanning them in concert with his lecherous grin.

His visits became more frequent. He would come up in the middle of the day and play with Anusha; Deepa would watch him. Then, one morning, when Anusha was at her play school, Deepa led him into the bedroom and took off her clothes.

Mukesh looked on from the door, hard, amused. Her nakedness made him aware of his own clothes: a checked half-sleeve shirt, loose gray pants, black Batas.

She sat down on the bed, her buttocks on the sheet, and began to read a gray dusty book titled *The Magic Mountain*, which she lifted from the side table.

Mukesh sat down on the sofa in the room, clutching and mopping his brow. Now that he had what he'd wanted—now that he was so close to it—he had a mind to turn back.

After a while, he got up as if to leave, but then turned around and, still fully clothed—this is how he liked to do it—climbed onto the bed.

It was not love—what happened. Though she had opened herself to him in that bed, on that morning, she was not aroused when he speedily covered her body with his.

It was as if she would only let him have her by pretending to be dead.

Their passion took on the flat quality of those mornings with their archipelagoes of white light thrown on the floor, the bones of the windows visible and gaunt, Mukesh coming over and rummaging around in her life, her bed—she never thought of it as sex, but as *rummaging*.

She had long since evacuated the sphere of full feeling. In some ways Vikas had been right about her after she'd come back from visiting Malik—she was gone. What remained was a bright shadow, a disturbance of light intent on going on a little longer.

The trouble started when she began to fall in love with Mukesh, as she looked forward to these illicit visits, imagining the imprint of his hands on the old wooden railing that ran alongside the staircase—the hands with their blisters from breaking and peeling branches with Swiss knives on trips to Dalhousie; hands that dragged the sliding door at the entrance to the drawing room so it hung, like a man taken by the throat, a few inches above its rail on the ground.

That's when she asked him for money.

That had been the implicit agreement from the start—that he would give her money for Anusha; he had offered it after the first visit as he buttoned up his shirt and put on his brutal black shoes: the patriarch getting dressed before his family, entertaining petitions. And they never once talked about *his* wife and two grown-up daughters. "I should go pick up Anusha," she had said after that first time, still half-smiling, half-radiant, abashed, touching her hair, confused, scared. She too knew she had crossed a threshold and, having done it, could not say why. It was not out of attraction—she had no physical feelings for Mukesh, disliked his breath, disliked even the tender, consoling way he had held her, as if putting her in a hypnotic lock before committing his act—no, she felt only a warping stasis, the desire to be rid of a station of life, no matter the method or means. And Mukesh, with his kara-cuffed arms, his triple-ringed fingers with their superstitious ruby insets, his almost synthetic mustache, his filigreed eyes, was such a means—had become complicit with her mission even before she'd set out on it. So she'd let him play his part.

And putting on his clothes, offering to help with future school tuition, boasting about how the sale of the lands had swelled his bank account so much his kids couldn't even squander it on TVs and cars, he was not so bad. She accepted.

He kept giving her money, but it was to slap the relationship back into the realm of transaction that she began asking for it directly, her eyes hard. The more she liked him the more she hardened herself against him.

They lived in a crowded complex—how long before everyone was talking about it? The servants, with their practiced clairvoyance, probably already knew.

"This is the advantage of being a do-gooder type," Mukesh said. "They think I'm interfering with everyone's business and so won't think it's unusual I'm sometimes at your house." It was a shocking touch of self-awareness and Deepa saw now how being generally shameless could permit and cloak even more dire shamelessness. "I've told them I'm bringing homeopathic medicines for Anusha," he said. It was true: he *did* bring medicines, for Anusha's persistent colds, but Deepa didn't let him give her any. "I want Anusha to grow up free of all pollutants," she said, thinking suddenly of Tushar's pleading, brimming reactions to the tetanus injection brandished by the bespectacled lady pediatrician, or Nakul's habit of squirreling away homeopathic pellets for all kinds of maladies in a single bottle, so he could nibble on them every night till they were inevitably found and confiscated.

Vikas, cut off from family, knew nothing about this. He came home and saw his wife in the same pose with Anusha—scolding her for running around too much, for falling and injuring herself when she had been diagnosed with keloids.

"Why not restart your baking business?" Vikas asked, waking from the dead dream of his endless documentary about terror.

"I want to be there for her," Deepa said, eyes pouring toward some faraway spot.

Over the years Deepa had started to blame herself for the boys' visit to the market. If *she* had been present, if *she* hadn't been so dead set on making up the shortfall in the family income by furiously baking, if *she* had known to intervene when her husband, lazing around, doing nothing, had nevertheless sent them all away in an auto on an obvious suicide mission . . .

if *she* had asserted herself. "What are you doing that's so important that you can't take them?" she imagined saying to Vikas. She often shouted it out loud as she walked about the house on her increasingly troubled knees, hobbling quickly.

But it didn't matter what she said to her husband, now or then. He continued to slip further and further into his dream of self-abnegation that predated even the boys' deaths.

For a man who had dedicated his life to seeing, he noticed very little. What he was really good at was getting people to talk, but that was within the square jail of his camera lens.

She was alone with Anusha, always had been, so one day in 2002, when Vikas said they should invite Mansoor over for tea, that Mansoor had had a relapse of his bomb injury and was back in India, she said yes—what choice did she have?

This was before the association, before the Sarojini Nagar blast. But seeing Mansoor in their drawing room—young, able-bodied, grown-up, handsome, thin, holding out his wrists, his stormy eyebrows like two thoughts disagreeing with each other—freed something in both of them. After years, they began to talk to each other again. They remembered stray things about the boys—the way Tushar, the morning of the blast, had come into the bedroom soon after Deepa and Vikas had made love, looking hurt and surprised, unsure what had happened, but putting his hands on his hips in a school-ma'amish manner, intuiting something.

They remembered the high-pitched sound, like the Dopplering whistle of a train, that Nakul made during his imaginary cricket commentary as he ran back and forth in the bedroom, awaiting Mansoor's visit—Mansoor's visit, which the Khurana boys were always so excited about, as if having two of them wasn't enough. But introducing a stranger always altered things, threw you into a new mood, forced you out of yourself, your small battles and jealousies; a new person signaled play. Tushar and Nakul were always their shiny boyish best around Mansoor. They had probably taken him to the market out of love and enthusiasm.

For the first time, the Khuranas found themselves forgiving the boys themselves. They had not known till now that the boys had *needed* to be forgiven.

But the boys *had* ruined their lives. The boys, not the bomb, had been *their* killers.

A booming cord of light fell over their necks as they sat in the drawing room. They were together again. They hugged and held each other.

The next day Deepa told Mukesh she wanted to end the affair. He looked at her sadly, his gray eyelids like two slow sloping slugs, mollusks with their own squirming life. Then he rolled the buttons through the buttonholes of his shirt and left.

A day later, he was back.

Deepa knew she must end it but was also addicted to it—to the numb pleasure, the dark routine, the certainty of his devotion; it had given her life, a feeling of independence from the domestic sphere. She had a *secret*. She stalked about the house powerfully now, not doting excessively on Anusha as she had before. She was a person again. Vikas was a befuddled aspect of her life, a sick branch that barely held on. They began to discuss ways they could memorialize the boys.

Soon after 9/11 and the Parliament attack, the Khuranas had been visited by a journalist eager for their opinion about America's response to 9/11 and how they felt about the 1996 trial, which was still lapsing through the courts. Deepa and Vikas had tried to be objective but ended up frothing. "They should kill everyone in the Taliban," Deepa had said, sitting under two garlanded portraits of Tushar and Nakul. "Every single one." Vikas had added, "When we see what is happening in the West, we are glad. We are glad George Bush is going after terrorists. It should be a lesson to our country. We've been passive people too long. But this passivity and ignorance doesn't work before terrorism."

Afterwards, they were shocked at themselves. They were no longer liberals.

Soon after Mansoor's visit, they approached K. R. Gill.

Gill, a sardar in his forties, was a former Youth Congress leader who had survived three separate car bombings by Khalistan separatists in the 1990s and now headed an association of terror victims. This group, which supposedly had fifty members, lobbied for terrorists to be hanged. Gill, who had a personal investment in the cause, was a towering, swaying figure full of undistinguished rage. He tilted about on artificial legs—both legs had been blown off in separate bombs—which he dismantled and brandished at the slightest provocation from a journalist or judge. He gave medals to victims and shamed politicians. He was theatrical, morbid, explosive, full of hot tears. He threatened suicide in court. The Khuranas had come across him when he made a vehement appeal before a Sessions judge for Malik to be hanged.

They had been frightened by him then, but now they reached out with an idea.

Gill, who had been looking to energize the drooping association, was happy to induct such well-spoken victims into his group. Vikas and Deepa began working with the victims of small bombings. "The deadliness of an attack should not be measured by its size," Vikas told a news channel who interviewed him about the association. "In my estimation the small attacks are more deadly, because a few have to carry the burden of the majority. Then, as these victims' grievances get forgotten, as the blasts themselves are forgotten, the victims of these small bombs turn against the government instead of the terrorists. Is that a situation we want? No. That's why, along with Mr. Gill, we've decided to take matters into our own hands."

The Khuranas now went to hospitals right after attacks. Vikas talked to victims and their families in the hospital, listening sympathetically, nodding on cue, his long neck bent down in respect and his large hands tenderly mashing the dense, comforting, youthful patches in his hair. Deepa, more unsentimental and direct, was better at knowing how to boss the nurses around, at noticing what exactly the doctors were overlooking as the patients lay bloodied and bandaged and dazed in the hospital. "Please bring him water," she might shout at a nurse, taking the bridge of her nose between her fingers and stroking off the dust and sweat. Or, "For how many days has this sheet not been changed?"

Together, aged, having experienced so much, they cut warm, comforting, watchful figures in the hospitals. Often, they were observing not the victims but each other. How had they come from marriage to the death of their boys—to this? And yet, it gave them enormous solace to know that their suffering had not been for naught, that they had been able to eke a larger meaning out of it; they felt the closeness couples sometimes experience when they become rich after years of poverty, a mutual appreciation and gratefulness and wonder and an awareness of the depths of the other person—an awareness that is stronger than any affection or love.

These kinds of couples are at their best when they are silent together, letting the world do the talking; when the world ignores them, taking them wonderfully for granted, so that they are no longer an anomaly. This kind of love is shot through with the fire of long-vanquished sadness. Deepa and Vikas did not hold hands as they stood by the beds of victims, listening to the complaints of mothers, the women distraught beneath the head cover of their dupattas. But they may as well have been.

"Let me know if you need help with the association," Mukesh said one day when he was sitting with Deepa, having tea. Many of their trysts amounted to nothing more than this; the illicitness of the meetings themselves was thrilling, with Deepa finding an excuse to send the servant on an errand to a distant market. "I'm sure I could get Naidu-ji to come."

"No need," she said.

It was the last time she saw him.

But not everything returned to normal. Anusha became neglected. Whereas she'd once been a bright, soliloquizing, self-contained child, hopping and leaping about the place in her looped black shoes, shaking her hips to Bollywood tunes that were frozen from the 1990s, when the boys were growing up (Deepa had kept all their tapes—*Hum Aapke Hain Koun*, *DDLJ*, etc.), she now found she had no audience. A knowledge of loss entered her face as her parents came and went, busy with work and the association. She began to grow up.

Later, when she was older, she would tell her friends that she understood how such people, outwardly sensitive, could neglect their children to the point that they would go to a market and blow themselves up.

CHAPTER 30

"The association of small bombs," as the Khuranas called it privately, was a support group and forum for the grievances of victims. It was also an alternative family for Deepa and Vikas, a group of individuals with whom they could converse freely, of which they were the matriarch and the patriarch. Not only were they the oldest members, but—besides one family in which three of five people had died (a mother had taken her two children out shopping to buy birthday gifts for the other sibling; all three were killed)—they had suffered the greatest loss. Sitting up together in drawing rooms, they dispensed advice on compensation and injuries and medical bills. Gill, meanwhile, dealt with the issue of the terrorists themselves, lobbying for the terrorists to be stripped of all rights. This put him in direct opposition to Tara and Ayub's NGO. "You people support terrorism," he'd shouted at Ayub some years before. "All the evidence is there—we need the trial to happen faster."

The way the association was structured—dependent, in a way, on the inflow of victims—also made the Khuranas perversely eager for new bombings. Soon after they heard about the blast in Sarojini Nagar on TV, they headed to the hospital.

It was in the hospital, amid the chaos and stinking blistered bodies and nurses pushing trolleys full of IVs and bottles and news crews thuggishly infiltrating the wards, that Deepa and Vikas met Ayub, though they had no idea who he was. He lay in a bed with a patch over his left eye and legs tightened in bandages. The blast had caused lots of lower-extremity injuries, the doctor said, talking to the Khuranas, but this particular man had been spared the worst. Instead a piece of shrapnel had bounced up and penetrated his left eye; the bomb had been packed with industrial nails and ball bearings. "Many of these people," he said, gesturing around the room, "have wounds that look like bullet holes."

"Better to have lower- than upper-extremity injuries," Vikas said.

The doctor looked at Vikas as if to say, "You know a lot," but then, pointing to Ayub, went on, "He'll be fine. If he had been closer he would have died instantly of an internal hemorrhage, so you're lucky." The Khuranas had pretended they were relatives of this boy on the bed. This was their usual ploy to get access to hospitals right after a blast.

What was it about such a morbid war zone that energized Vikas? Once, on a trip to France to screen a documentary at the Aix-en-Provence film festival, Vikas had peeled off and visited a chateau in the Loire Valley. Stony and hard skinned, the chateau consisted of two towers connected by a covered bridge that ran over a river. During the Great War, his guide had told him, the battling armies shared the bridge as a common hospital. Vikas had been stunned by the idea of wounded soldiers—who may have wounded each other—lying bed-to-bed in the same ward. What horrified him was the fact that injury, its violent horizontal stasis, revealed the complete *artificiality* of war.

He remembered seeing Tushar and Nakul in the morgue and thinking: They belong to a different class now. The class of the dead.

He had never lost his urge for classification—this tyrant's urge for unity *and* separation. He knew everyone was different, yet he wanted them to be the same. Hence his obsession with death.

Vikas had always been obsessed with death. In his youth, it had taken the form of constant anxiety and brooding, and he had always been fascinated by Deepa's star-crossed past, the way so many of her relatives had died young. And maybe he had taken satisfaction in the ruin of his own life, the way in which death had washed over him in an equalizing wave. Maybe if he had not thought so much, worried so much about death, it would not have come for him.

And yet, death could not get him now. Everything had been taken away from him. Even his wife, to a degree, was gone; he knew (vaguely) that he didn't have her completely. He had made himself immune to the only disease without a cure.

CHAPTER 31

Mansoor heard about the blast the day it happened, but he didn't learn that Ayub was among the injured till he saw his face a day later on TV—Ayub, swaddled in blankets, on a rusted bed, croaking a few words into the microphone, the groove above his nose deepening; then Vikas Uncle (of all people!) taking over the proceedings with his trademark fluency and rapid-fire way of speaking. "The government has promised compensation," he said. "But so far no one has even visited these people in the hospital. Nor has the emergency protocol changed and improved—it took two hours for an ambulance to come to Sarojini Nagar and then too it was not equipped with the right emergency machines."

"Mama," Mansoor said, muting the TV.

"Yes, beta," she said from the other room.

"Something very bad just happened."

When his mother saw Ayub on TV minutes later, the news segment recycling itself, she shook her head sadly, but also, Mansoor felt, not urgently or empathetically enough.

"I've had a feeling that something bad was about to happen," Afsheen said. "I've been having headaches." Tears sprang to her eyes. "Do his mother and father know?"

"I don't know if anyone knows," Mansoor said. "If *he* knows. I should go right away to the hospital. But it's good that Vikas Uncle and Deepa Auntie are there. Poor fellow—he's about to get married, and Papa said he came only two days ago to the office and was wondering why he hadn't phoned." He could understand now, in a way he couldn't before, the point of Vikas Uncle and Deepa Auntie's association. He hadn't known they got involved *this* early in a bomb's unraveling.

His mother insisted on coming along with him to the hospital and he didn't refuse.

In the car, Mansoor, resting against the door, marveled at the oddness of the situation—the way in which life had come full circle, so that he was the well one now, with strong arms, a skullcap on his head, a prayer on his lips, visiting *someone else* who'd been injured in a blast. He must have met thousands of people over the course of his life and none, save for Tushar and Nakul, had been injured or killed in a blast. Ayub, as the poorest of his friends, was the most likely to end up in a public space overrun with flames.

Of course, by the time Mansoor got to the hospital, propelled forward in his car by the driver, the city comforting him with its exciting colors and music—the soundtrack to *Godzilla* on the stereo casting its own spell—he'd forgotten all about this circularity and was taken up with parking, finding the reception desk, moving to the right ward, behaving like an adult to the correct degree. His mother was beside him, covering her mouth, put off by the hospital.

"I was also in a hospital like this and I was OK," Mansoor said, referring to his first visit to the hospital after the blast to get the shrapnel out of his arm.

"But you didn't *stay* in the hospital, beta. We took you home. These days a lot of antibiotics are being dumped in our rivers—I've read drinking river water is like drinking Crocin. All the bacteria are resistant to medicine. You should cover your nose. Most people die in these hospitals from staph infections and pneumonia."

You should have been a bloody doctor, he thought, but kept his mouth shut. He noticed people staring at him because of the skullcap and broadened his chest in defiance.

Passing through the ICU, they found Ayub lying on his own bed (most of the other victims were doubled or tripled, head to foot, on beds). "Ayub bhai," Mansoor said.

Ayub smiled weakly from his metal bed and held out a bandaged hand. He did not actually feel so weak anymore but knew it was crucial to act the part. After the explosion, the pain, the loss of his left eye, which had sliced the world in half, tunneled it, he'd woken up in the hospital surprised and frightened—though he'd been told, during training, that such an outcome was far from extraordinary. Terrorists were always being blown up by their own bombs; if he were injured, he'd been told, he was to play a confused victim and supply a Hindu name.

Now he waited, in panic, for communication from Shockie or Tauqeer.

"Do you know they're calling you Mr. Galgotia?" Mansoor asked. (Ayub had named himself after his favorite bookstore, Galgotia & Sons.)

"They're confused about everything." Ayub waved it away. "Hello, auntie."

"Hello, beta," she said. After ascertaining he hadn't talked to his parents, she said, "Do you have your mummy and papa's phone number? We should call them. Otherwise your pain's under control? We can make arrangements to transfer you to a private room."

"That's a good idea," Mansoor said. "The state you're in, it might take you ten more days, and you'll feel better if you have a room of your own." He felt self-conscious offering this privilege to his Gandhian friend. He sighed. "I couldn't believe you were in a blast, yaar. I thought I was imagining it. But your eloquence was undiminished."

"It's like what you had said. One remembers nothing."

"Something about the intensity of the sound and the speed with which things get rearranged," Mansoor said, stroking his chin thoughtfully. "It's like being sucked into a tornado. The mind doesn't know how to process it. But you should have phoned us, yaar. That couple who came, the ones who run the association, they're family friends."

Ayub's neck twitched. He had recognized the couple—but they had not recognized him—and he'd been very uneasy the whole time he'd been speaking to them and into the camera. Yet he'd gone ahead with the interview in hopes that his comrades would see that he was injured and that he'd given away nothing. At the same time he worried about his parents watching him on TV. "I would have called but I couldn't remember the number and my mobile—I don't know where it is."

"The hospital has a directory," Mansoor said. "But believe me, I understand. I couldn't remember my own home number when the blast happened," he said, looking triumphantly at his mother. All these years and they had never believed his story!

"Your mummy and papa's number?" Afsheen repeated, sitting on the edge of the bed and looking around the shabby ward. The place was heady with the stink of sweat.

"Even that I can't remember," Ayub said, smiling.

"We'll talk to the doctor and get you moved," Afsheen said. "If you give me their name—"

This was the thing about his mother, Mansoor thought. Financial troubles or not, she was extremely generous.

"Mr. and Mrs. Azmi," Ayub said, unable to lie anymore. "Of Azamgarh. And no need for the room, auntie." But he did not push hard. Better to be put out of public view.

"What was he doing in the market?" his mother asked as they left the hospital in the car.

Mansoor knew there was a kernel of suspicion buried in her generous soul. He coughed. She'd never really cared for his friend, had been suspicious of his antecedents, his needlessly long stay. "He's not from a rich background," Mansoor said. "That's why he was shopping in Sarojini Nagar. I told you—he's a very impressive guy. He did his engineering and then he came to Delhi and decided to do social work. Can you imagine someone from our background doing that?"

She smiled and shook her head absently. Noticing her nervous tremor, he was angry, sad, afraid. Life was an endless parade of tragedies: solve one thing and another rushes to take its place. He was consumed by the idea that his mother, this noble creature with her dark thick skin and mauve lips and particular motherly creases, was going to die. He put his hand over hers. "But it's bad luck for him," Mansoor continued. "He doesn't have much of an income and I think he's the only son in India, so it'll be tough for his parents."

"We'll take care of him," his mother said, smiling.

"It's so ironic," he said to her. "He was the one in my NGO who was the most staunch believer in nonviolence. He's the last person it should have happened to."

Ayub, left alone in the ward, began to palpitate and lose his nerve. He'd always had a weakness for mothers, feared their telepathic abilities and felt that no matter what he said, Mrs. Ahmed would see through it. "She knows," he thought. "That's why she wasn't smiling, and that's why she came—out of curiosity."

Before, for all his planning, he was an innocent, pure potentiality. Now, he was a murderer and a terrorist—worst of all, he was injured and in pain, which prevented him from thinking clearly about what he'd done. Why had the bomb gone off so quickly? He'd been told Shockie was the greatest bomb maker of his time.

Thinking of Shockie, he got inexplicably angry for a second and clutched the rusted nail.

Then he turned over on the bed. He knew that the people around him were here because of his efforts, that their wounds and tears were *his* doing—he'd heard the fat man who'd been talking on the mobile in the market moaning—but for that reason, it was satisfying that he too was hurt. He hadn't exempted himself from the suffering he'd caused others.

The doctor had told him he would make it out with a slight limp if he did the right exercises. Ayub had smiled through his comments, aware of having hardened. So this is how it feels to be bad. Cold and sober.

Riding the flare of this feeling now, he got out of bed and started walking away. "Where are you going?" a nurse asked, calming another patient, but when he put up his pinky in the universal salute of wishing to pee, she

looked away and he kept trudging. He came to a door that led out of the
ward, amazed at the blindness of the doctors and the patients—a blindness
like that of the shoppers he'd killed. He slipped out of the main entrance
into the shameless afternoon light.

Buses, angry and green and gray, with oleaginous windows and robotic
grimacing grilles, were blowing lightly down the road.

Originally, he was supposed to meet Shockie at the park after the bombing; he wondered how Shockie had responded when he, Ayub, hadn't
shown up. Did they think I was a double agent, that I went to the police?
But, then, the bomb did go off—surely they heard about that. Would a
double agent really set off a bomb?

The bomb had only killed fifteen and injured thirty. He wasn't sure how
to feel about it, except to say to himself, "It's Indian propaganda. It was
much bigger."

Ayub passed a phalanx of dozing ambulances. But when he got to the lip
of the hospital complex and hailed a rickshaw, he realized, with the despair
of a man who has almost escaped, that he had no money. Someone had
taken it from his pocket when he was lying in the mud, bleeding.

Mansoor came again in a few hours with his father, who fussed over Ayub
and had him moved to a private room (Ayub had come back to the ward).
"They've started making arrests already," Sharif told Ayub. "The Indian
Mujahideen has taken credit." It pained Sharif to have to talk about yet
another group of Muslims responsible for terror. He really did feel, as they
moved Ayub to his room, that the world was closing in on him and his
family, that it was bad luck to be back here again.

Ayub was frightened to hear about the arrests. "Did they say who did it?"

"You think there's a reason?" Sharif said, mishearing. "They hate everyone, especially themselves."

"You'll appreciate this, uncle," Ayub said, settling into his new bed, now
echoing Mansoor's statement to his mother. "I fought for the rights of
people arrested for terror but I've never been on this side." Suddenly, seeing
his body, the whole injured extent of it, he was comforted. "One under-

stands how the victims must feel about terrorists. They're looking for revenge. They don't want to listen to reason. What happened is so irrational
that it makes people irrational."

"Which is exactly what the terrorists want," Sharif said. "How's your
eye?"

"It's OK, uncle. One eye is nothing."

"Better than the brain, I suppose." He smiled weakly, saying the wrong
thing as usual. "I should have had you start work that day itself—then you
wouldn't have had time to do shopping." Sharif smiled again.

"I only went because I had to buy gifts for my family. They all like
brands. Maybe this is a lesson for me not to buy brands," he said, smiling.

"My missus called your parents," Sharif said, remembering what he'd
been told to say. "They said they're coming. I made a booking for them
through my travel agent." He didn't mention how surprised Mr. and Mrs.
Azmi had been to hear their son was in Delhi, how they hadn't heard from
him in weeks.

"They're both becoming blind," Ayub said sadly, his eyes curdling with
tears. "They won't be able to come."

"They didn't tell me that."

"They're very polite."

Seeing them now in his mind's eye—seeing the disappointment they
would feel if they ever discovered he was a terrorist, his heart crumpled. I
hope the train crashes and they die happily, he thought.

When Sharif went out to make a call—he was always making calls on his
mobile—Ayub said to Mansoor, "I have to tell you something. Close the
door for a minute."

Mansoor lowered his big head and shut the door.

Ayub said, "I'm going to be arrested."

"What?"

Ayub craned his head toward the door. "I don't want your father to
know." Now he told him a story he'd thought up earlier. For all his pain,
Ayub's ability to fabricate hadn't gone away; it had got better with desper-

ation. He said he had enraged so many policemen over the years with his activism that they had vowed to take revenge on him; one had come by and threatened him with arrest.

"Which one?" Mansoor asked.

"I wish I knew his name. He was a sub-inspector with the Delhi cadre. But he said they can take me away under POTA anytime."

"But I have a connection," Mansoor said, thinking of Vikas Uncle.

"The connection won't help. It's a deep issue. I've revealed too much corruption in the police."

"We can go to the press," Mansoor said.

"Mansoor bhai, you have to trust me. This is the one time none of this will help. You saw how the press reacted to our rally—why will they come help us? And a Muslim injured in the blast? They can easily pin it on me. Religious, young—they don't need evidence."

"I was also injured in a blast."

"That's different. You were little."

Mansoor paused. He was wondering at this story.

Soon after, Sharif came in and asked Mansoor to accompany him to the photocopier in the hospital complex to make a copy of Ayub's prescription. Mansoor, nodding to Ayub, went out with him. He had assured Ayub he wouldn't tell the secret, yet he wasn't sure why he should keep it from his father. Still, as he walked with his father, he became aware of how burdened Sharif had become, a neckless man sunk in the worry suit of his body. Mansoor decided to help his friend.

Going back to Ayub's room—his father was now on the phone talking to a business contact in the lobby of the hospital—Mansoor said, "What do you need?"

"Honestly? Thousand rupees."

"That's easy. Here's six hundred." Mansoor's pulse raced. Would he be arrested too?

"You don't need to worry," Ayub said. "They won't do anything to you. Their issue with me is personal."

"It still sounds dangerous. We should tell my family friend."

"If you tell them, it'll only cause more drama. Believe me, the best situation is for me to go." At that moment, stuffing the money into pajama pockets, Ayub smiled. In that smile Mansoor suddenly knew that Ayub had done it, that he'd planted the bomb.

Mansoor was thrown out of himself. His emotions and facial gestures got scrambled. He smiled and blinked and frowned and twitched; he didn't seem to have control over his hands, which felt around his face as if for the first time, as if touching the face of a lover in the dark and discovering it is your enemy, or worse: a cold corpse, the corpse of a loved one. His stomach muscles cramped. The food he'd eaten earlier that day troubled the top of his throat.

Ayub stood up jauntily and put a friendly hand on Mansoor's shoulder. "You'll be OK."

"Yes." Mansoor smiled.

"Good. You go from the stairs," Ayub said. "I'll take the lift." They walked out into the corridor in opposite directions.

But going down the stairwell, that pouring cuboid of negative space, the undersides of the zags of staircase above furiously black with beards of dust, Mansoor became worried. Everything swirled in the stairwell; a bat flew up, circling, wafting through the unmarked stories. Mansoor sweated, his heart beating weirdly

When he came to the lobby he half-expected to see his father and Ayub chatting. But neither was there. His father, it turned out, was already in the car, getting lathered with the aftershave of air-conditioning; he had left Mansoor missed calls to join him in the car.

So Mansoor walked across the lot to the pale blue Honda City and got in.

His father was sitting in the back, scratching his stubble like a happy animal, playing "Yeh Shaam Mastani" on the stereo—his favorite song, partly because it was the only one he knew how to play on guitar; late in life, Sharif had developed a fixation that he ought to learn one musical instrument.

As the car started, Sharif unconsciously put his thick hand on his son's—the hands were plastic and large, puffy, covered in ridges, fair. His fingers were so much fatter than Mansoor's. He seems to be made of a different material from me, Mansoor thought.

But they did not talk the whole way home.

At home Mansoor was disoriented, unable to speak at dinner, which was illuminated by the faint light of the generator—the electricity had gone. "Poor boy, you're tired," his mother said. Mansoor, smiling sweetly and dumbly, neither agreed nor disagreed.

It was only in his room that night, in that palace of air-conditioning, that he began to shiver. The shivers were uncontrollable. His ribs hurt. His teeth clattered and sang and slid against each other, testy with enamel. His body was out of control. He got up and sat on the desk but his palm vibrated on the table like a mobile. "No," he said out loud.

He thought of Ayub and wondered where he was now. But it was no concern of his. He was just Ayub's friend. He had only come to see Ayub in the hospital. It was Ayub's free choice to go wherever he wanted. This relaxed Mansoor. Then the shivering began again.

"Are we going to go today to see him?" his mother asked in the morning.

She was clearly enjoying this routine of spending time with her son.

"Let me call his room in the hospital and find out if he's awake."

"He'll of course be awake. They wake you at six in the hospitals and they keep you up the whole day with checkups and plates of food. That's what we're being charged four thousand per day for." Her generosity did not preclude harping.

Clutching his Nokia, Mansoor called the hospital. After an interminable wait, the receptionist came back to him and said, "He's not there."

"Oh?"

"He's gone. There's no one in that room. Has he checked out? We have a queue of patients." He was surprised by her lack of concern.

"He's left the hospital," Mansoor told his mother.

She crinkled her expressive moon-shaped forehead in surprise. "Very strange."

"He's like that. I knew he would behave this way if you got him a room. He's too self-respecting. It's how he left after we offered him a job."

"I only hope he gets better," his mother said. "And his poor parents are coming also."

Mansoor prayed that nothing had happened, that Ayub had not been caught, that all of this fell behind them.

Then, the unraveling began—but in the strangest way.

CHAPTER 32

For years, the Delhi police, as well as Khurana and Gill—first individually, then collaboratively—had been tracking Shockie. Three years after the 1996 blast, Malik had actually broken down and fingered Shockie, though he had returned quickly to a contrite silence.

Ever since then there had been a bounty on Shockie's head and a great deal of intelligence expended in failing to capture him. So it was a surprise when, a few days after the Sarojini Nagar blast, he was arrested.

It was a triumphant moment for everyone. A flighty, bald, wet-eyed man was produced in the lockup. He looked like an electrician—like someone you might hire for handiwork at Lajpat Nagar. There was nothing terroristic about him. Gill and the Khuranas watched with delight from behind a glass window as he was interrogated and beaten.

After three days of torture, he angrily confessed. "The real mastermind is Ayub Azmi. He's done the last ten blasts. I've been his servant."

"Who's that?"

"A young man," Shockie said. "An activist from Azamgarh. That's why he was never detected. He was injured in the Sarojini Nagar blast." Shockie secretly blamed Ayub for his arrest. Actually, he had become quite attached to Ayub, the way he had been attached to Malik, and had stayed on in Delhi hoping Ayub would reappear at the park. But it was Shockie's constant presence in the park that had attracted the attention of a paranoid man who lived on the periphery. Soon after this man had contacted the police and a policeman had matched Shockie to his photo.

After escaping from Delhi, Ayub went to the base near Hubli. But when he got there, exhausted—his exhaustion only fully expressing itself now, as it does at the tail end of journeys that have been soaked and powered by adrenaline—Tauqeer, looking gaunt and ill, only wanted to know where Shockie was.

"I thought he had come back."

"Obviously he didn't."

"I assumed he had." Ayub unconsciously covered his gashed left eye; it was lacking a patch now. No one in the group appeared to notice or care.

Soon after, the group learned Shockie had been arrested, and in a panic—but a smooth one; the group was made for panicky situations, even looked forward to them—split up into cells and went in different directions. Shafi and Rafiq went north, to Kathmandu. Waris and Karim headed to Gujarat. Ayub and Tauqeer hurtled overland, in the back of a truck, to a secluded beach in Kerala. Once there, Tauqeer and he settled into a hut on the beach.

The first two days were almost pleasant. Ayub liked Tauqeer now and they talked about Palestine and Carlos the Jackal. Then one evening, after going out for a walk, Tauqeer vanished.

The problem with this was that Tauqeer locked the door whenever he left; Ayub couldn't get out of the hut. For a few hours he sat cross-legged in the sand.

He could hear the ocean susurrating beyond and after a while, he pounded the door and threw his bulk against it but the force was useless; the door was metal, clasped with a chitkani outside.

He sat back down in the sand and told himself not to worry. Tauqeer would come back for him.

Night came—no Tauqeer. He drowsed and drooled, hungry. He hadn't eaten in a day. He was thirsty too; to get to the water under the sand, he began to dig.

He passed out. When he woke the next day, he was in another hut, on an operating table of some sort. "I'm glad you found me," he said with a smile, still surprisingly weak. "Is there a drip here? Some glucose?"

He had a vague memory of waking and trying to open the door of the hut and then passing out again.

The doctor, who was wearing a face mask, said to another man in the dark corner, "Our friend is awake." He had kind eyes that closed into slits.

"Tauqeer bhai?" Ayub asked. "Are you there? Was the key to the hut lost or what?"

The man in the shadows did not answer.

Ayub became aware that he was undressed to his waist. More to the point: there was a strange square scar on his chest, where a scalpel had been recently applied. The skin was reddish, welted, peeling.

"Did I need to have surgery? Was I very sick?"

"You are the bomb," the doctor said.

Ayub moaned and tried to turn over.

The doctor tapped his chest with a blunt cold metal instrument. "We've put a bomb in you. It's a new kind of bomb, since you're curious. It isn't timed. It goes off when you move your body in a particular way."

Ayub's broad shoulders shook and compressed. His leg muscles tensed. "What did I do?"

"We know who you're working for," the man in the corner said. It was Tauqeer after all.

The doctor helped Ayub off the table. "It's OK," he said. "You can walk. Here," he said. "Put this shirt on." Ayub complied, hunching himself to accept the shirt. He was very weak.

He must have been walked some distance in this drowsy state, because when he came to, he was on a deserted beach.

Tauqeer and the doctor were gone. The hut was gone. The birds struggled in the wind like flies in honey. The sounds were enormous, the ocean regally hushing the beach. It was beautiful. He tried not to move—to avoid the secret configuration that might set off the bomb. With one hand he picked at the sand, kneaded it. What a waste of a life, of talent. Did he be-

lieve he would explode? Of course. Stranger things have happened. He had
never experienced such a fear of the body before, not even with his back
pain, or the bomb he'd planted in Delhi. The body itself was abhorrent. It
could be made subservient to anything. It could work for despots, tyrants,
fascists, terrorists—it could work for machines. He realized the pointlessness,
at a time like this, of having a mind. He kept imagining the form the explosion would take, how it might gush out of him like a white star, pelting the
ocean with soft embers and pieces of his skin. What was a bomb, really? A
means of separation, of opening. A factory of undoing. It took the violent
forces of civilization and applied them to the very opposite aims with a
childlike glee. A bomb was a child. A tantrum directed at all things. A wail
of a being that hadn't got its own way. The choice of suicide over defeat.
Ayub, in his reading of Marxist history and leftist theory, had always been
interested in the role of bombs; now he too was a weapon, part of a long
evolution of revolution. In that instant, he was connected to the bomb
throwers of the past and the bomb men of the future. Entire cities of exploding people might exist someday. He saw a hut in the distance. Casting
aside fear for an instant, he got up and ran.

He punched out holes in the sand with his feet, breathing, hyperventi-
lating. His pellucid, cellophane-like toenails, advancing feelers of dead skin,
were small helmets of death on the living crab of the foot. The metal object
implanted in his chest rattled. His body, for all its glaring tension, was free
of pain. Arriving at the hut, he panted and waited, hoping someone would
show up. But it was a bombed-out husk. No one was there. He saw an entire village of husks leading up a hill.

He wondered if this was a place that had gone extinct in an experiment
of the sort that was being carried out on him. Tired and hungry, his eyes
fastened on a glistening mound of coconuts—green balls with flattened
heads and straws sticking out of them. The hunger was so bad, it overrode
his fear of dying. On his knees he got before the mound of coconuts and
sucked the tart juice from the used husks. It came out one drop at a time.
It was pink overhead, the sky. He knew he had to go to the police.

Whatever had been done to him had weakened him. He thought of how far he'd come, once again—from Tara to Azamgarh to Delhi to this beach, destined to perish and vanish the way the whole village had vanished. Had the villagers been taken out by dacoits? By bandits? By the government— cleared for some massive project? He became impatient for the bomb to go off. The coconuts yielded very little. He got up abruptly, gnashing his teeth, the muscles in his legs squeezed. He had the distinct feeling that he was in a dream—a hallucination like those he'd had on drugs.

This village at the edge of India, the complete absence of living things save for the jutting birds overhead, the mysterious mound of recently drunk coconuts—complete with the twisted straws brutally stuck back into the maws of the fruit—the bomb in his heart, the shabbiness of his clothes: none of it felt plausible, connected to the reality he'd known. He hoped he might fall asleep and wake up corrected. He put his fists against his blackly circled eyes. Twenty feet from him, water gushed on crumbling soil. His systems were shutting down; he could feel it—and it was right before he fell into sleep that he realized: *sleep* might trigger the bomb. He jerked awake. Brilliant. A person exhausts himself trying to avoid obvious postures only to fall into the default position of nature. Sleep. Everything major happened when you were sleeping. Plants grew. The earth, browsing the aisles of the sun, renewed itself. The truth about a place—its dangers, its crimes— came out. Why shouldn't the bomb in me work the same way?

Suffering a fit of mania, he began to believe he controlled how the bomb worked. That he could turn it on and off with his mind. One with his body, he breathed deeply, yogically. Waves of tension passed up through his legs.

Suddenly feeling watched, he cast his gaze behind him, in an arc. He felt he was bringing the bomb up with concentration. Instead he vomited—a thin, colorless, sleek fluid. His system emptied itself out. Hunger, mania, vomiting—he didn't understand. He was certain he would go off now. He was hungry for it.

He began singing. *Haathi ka anda la. Aati kya khandala.* A favorite of his and Tara's. He was losing his mind. It was like that time in the fields of Azamgarh soon after he'd heard that Tara was going to America. This was the absurd singing of a man near death. A man looking to be finished and still throwing notes into the void. He let out his high-pitched laugh. It was like a tennis ball thrown high over a sparkling, waiting field. He got up suddenly and ran again. He ran through the town, past the shattered huts, huts that seemed bashed softly, rattled by the ocean, the wood fungal and ancient, the objects scattered around with such basaltic, modern randomness—plastic buckets, plastic bats, a bansuri—that he could make no sense of the people who'd lived there except to say they must have been happy and they must have used plastic.

The ocean had come into these homes and dragged the people away. The floors of cement, where they existed, had busted through to reveal black melting radiant damp soil. Somehow the plastic objects had been spared. It was as if the dragging bag of the blue ocean had known to reject certain things. A skeleton of a small dog grew bright with age. He moved up the winding streets. I have to find someone, he thought. Nothing is lost yet. I am only twenty-seven! I have sixty more years—years in which to decide what I wish to do, to make incremental change. I will dedicate myself to normal life. This will be a turning point.

An explosion threw him to the ground.

No—he was alive. It was just a rotten branch falling off a tree. He tore open his shirt and looked at his chest. The scar, shaped like a square, was like a space demarcated for punching. "Help!" he screamed. "Help!" His voice went far and deep, tearing up his larynx, knotting and releasing it. "Help!" Deep, large, explosive sounds. "Help!" Where did this strength come from? Whom was he beseeching? "Help!"

Afterwards he became very tired and despairing and he sat down by a crooked doorframe and wept. "I am sorry, God," he said finally, recalling his oldest companion—one he had forgotten. "Take me back."

He was found dead on the beach a day later, from hunger and exhaustion.

The police back in Delhi, of course, did not know any of this. They went to the hospital and followed the trail of documents and paperwork to the Ahmeds' house.

Mansoor was taken from the house while still in his morning Adidas shirt and Bermuda shorts.

"Do you know why they think Ayub is a terrorist?" his father—jogging down the driveway, sweating, hair scrambled on his head—asked Mansoor, as he was led away in a knot of policeman on a thin colony road. The neighbors, arms folded over low walls, watched.

Mansoor's shame kept him from speaking. "No, nothing," he said, hoping that his father's plastic business, which could so easily be linked to bombs, wasn't held against him.

That first night, Mansoor was taken to the thana and beaten on the back and legs with a hockey stick by two policemen on a broken concrete floor. As he whimpered and cried and begged for his parents—as he thought of his days in California—he never denied knowing Ayub, or the fact that Ayub had stayed with them, or that they had taken care of him in the hospital.

Wouldn't this string of charitable actions only exonerate them?

"The person who helps a terrorist—he's even worse than a terrorist," a young policeman, who at first had seemed as afraid of Mansoor as Mansoor was of him—the man could barely grow a beard—screamed. Over the next few days, Mansoor became very frightened of this sociopathic policeman with no sideburns, this eunuch of an angry policeman. He seemed unafraid and undeterred by threats. He didn't care a jot for Mansoor's "connections," and when his parents and Vikas Uncle visited the station, pressing the police for his release, for bail, Mansoor was beaten even harder and not allowed to meet them. He wanted to meet them to tell them *not* to come. He was too sensitive to physical pain. Oddly, though, his wrists did not hurt; it was his neck that sent out shockwaves of pain.

Usually you could meet family but under the terrorist law all restrictions were permitted. He sat in the cell and wept.

Eventually, Mansoor confessed to setting off the Sarojini Nagar blast with Ayub.

The Khuranas had, of course, become involved—they told the Ahmeds they thought of Mansoor as a son and couldn't believe that the good news of the 1996 accused arrest had led to this.

Now that arrest, that search, seemed hollow. The obsession with the bomb, with terrorism, seemed hollow. But there was nothing to say. Only actions counted.

And in this the Khuranas, who claimed to be so involved in the world of terrorism, failed to make a difference, discovering that they too, at the end of the day, belonged to an NGO.

Mansoor sat crumpled against a wall of a cell. He knew he had brought this upon himself—upon his parents—and he shivered. He felt bad for them—for how much they loved their son, for how easily it could have been avoided. If he had only . . . but what would he have done? It was a closed loop. His life had ended as soon as Ayub had come into it.

How long had Ayub been a terrorist? Probably from the start. Is that why he converted me? Mansoor thought. And Mansoor began to shed religion, grew angry at it. "I hate religion," he wrote on a notebook he was allowed when he was transferred to Tihar. "It's what I hate most." After the 1996 bomb, it was the second thing that had blinded him.

The Khuranas promised the Ahmeds that Mansoor would be out soon, but then months and years passed and nothing happened and Mansoor got used to his new life in Tihar Jail. He rose with the light and was locked down at four p.m. and spent the nights under a thin blanket on the floor of the roza ward, the Muslim ward, where, as if taunting him, everyone was highly religious, constantly putting their heads to the ground, staying there for hours in a retreat of penance, boredom, meditation. For an accused terrorist—his trial, of course, was still going on—he was allowed an unusual degree of freedom, not confined to the Anda cells, the solitary egg-shaped areas. It was as if the police knew he was no danger and so allowed him to interact with the general populace. The other prisoners, mostly poorer men, the sort he would have hired and fired in real life—it took Mansoor years to shed his classism—were impressed with him. Being a terrorist gave you a certain respect; it meant you had connections, and people asked him for help. But the real help he provided was with English, with reading legal documents, rewriting petitions, translating letters. He became known as "padhaku," the "studious one." His eyes got weak. He still hated religion but he saw it from a wise remove. Yes, he had become wise. He got up every morning and wrote of his boredom in a Bittoo notebook and thought of his life and came to the conclusion it couldn't have gone any other way; he was still living out the phase that had started with the 1996 bomb; his mistake had been to think that it could go away overnight. But nothing did. You had to settle into tragedy as you settled into love or death. And he had settled. He was living at the bottom of the ocean of society. Sometimes, when the weather was good and he had come early to the hand pump where everyone washed and had traded his homemade rotis for a better place in the toilet queues and had found the one Chetan Bhagat novel in the library to read and had been able to garden and had received his thirty-rupee income for the day, he would feel almost happy.

Delhi was just beyond these burning coil-wrapped walls. He was still inside Delhi.

His mother came to see him often. She would sit across from him, separated by two layers of barbed wire, and cry and he would too.

Tragedy had given her a certain physical strength even as it eroded her mind. Her forehead seemed oddly free of lines—or that's how it seemed through the spiky wire.

"Crying won't solve anything," he'd shout at her. "Don't come here if you're only going to irritate me with *your* grief."

Of course he was only angry with himself. He would only understand this after she had gone away.

Nevertheless, he wanted to hurt her again and again. This was his purpose on earth.

For having given birth to him.

One day, after many months of silence, Vikas Uncle came to see him in the prison. Vikas Uncle had developed some kind of rash on his face—it was raw and pink. He told Mansoor, his voice lilting with emotion, that Mansoor would be out in six months, that he was doing everything he could, that he had given his epic film about terrorism a narrative that started and ended with Mansoor and that he was confident its public release would speed up the process.

In fact, Vikas had become a broken man. His visit to Mansoor had been one of the lowest points of a long-simmering nervous breakdown.

When Mansoor had been arrested, he had thought he could get him out but had in fact discovered he was as powerless as before. He was hindered at every step, and often by people he knew. Gill, for example, had said, "He's pukka a terrorist; don't be fooled."

"He's like my son."

"He's a Muslim," Gill said.

"He was injured in a blast."

"Psychologically speaking that makes the most sense. You turn into what you hate," Gill said, caressing his beard and seeming oddly, in that moment, like Sharif Ahmed with his glorious almost-autistic surety.

Vikas never saw him again.

Vikas left the association too. He was surprised by how callous his wife was, in the end. "I have to live my life," she said when Vikas said they ought to do more—that they ought to sell their property and support the Ahmeds in their multiple cases because they were running out of money.

"Deepa."

"We can't live like paupers. We've suffered enough already. And what about Anusha?"

Anusha—Vikas turned to her and saw that he . . . felt nothing. She was a corridor down which he never should have gone.

He felt the blast had made Deepa selfish in a way he had never expected. She wanted only to live in a nice home and to take care of Anusha and to take trips with her. She wanted no traffic with the larger world. Whereas tragedy had only opened Vikas's eyes.

They tried for a while to reconcile but in a fit of rage she told him about Mukesh. That was the last provocation for Vikas. Rushing down the stairs, shouting at Mukesh in his construction office, causing a scene on the property, he soon left Maharani Bagh for good.

He moved into a small flat in Sukhdev Vihar. There, alienated from everyone, he worked day and night on the documentary. But he also starved himself, subsisting only on bananas.

It would have amused him as he died, a year after he moved out—from a potassium overdose—to have discovered he'd suffered a fate of semi-starvation similar to Ayub's.

His body was found in the flat by the sweeper and for a while people thought he had been murdered and there was a lot of talk about Deepa and Mukesh being involved. But then that too was forgotten. Deepa and Mukesh had long since stopped seeing each other.

Deepa returned to Bangalore with her daughter.

The Ahmeds lived lives of quiet, drowning desolation in those years when their son was in prison. They had lost the property case, of course—the minute the arrests hit the papers, the Sahnis had swooped in and the judge had turned against them—and having been bankrupted, had moved out to a tiny place in Batla House, not far from where Mansoor had visited the women in the "VC fund" years ago.

Living together, having lost all their friends, they became quite religious,

praying and spending time doing charitable work with the Zakat Foundation.

Then one day, driving to an orphanage, Sharif felt the steering wheel of
the car turning and banking away from him, as if the road were an ocean
that could grasp and torque your rudder. He pushed the brake pedal. Nothing. He took the car to the mechanic. But the car kept disobeying him.
Around the same time, Afsheen discovered that all the buttons on her kameezes were vanishing, even though the clothes were under lock and key
in a Godrej.

It was when she found a lemon filled with blood behind a photograph
of Mansoor that she became convinced someone was trying to drive them
out of the property with black magic. Sharif and she began seeing a black
magic expert who would help counter this force.

They knew superstition was against religion, but what choice did they
have? And so they became wrapped up in this new religion of terror, till
twelve years after his arrest, Mansoor was finally released for lack of evidence.

By this point much had changed. Shockie had been executed—
controversially—and Malik had been hanged too. But the Ahmeds could
never take joy in these kinds of executions. They wanted only to see
their son.

Hobbled and old, they drove to the jail—the car now obeying them—
on a gray day livid with dust. When they got to the entrance of the
prison, the loo wind was slapping curtains of sand toward them and they
couldn't quite see Mansoor's face as he came up to them with a plastic
bag full of his things. But they all stood within the two flare-ups of par-
ticles, embracing.

At home, Afsheen fed her son his favorite mix of bhindi, gobhi, and khichdi
and asked him a thousand questions. Sharif was dumb and silent. Mansoor
was dazed to be home—in this new place, with all the old photographs and
leftover Oriental curios galaxied around him. All these years he had been

imagining returning to the old house in South Ex—it had taken his parents years to admit they had moved.

"And remember Sultan, Farhan Uncle's golden Labrador? He wanted to give us the puppy," his mother was going on, as if he'd been living with them all these years. "Do you want to go out?" she asked finally.

"No," Mansoor said. "I want to stay here with you."

He never went out again.

ACKNOWLEDGMENTS

Thanks to: Alexander Benaim for his intelligence and offhand erudition; to Alice Kim, Nicholas Casey, Altaf Tyrewala, Ross Perlin, Thomas Meaney, and Masooma Ali for close reads; to Laura Davis for kibitzing; to Corey Miller for line edits; to Jin Auh at the Wylie Agency for her deadpan humor and literary decisiveness; to Jacqueline Ko at the Wylie Agency for her backstage ministrations and friendship; to Catrin Evans, Tracy Bohan, and Ella Griffiths at the Wylie Agency for their foreign sagacity; to Allison Lorentzen at Viking for her editorial brilliance and suaveness; to Diego Núñez at Viking for his jugglery of the aspects of production; to Karthika VK and Ajitha GS at HarperCollins India and Juliet Brooke at Chatto & Windus for shrewd edits; to Suhani Mahajan, Rafaqat Ali, Sudhir Aggarwal, Mahtab Alam, Gurdial S. Mander, Pulkit Sharma, Ankit Pogula, Zubin Shroff, and Tvisha Shroff for top-notch information; to the Michener Center, the Keene Prize for Literature, the MacDowell Colony, the Corporation of Yaddo, and the UCross Foundation for literary and financial support; to Jim Magnuson, Elizabeth McCracken, and Michael Adams for mentorship; to Jim Crace, Joshua Cohen, Adam Johnson, and Norma Rush for their early endorsements; to Samyuktha Varma, Narayana Murthy, Karim Dimechkie, Travis Klunick, Tom Rosenberg, Tory Stewart, Greg Wayne, Amelia Lester, Ben Lytal, Anthony Ha, Tony Tulathimutte, Vauhini Vara, Jenny Zhang, Rachel Kushner, Marla Akin, Debbie Dewees, and to all my friends in Delhi, Bangalore, Austin, and New York City for their support. Finally, to my parents and brother for their unbending love. To Francesca Mari for everything.